Robert Charles

Flowers of Evil

Macdonald Futura Publishers

A Futura Book

First published in Great Britain in 1981 by
Macdonald Futura Publishers Ltd

Copyright © Robert Charles 1981

This book is sold subject to the condition
that it shall not, by way of trade or
otherwise, be lent, re-sold, hired out or
otherwise circulated without the publisher's
prior consent in any form of binding or
cover other than that in which it is
published and without a similar condition
including this condition being imposed on the
subsequent purchaser.

ISBN 0 7088 2004 2

Typeset, printed and bound in Great Britain by
Hazell Watson & Viney Ltd,
Aylesbury, Bucks

Macdonald Futura Publishers Ltd
Paulton House
8 Shepherdess Walk
London N1 7LW

CHAPTER ONE

Babushskaya was a village on the edge of a wasteland, the last human habitation before the potholed road entered the forbidden zone. Galina Savenkova watched it disappear behind her with growing apprehension and a fluid, sick feeling deep in her stomach. The faces of the villagers who watched the convoy pass from the doorways of their poor wooden buildings were guarded and expressionless. But Galina knew they were afraid. They were silent, peasant faces, heavily wrinkled by age, toil and weather, fading quickly behind the thick dust clouds whipped up by the wheels of the expedition vehicles. From the fleeting glimpse she had, Galina formed the impression of cowed faces, faces with hollow eyes, the faces of people who had learned to live with nameless fears.

She noticed there were no young faces among them. Perhaps the young people were out in the fields, tilling the land, hunting, fishing or cutting wood, following the traditional patterns of village life in rural Russia. Perhaps. In almost any other village – yes, but in Babushskaya Galina knew it was not so. There was no market which would accept the tainted crops grown in the nearby fields; there was no animal or wildlife, and the fish in the polluted rivers were radioactive. The young men had all moved away to find work elsewhere. And the young women had gone with them, to marry and bear their children – if they dared to bear children at all – as far away from Babushskaya as possible.

Galina was disturbed. But the dull, staring faces of the villagers had no effect on the two scientists squashed into the front seat beside their driver. Professor Leonid Shumilov was a distinguished botanist, and Professor

Ivan Martov was one of the Soviet Union's leading geologists. Both men approached their work with the total dedication expected by the Soviet Academy of Sciences, and showed far more interest in their own fields of specialized study than they would ever show in the drab lives of ordinary human beings.

There were four vehicles in the small convoy, each one the same four-wheel-drive model built for rugged cross-country work. They had been built in a Soviet factory to a proudly proclaimed Soviet design — which just happened to be a close copy of a British Landrover. In the first vehicle, with a driver and two other soldiers, rode the brisk and efficient young army captain in charge of the expedition's military escort. In the second vehicle rode Professor Pavel Kasnovetsky, the high-ranking nuclear physicist who was the leader of this select expedition into the remote Ural mountains.

Kaznovetsky had with him another Russian soldier as driver, and a more recent addition to the party whose name Galina did not yet know. This man had not accompanied them from Moscow, but had joined the expedition *en route* when they had detoured to call at the huge Beloyarskiy nuclear power station a few hours before. The new arrival had been introduced to his fellow-scientists but not to Galina, who was only a lowly secretary. Galina had, however, gained the impression that he was another nuclear physicist. He and Kaznovetsky had elected to share the same vehicle, and from their close conversation Galina had concluded they had much in common.

Galina herself travelled in the third vehicle with Shumilov and Markov. The fourth vehicle, the last in line, carried three more soldiers. All four vehicles were heavily loaded with camping and scientific equipment.

They drove through Babushskaya without stopping, and at the same unchecked speed swept past a large roadside sign which proclaimed that beyond was a prohibited zone forbidden to all unauthorized persons and vehicles. The road here was narrow and crumbling, the old tarred surface breaking up into numerous potholes. It had not been used for more than twenty years.

The road led to Khyshtym – or rather it had once, for the small town no longer existed. In 1958 something terrible had happened at or near Khyshtym. Even today, more than twenty years after the event, the true nature of what had happened had not been publicly revealed, and remained a closely guarded state secret. Galina only knew the rumours, which spoke of a huge explosion, a gigantic blast which had devastated hundreds of square kilometres. Khyshtym had been destroyed, or perhaps only evacuated; the rumours were vague. Thousands of people had been killed, or perhaps it was only hundreds; the rumours were liable to exaggeration. The only thing that was certain was that there had been a catastrophic disaster and that a huge area of land east of the Urals had been turned into an empty, blackened wasteland.

The size and force of the explosion indicated that it must have been nuclear. One rumour spoke of a new weapon being tested by the military, or detonating through accidental damage in transit. Another whispered of a secret military plutonium plant. The most widely believed laid the blame on waste fuels from the Beloyarskiy power station. It was said that the waste fuels had been buried, but not deep enough. The burial grounds were shallow and unfortunately sited over previously undetected sources of underground water. The heat generated by the still-active nuclear waste had turned the underground streams to steam, building up a monstrous pressure which had finally exploded upwards like an atomic volcano. Whatever the cause, the blast had laid bare the surrounding landscape, and the clouds of poisonous radiation released by the explosion had kept it devoid of life for two decades.

Galina had been Shumilov's secretary for five years, and when she had been told that she was to accompany him on this expedition she had naturally been curious. Shumilov had merely told her, more curtly than usual, that she must not ask questions. Now she began to wonder if even Shumilov knew the answers. He and Martov were to study the effects of the disaster twenty years after. Perhaps it was not considered necessary for them to know the precise nature of what had occurred twenty years before. The Soviet state was extremely jealous of its secrets. Perhaps only Kaznovetsky really knew; he was the expert in nuclear physics and the leader of the expedition.

After Babushskaya the landscape quickly became flat and more barren. The uncultivated fields grew wild tough grass and were broken up by patches of sparse birch and pine trees rooted over the past twelve to fifteen years. Half-hidden in the copses of sickly new trees were the blackened stumps of old trees that had been broken down. As the miles bumped by, the stunted trees grew smaller and eventually petered out altogether. A few tough shrub bushes had managed to struggle up over the next mile, but they too disappeared with the last straggling clumps of grass. The vehicles slowed to a more cautious speed and then stopped. Ahead, as far as Galina could see, there was nothing but black, scorched earth, horrible in its silent emptiness.

Kaznovetsky and the scientist from Beloyarskiy climbed down from the second vehicle. Kaznovetsky carried a black box device and he and his colleague studied its dial readings and conferred in low, serious voices. Galina guessed that the box was a geiger-counter for measuring the level of radioactivity. The two men seemed satisfied and made a decision. They spoke to the captain of their military escort who promptly relayed orders to his soldiers. The expedition began to set up camp.

While the soldiers worked, the scientists withdrew to a discreet distance to debate what they had seen so far.

For Galina, there was nothing immediate to do. She climbed down from the vehicle to stretch her cramped limbs and watched as the tents were erected. The young captain smiled at her. He was quite good-looking, and had blue eyes. Hesitantly she smiled back. Galina was twenty-five; she was modestly satisfied with her own face and figure and knew most men found her attractive. She wondered if the captain hoped to flirt with her and decided she would not be distressed if he did. She would be faithful to Ilya, of course, because she loved him and hoped to marry him soon. But Ilya was far away in Moscow and a mild flirtation would not do any harm. It might even take her mind off the awful, dead landscape around her. Every time she looked beyond the campsite she could feel the sick chill creeping back in her belly. She sensed something frightening in its bleak, lifeless desolation.

The expedition stayed for six days, and, once the work routine was established, Galina found she had no time left for private affairs. Although strictly speaking she was Shumilov's secretary, she soon learned that she was expected to type out notes and keep paperwork in order for all of the scientists. Four secretaries would have multiplied the potential for gossip, and to maintain the high level of secrecy it had been decided that one secretary could be shared between the four men. The work kept her busy virtually from dawn to dusk.

Each day three of the vehicles would depart on short field trips, always in different directions. The two nuclear physicists invariably travelled together, never without their geiger-counter, and Galina concluded that the reams of figures they brought back were mostly radiation readings and map references. Later Martov would return with samples of soil, rock and minerals, all to be labelled, dated and recorded as to exact location; he too carried a geiger-counter at all times. Shumilov's initial trips were fruitless and he scoured the central area of the black wasteland without finding any plant life at all. However, as he began to range in wider circles he slowly began to locate samples of more hardy plants and grasses which had begun to re-establish themselves. Here and there he was rewarded with an interesting mutation.

Many of the facts and figures Galina had to type out from the hand-scribbled notebooks were meaningless to her, but it was obvious that the four scientists were studying the after-effects of an atomic explosion. Once she dared to ask Shumilov directly what had happened here, but he quickly crushed her inquisitiveness.

'It is not for you to know,' he told her sternly. 'Remember, you are only here because I felt able to give you my highest personal recommendation. I have always found you to be a good worker; you type fast and I trust your discretion. That is the important thing – discretion! You must not ask questions now, or talk afterwards about what you have seen. Please do not fail me. It will be bad for me if you do.'

Galina promised to say no more, but her curiosity continued to burn inside her.

On the fourth day Galina made a small discovery of her own. She had typed up all the reports from the previous day except a few pages belonging to Martov, whose handwriting she found the most difficult to decipher. These pages were even more spidery than usual and she was stuck until he returned from his latest field trip and explained them. Wearily she pushed up from her chair, stiff and tired and thankful for an excuse to leave her typewriter, and decided to take a short walk to stretch her legs.

There was nowhere to go except to walk in a circle around the camp, for although she was uncomfortable in the presence of the soldiers, she was reluctant to stray too far. This was a grim, silent world, utterly devoid of animal and insect life. Nothing moved. Except when the odd breeze stirred up the dust, it remained a frozen landscape of grey rock and black earth, utterly still and featureless. There was no pleasure in the walk except to exercise her cramped muscles.

And then, totally unexpectedly, she found a source of pleasure; a hundred yards from the camp, a microscopic flash of blue caught her eye. She moved closer to investigate, and discovered a small cluster of tiny, blue-flowered plants nestling in shadow beneath the overhang of a large, flat rock. To find one glimmer of beauty in the whole of this nightmare world gave her an almost ecstatic thrill, and she knelt to examine the plants more closely.

She was fond of flowers and plants. There were more than a dozen varieties in pots scattered around her Moscow apartment, and her genuine interest in botany was one of the reasons why she had made Shumilov such an excellent secretary. However, this particular plant, although delicate and beautiful, was quite unlike anything she had ever seen before.

There were six of the small plants, the largest no more than three inches high. Each plant had two or three of the bright blue-petal flowers, no bigger than her fingernail, and the emerald-green leaves had the rich texture of velvet. They were deeply rooted in the poor soil and looked sturdy and healthy despite their hostile environment. The most unusual thing which Galina noticed was that each plant possessed very fine, long tendrils. On the smaller plants they were no thicker than the strands of her own dark hair.

Dutifully she called Shumilov's attention to the plants

FLOWERS OF EVIL

as soon as he returned, and was disappointed to learn that she had not made an original discovery. Shumilov had collected samples of the plant and its seeds from other sources along the edge of what they now called the 'total devastation area'. But he was gracious enough to admit that he had overlooked this particular grouping.

'They are a mutation,' he explained to her. 'But of which plant I don't yet know. It certainly doesn't seem to be any plant native to this area. Perhaps we shall learn more with study.'

Martov returned and Galina had to go back to typing his notes, but later she decided that if Shumilov did not want her plants she would keep them for herself. They were pretty and unusual, and they would look nice on her apartment windowsill beside her cacti.

The next day, when all of the scientists were again absent from the camp, she borrowed a trowel to lift up two of the tiny plants, transferring them into a plastic bag with plenty of soil still clinging to their roots. It was a hurried task. She hid the bag among her personal belongings and hoped the plants would survive the journey back to Moscow without being crushed.

On their last day the expedition not only ran out of fresh water, but also found they were running low on stocks of canned and powdered food. So the ever-efficient army captain took one of the vehicles and two of his soldiers back to Babushskaya to procure more supplies. They returned late in the afternoon in high spirits with full water containers, fresh-baked bread, fresh vegetables, and six live chickens.

The chickens were somewhat small and scrawny, but were expertly killed and prepared and served up for the evening meal in what proved to be a delicious chicken stew. It was the party's last night under canvas, and to celebrate the successful completion of their objectives, Kaznovetsky produced three bottles of vodka. Galina permitted herself two small glasses of the fiery spirit and an exchange of smiles and pleasant words with the captain, and then retired early to her bed. She was happy to think that in the morning they would all be returning to civilization.

Twelve hours later the four expedition vehicles were again speeding through Babushskaya, and once more smothering the helpless, watching villagers with fine clouds of dust thrown up by their wheels. But this time it was dust mixed with particles brought back from the wasteland, including deposits of the tiny seeds of the strange new plants, which had clung to one of the vehicles and then been shaken loose as it jolted over a particularly large pothole on the edge of the village.

Before the party struck camp the campsite had been cleared, the rubbish buried and the latrines filled in, and practically no trace of their visit remained. Except the chicken heads and offal from their previous night's meal. The soldier who doubled as cook had been busy preparing his menu, and the man detailed as his kitchen assistant had been one of the lazier soldiers. He had not bothered to bury the offal. Instead, he had simply walked a short way away from the camp and hurled the unwanted pieces of meat and intestine out into the night.

By chance two of the chicken heads had rolled close to the tiny plants Galina had discovered growing under the shelter of the flat rock. Unseen in the darkness, the tiny tendrils had stretched out and curled around the chicken heads, drawing them into two of the nearest plants. The tendrils had slowly tightened, crushing the dead chicken heads until the last dribbles of blood had dripped out on

13

to the black soil at their roots. During the night the roots had hungrily absorbed the spilled blood, and by dawn the two plants had visibly grown.

CHAPTER TWO

Galina occupied a small, two-room apartment in a large block in one of the residential suburbs of Moscow. It was quite close to the Gorky Recreation Park, where she liked to spend much of her free time when the weather was warm, and within easy reach of a station of the underground railway line which took her to work each day. The apartment was cramped and state-owned, but Galina considered herself fortunate to have the place to herself. A flatmate might not have been prepared to put up with her pets and her plants.

Her pets numbered two: a kitten called Misha, who was white and fluffy, and still small enough to be cradled in her two hands; and a canary. Misha was a recent addition to her household, and she had fallen in love with him at first sight. She hoped that by the time he grew larger he would have learned to live in harmony with the canary, who watched doubtfully from its cage on the kitchen wall.

Her plants were more numerous. On her bedroom windowsill were potted azaleas which bore bright red flowers in winter, a purple flowering cineraria, and her favourite – a zebra plant with pale-striped leaves and striking yellow flowers. The kitchen windowsill was given over to a collection of cacti, and wherever the kitchen shelves afforded space there was a potted begonia or gloxinia. The two nameless blue-flower plants from the Khyshtym wasteland had survived the journey back to Moscow and she had potted them carefully, placing one among the cacti and the other on one of the cooler shelves. She was not sure whether the plant would thrive best in or out of direct sunlight, but she would soon know if one fared better than the other.

She was pleased to be home, having decided she was not really the outdoor type. She might have enjoyed a camping trip with a group of young people in a recognized holiday area, but the Khyshtym trip had been a depressing experience. Also, she had worked hard. At least Shumilov appreciated her efforts and had permitted her a few days' rest before she resumed work.

After watering her plants, and ensuring that the neighbour who had fed Misha and the canary would continue to do so, Galina departed to spend some time with her parents in her home town outside Moscow. When she returned again she was delighted to find that her blue-flower plants were both thriving. They were healthy and succulent and appeared to have recovered quickly from their uprooting.

Shumilov's laboratory facilities were on the outskirts of Moscow, not far from the university, where he frequently lectured on botany. During Galina's absence he had begun his closer study of the various mutated and normal plant forms he had brought back from the area around Khyshtym. Some he had dissected for study under his microscope; others he had replanted in order to watch their pattern of growth and reproduction. Galina noted when she entered the laboratory that the official samples of the blue-flowered plant were also thriving. Shumilov was experimenting by feeding them with different forms of liquid plant food, but so far none of them had attained a height of more than three inches. It gave Galina added satisfaction to see that her plants were doing as well as those in the labs.

During the evening of her first full day back in Moscow Galina received two visitors. The first was expected, and her preparations were made well in advance. The flat was tidied for the occasion, and she spent an hour brushing her hair, choosing her clothes and applying her make-up. She wore her best blue woollen dress, the one which rather daringly hugged her figure, together with the string of white pearls he had bought for her last birthday. As a final touch, she dabbed discreet spots of perfume behind her ears. When the familiar knock sounded on her door she flew to open it.

Ilya Kachenko smiled at her from behind a large bunch of yellow and white chrysanthemums and welcomed her home. Galina drew him inside and kissed him, and then hurried to find a vase for the flowers. By the time she had arranged them in water, Ilya had taken off his topcoat and his arms were free. She went back to him for a more satisfying embrace and a longer, less hurried kiss. They were lovers, soon to be married, and her heart beat fast in her breast. Happily, she could feel that Ilya's heart was beating fast too.

Ilya had brought along a bottle of vodka to celebrate their reunion. Galina produced glasses and they sat down to toast each other and exchange news of the past two weeks. Ilya was three years older than Galina, a clever if rather serious young man who was already making good in his chosen career as an architect. He was able to tell her that his designs for a new school to be built in one of the small towns outside Moscow had met with cautious approval from the authorities. Galina gave his hand a squeeze of congratulation, knowing that every success he achieved brought their wedding day one step nearer. She knew he was only waiting for another increase in his salary before naming the date.

Galina told her own news briefly. Not because Shumilov had warned her against talking about the expedition – for there was no secret she would not have shared with Ilya – but because there was really not very much to relate. She described the strange new plants they had found, and showed him the two samples she had brought back to add to her own collection.

Ilya frowned for the first time that evening.

'Was this wise, Galina? If Professor Shumilov, or anyone else, were to find out that you have brought these back from the forbidden zone, then you could find yourself in serious trouble.'

Galina felt a small twinge of annoyance. Her one complaint against Ilya was his constant fear of offending the all-powerful authorities. Though she knew she could never live with a firebrand counter-revolutionary, or even a modest dissident, she sometimes felt Ilya went too much to the other extreme.

'Shumilov will never find out,' she said confidently. 'And no one else would ever recognize where they came from.'

'Even so,' Ilya insisted, 'it would be best not to show them to anyone else.'

Galina made a pout of annoyance, but decided she did not want this evening spoiled. 'Very well,' she agreed. 'But you must admit they're very pretty. The blue of the flowers matches the colour of my dress.'

Ilya nodded and smiled, and they held hands again as they returned to the table and the vodka.

Before they could develop another line of conversation, Galina received her second visitor of the evening. This time she answered the knock on the door with less enthusiasm. But there was a pleasant surprise in store for her. The young man who smiled at her this time wore the uniform of the Soviet Merchant Marine, with the gold bars and sleeve rings of a second deck officer.

'Aleksandr!' Galina cried, and threw her arms around him in greeting.

'Hello, little sister.' Aleksandr Savenkova lifted her off her feet and whirled her around gaily before noticing Ilya. He set her down unabashed and advanced to offer

FLOWERS OF EVIL

a firm hand. 'And hello, architect. When are you going to build my sister a fine house and marry her, instead of calling round every evening like a sailor between trips? Think of the money you could save on metro fares, hey?'

Ilya rose to answer the greeting with good grace. The two men were by now well known to each other and viewed each other with cautious approval. Ilya was sometimes embarrassed by Aleksandr's exuberance, but he put it down to the relaxing of all the tensions of living and working at sea. He was also beginning to get used to Aleksandr's boisterous sense of humour. For his part Aleksandr considered Ilya to be rather dry and colourless, but a decent enough fellow underneath. If he couldn't quite understand his sister's choice, at least he could see that she was happy with it. Besides, the architect obviously had enough affection for her and would treat her well.

Ilya offered the vodka, which Aleksandr accepted cordially. Galina brought another glass and sat between them, and spent the next hour happily listening in turn to the two men she adored most. Aleksandr's ship was the *Yenisei*, a 600-ton diesel-engined trawler of the Soviet fishing fleet which was at present moored at Riga. She had put in for minor repairs, Aleksandr explained, giving him a few days' unexpected leave and the opportunity to visit Moscow.

The time fled all too quickly, and soon Aleksandr announced that he had to leave them. Galina protested, but Aleksandr pointed out that he had to reach their parents' home before it was too late, because he was planning to spend the night there. Although Ilya was too polite to drop any hints, the sailor had also realized he was intruding. Abiding by his own 'love and let love' philosophy, he had no wish to spoil whatever plans his future brother-in-law might have for the latter part of the evening.

Before he left he noticed his sister's latest acquisitions. The kitten purred around his leg and he picked it up and fondled its ears. Then his glance rested on the windowsill.

'And some new plants,' he observed. 'This is one I haven't seen before.'

Galina responded to his show of interest and told him where she had found it. Ilya's brows furrowed slightly for the second time that evening, and so she added:

'Ilya has warned me to keep quiet about it. He's worried I may get into trouble.'

'Perhaps he's right,' Aleksandr said diplomatically, knowing the other man meant well. 'But it's a very pretty flower. I can see why you were attracted to it. I've never seen quite this shade of blue in a flower before. It matches the colour of your eyes.'

Galina was intrigued and studied the plant anew. Of course, she had bought the dress to match her eyes, so if the bright blue flowers matched the dress, then they must also match her eyes as well. She had not realized it before. Ilya had not noticed either, but Aleksandr had spotted it almost immediately. She felt a wave of fondness for her brother. After several glasses of vodka, her moods were fast becoming uninhibited.

'If you like it, then take it,' she offered. 'It'll brighten your cabin on that dull old ship, and it'll be a memento of me.'

Aleksandr smiled and protested.

'I couldn't take it. It's yours. It belongs here with all your other flowers.'

'Take it,' Galina insisted. 'I have two, and when the other seeds I can grow more.'

Aleksandr possessed a streak of flamboyant gallantry, which he had polished as soon as he had learned that women were impressed by it. It never did any harm to humour their little whims, and he had found that the returns in goodwill were often quite rewarding. Galina had obviously made up her mind she wanted him to have the plant, and to please her he finally gave way and allowed the gift to be pressed upon him.

He took his leave, kissing Galina and shaking hands with Ilya, and when he reached the pavement outside the apartment building he stood for a moment to breathe deeply on the cool night air. Ilya had been generous with the vodka and he was feeling just a little bit fuddled.

He looked down at the carrier bag in his hand which now contained one of the little blue-flower plants in its pot, and shook his head. It was going to be an embarrassment when he returned to his fellow sailors on board the *Yenisei*, but he didn't have the heart to throw it away. Perhaps he would leave it at his parents' house.

He began to walk briskly toward the metro, swinging the carrier bag and the plant and whistling cheerfully as he went.

In the apartment Ilya was pouring more vodka, while Galina put on a record of Tchaikovsky's *Swan Lake*. They had watched the ballet several times together and the music brought back pleasant memories. They were no longer at the kitchen table, but had moved into the small bed-sitting room to make themselves more comfortable. There was space for just one armchair in which Ilya relaxed, and Galina curled up on his lap.

They listened to the music for perhaps ten or fifteen minutes, until Galina became aware that Ilya's hand was resting on her breast. She sighed with contentment and covered his hand with her own, pressing him closer. They were in no hurry, and another minute passed before Ilya began to gently nuzzle her cheek and the side of her neck with his lips. Galina smiled and closed her eyes, and finally turned to offer her own lips in happy surrender.

Soon the pleasure of the music was forgotten as they rediscovered the even more delicious pleasures of each other. The games which began on the armchair were soon transferred in a laughing, rolling embrace on to the bed, where there was room for more abandoned passion.

Ilya may have been serious and cautious in other fields, but when his sexuality was aroused, he could discard his inhibitions as quickly as he discarded his clothes. He kissed her in ways that made her squirm with ecstatic, shuddering sighs – and her responses were equally hungry. He kissed her breasts and teased her nipples with his tongue, and when it became unbearable she pulled at his head and began to kiss and nibble at his ear. Ilya kissed the hollow of her throat and his kisses moved eagerly round the side of her neck. Galina bit gently on his earlobe. Ilya bared his teeth and made a mock-ferocious bite at her neck. Galina wriggled and bit his ear again, more sharply than she had intended. Carried away by his aroused passions, Ilya gave her neck a love-bite.

Galina yelped with the sudden pain. Ilya realized that he had gone too far and drew back to apologize. The last thing he had wanted was to hurt her.

'You idiot!' Galina scolded him. 'If you've marked my neck I'll kill you.'

'It isn't marked,' Ilya lied hopefully, not wanting to ruin the moment. But Galina would not believe him. She jumped up from the bed and went to her dressing table to examine the damage for herself.

'It *is* marked!' she cried crossly. In her mirror she could see the brownish bruise just below her jaw line. It was quite large, almost in the shape of his lips, and where his teeth had penetrated the skin had broken to show a trickle of red. 'And you've drawn blood,' she

FLOWERS OF EVIL

accused him. She found a tissue and began to dab gently. 'Ouch, it hurts.'

Ilya got up from the bed and went to her, still making his apologies.

'You are an idiot,' she told him again. 'Why did you have to bite so hard?' She stared at the bruise in the mirror and stamped her foot in anger. 'It will show! Everyone will see it. I have a good job and a responsible position, and you have to go and mark my neck like some common factory girl.'

'It won't show.' Ilya tried to soothe her. 'You can wear one of your sweaters with a high roll neck. That'll cover it up.'

'Everyone will guess,' Galina insisted dismally. 'The weather's still warm. Nobody's wearing high sweaters yet – unless they have love-bites to hide. Ooh, I could kill you!'

Ilya began to kiss the other side of her neck very gently, and she became aware of his nakedness pressed behind her. She turned, her anger already melting as the waves of desire returned. He was still hard, and she put her hand down to grasp him.

'I ought to break this off,' she threatened, but he winced with such sensitive anguish that she immediately became sorry for him. After a few more minutes of soothing she allowed herself to be drawn back to the bed.

It happened very quickly then. Her need for him built into hot, unbearable flames in her loins and her legs opened wide to receive him. Ilya entered her, a little clumsily at first, but then with deep, satisfying thrusts as she lubricated. Swiftly their love-making built up to a climax.

They were so totally absorbed in the ultimate shared experience that neither of them noticed the reactions of the little blue-flowered plant on the kitchen windowsill, just beyond the open bedroom door. The bruise on

Galina's neck was still bleeding slightly, and scenting the microscopic trickle of blood, the plant was waving its fine green tendrils in intense agitation. It was observed only by the sleepy kitten, curled up on a still-warm chair, and by the beady, watchful eye of the caged canary.

CHAPTER THREE

Barry Gordon was in an exuberant mood as he drove out of London on the A23 in his cluttered and briar-scratched blue Cortina estate. Normally he hated London and all other big cities, preferring the freedom of open fields, woods, and cloud-tossed country skies, but today's visit to the rat race had been an outstanding success. He had enjoyed lunch in one of the West End's plushest steakhouses at his publisher's expense, and at the end of a long discussion Brian had finally accepted Barry's ideas for his new book. *Winged Skyways* was now commissioned, and as soon as the contracts could be exchanged a cheque representing a handsome advance on royalties would follow in the post. The sun was still shining at the end of a fine September day, and Barry's spirits were soaring.

At thirty-eight, Barry Gordon was a full-bearded outdoor man with a passionate love of wildlife, especially birds. He was already noted as an ornithologist and author, having published several books of his own as well as making major contributions to one of the country's best-selling field guides. In addition to his writing talent, he was equally skilful with pencils and water colours, and behind the lens of a camera. Most of the line sketches and photographs which illustrated his books were his own work. The clutter on the seats behind him consisted of notebooks, sketch-pads, binoculars, camera, rucksack and walking boots; and the multitude of scratches on the outside of the vehicle came from driving down woodland tracks, or parking too close to leafy hedgerows in narrow lanes.

Today, as a reluctant concession to the city, he wore a

dark blue suit usually reserved for weddings and funerals. But as soon as he had climbed into the car to begin his return journey he had thankfully hauled off his necktie and thrown it on to the back seat. Now, with no more restriction around his throat, he was singing in a hearty baritone.

Before he had married Valerie and the children had come along, they had spent most of their weekend evenings in folk clubs and pubs, and he had picked up an extensive repertoire of traditional English chorus songs. He had sung his way through a dozen sea shanties by the time he made his exit from the city, and when he turned off the A23 on to the last lap of winding country road he was already on to the second verse of *The Whistling Gypsy*. He was very much an independent and self-contained man and he had no need of a car radio. He created his own music.

The cottage was a mile from the nearest town, set among rolling hillsides divided by hedgerows into fields and woods. It was an old building of red brick and brown roof tiles, which had been somewhat leaking and dilapidated when he had purchased it ten years before. Since then he had transformed the place, installing central heating and a bathroom and adding a new sun-lounge extension. At the back were rambling outbuildings, a small orchard, and an extensive beech wood where squirrels played and the birds heralded each day with an ecstatic dawn chorus.

He noticed smoke curling from the tall chimneys as he approached and smiled with satisfaction. He liked to see a natural coal or log fire in the old-fashioned fireplace. It made the house cosy in winter and took the chill off the late summer evenings. In his view real flames gave off a warmth with which the artificial effects of gas and electricity could never compete.

He stopped the car in front of the house, not bother-

FLOWERS OF EVIL

ing to drive round the side and into the garage, and turned to gather up the parcels he had bought from Harrods, which were scattered in the back. Jonathon had heard the sound of the engine and came running to open the car door.

Jonathon was ten years old, tousle-haired, bright-eyed and full of energy. He was at that enquiring, challenging age, forever asking questions and seeking adventures, which some parents find exasperating or nerve-wracking, but which Barry found a constant delight. He had a tear in his jersey and mud on the knees of his jeans, and his face was full of the excitement of the day.

'Dad! Hey, Dad, guess what I saw today. Down by the big field on the other side of the beeches. You'll never guess what I saw.'

He shouted the words as he pulled the car door open and Barry got out and ruffled his son's hair, a gesture of affection which in no way altered its appearance.

'I won't guess. I'll let you tell me. I can see you're itching to anyway.'

'An eagle,' Jonathon announced proudly. 'Not a very big one, but it was an eagle. It had a hooked beak and everything.'

Barry smiled. 'It couldn't have been an eagle. The only eagles left in the British Isles are golden eagles, and they stay up in the mountains in Scotland. If it had a hooked beak, it was probably a merlin, or perhaps a kestrel.'

'No, Dad, I've seen a kestrel. You showed me one in the big elm near the village last summer.' Jonathon had a faultless memory for detail. 'This was bigger than a kestrel.'

Barry thought for a moment, trying to deduce what his son had actually seen. 'A buzzard,' he decided. 'Come inside and we'll find a picture in the field guide. I'll bet you it was a buzzard.'

'It *looked* like an eagle.'

Jonathon sounded a little forlorn, unwilling to be robbed of his triumph. Barry ruffled his hair again and grinned.

'Give me a hand with these parcels, and then I'll tell you some good news. Soon you'll be seeing lots of birds you haven't seen before, and on the way we just might see a real golden eagle.'

They walked up to the house together. The door opened and Julia appeared to meet them. She was fourteen years old, with her mother's blue eyes and golden hair, and growing up fast into a beautiful young woman. Too fast, Barry thought sometimes.

'Hi, Dad,' she greeted him warmly. And then more sternly to Jonathon: 'Where have you been? Mum wants you to do some shopping for her.'

'What's wrong with *you*?' Jonathon retorted stoutly. 'Broken your legs or something?'

'Mum says you're to go. It gives you less time to get dirty.'

'At least I don't smell of horses.' Jonathon sniffed pointedly and eyed his sister's jodhpurs, which showed that she had been for a riding lesson since finishing school.

'You horror.'

Julia flushed as Jonathon dodged out of harm's way behind Barry's back. She spent much of her time trying hard to be a lady despite her younger brother's provocations, and frequently she fought a losing battle. Barry reached back to give his son a gentle cuff to terminate the issue before it got out of hand, and then dumped his share of the parcels on the dining-room table.

'That's enough,' he told them. 'Where's your mother?'

'In the kitchen. You've had a good day, Dad.' Julia knew the signs. 'Did they buy your book idea?'

'They did indeed.' Barry hugged her with one arm and

kissed her forehead as the sound of their voices brought Valerie to join them. He held up two bottles of wine in his free hand and said cheerfully, 'Tonight we celebrate, my love. We're back in the money.'

Valerie came forward doubtfully to be kissed. At thirty-six she was still a handsome woman, and in many ways more wonderful than when he had first met her in her late teens. She wore her hair down to her shoulders like Julia's, but in a more elegant style. Her complexion was still smooth and free of wrinkles and, even after the two children, her body was still supple and firm. Their marriage had seen its share of storms and calms, but until a few months ago they had been well on the credit side of happiness. But recently unspoken strains and tensions had intruded, which Barry pretended to ignore.

She was pleased about the money, he knew. The often alarming fluctuations of his writing income had meant many financial crises, and recently they had just struggled through another. At the same time he knew she was not entirely pleased about some aspects of this new book. She smiled for the benefit of the children, but he could feel the stiffness in her. Her kiss was not as warm as it might have been.

'The book about bird migration?' she said. 'The one you have to go to the Shetlands to write?'

He nodded. '*Winged Skyways*. It's about the flight patterns and aerial routes of the millions of birds who move annually between Scandinavia and the Arctic and Southern Europe and North Africa. Brian thinks there's a gap in the market – he thinks they can sell it as one of those big coffee-table books. You know the sort of thing – not too technical but well-informed, with plenty of first-class glossy photographs. We want to make it the sort of book that even a person with absolutely no interest in birds can still pick up and be impressed by.

Brian hopes to publish it in time for Christmas next year.'

'So are we really going to the island?' Jonathon demanded eagerly.

'Yes, we are!' Barry reached to a wall unit full of books and took down a large-scale map of Scotland and the northern isles, opening it with a flourish on the table. His finger pointed. 'Here we are, Lairg Island. It's not very large. There are only two cottages on the whole island and only one of them is occupied all the year round – but it's one of the most important landfalls for millions of migrating birds. We can spend a couple of months in the second cottage; I've already checked that it's vacant and I'll telephone to make a positive booking tonight. I can study the birds and research the book, while the rest of you enjoy yourselves and have a long holiday.'

'How do you enjoy yourself on a rock in the middle of nowhere?' Valerie asked gloomily.

'It's more than just a rock,' Barry insisted. 'There are beautiful sunsets and seascapes, and adventure walks along the cliffs and the beaches. The bird life will be fascinating for you too, and you know how you love the sea. You were thrilled by the thunder of spray breaking over the rocks at Cornwall last year. Parts of Lairg will be much the same. The cliffs and stacks on the north side are supposed to be stupendous.'

'Are there any horses?' Julia wanted to know.

'Er – I don't think so,' Barry had to admit. 'But on an adventure like this you can manage without horses for a few weeks. I know there are sheep on the island, because the only chap who lives there all the year round is a shepherd. You always loved sheep when you were little.'

'But I'm big now,' Julia reminded him. 'And I'd look pretty silly trying to saddle up a sheep.'

FLOWERS OF EVIL

At that she and Jonathon both laughed, and Barry knew the children were with him all the way.

'It's the land of the midnight sun,' he told them. 'In summer the daylight never fades. And the islands are steeped in history. They were the haunt of the old Vikings. The whole place is alive with seabirds and there'll be seals basking on the beach. We'll have a fantastic time!'

The word-picture he painted was so glowing that the children drank in every image, their faces full of enthusiasm.

However, Valerie had researched a few facts of her own.

'But it's completely isolated,' she pointed out, '– just a dot in the North Sea. It's bitterly cold, and there are more gales there than anywhere else in the British Isles, with winds howling up to ninety miles an hour. It'll be hell.'

'So it's wild and stormy, and a little bit windswept,' Barry admitted. 'But that only adds to the drama and the adventure. We won't be stopping for the winter, anyway. We'll get mostly fine weather. The rest will be an experience!'

One I could do without, was Valerie's secret thought, but she kept it to herself. Now the book was commissioned she knew Barry would follow his plans through, and the children would follow him to the ends of the earth, to Cape Horn or Outer Mongolia if he had asked. Barry, with his passion for nature in the raw, would convince them that any desolation was a paradise, and on arrival he would probably prove it. She watched them poring over the map, listening to their excited talk. Barry's eyes were as sparkling as Julia's and Jonathon's as he parried their questions. Valerie reflected. Sometimes she felt as though she was dealing with three children instead of a husband and two.

Her compliance was being taken for granted, despite her muted objections, and the annoying thing was that they did have a certain right to expect it. Up to six months ago she would have welcomed this working holiday, for there had been many bird-watching, nature-walking expeditions which she had shared and enjoyed with Barry. When the children were small they had carried them on their backs, well wrapped up in specially adapted rucksacks, and so the whole family had grown up to love the open country, its wildlife and its ever-changing skies. Barry's life-style and his seemingly encyclopædic knowledge gave every aspect of it a greater depth and wider scope and made it more rewarding for them all.

But now something had changed. Something inside her had changed. After fifteen years of marriage she had suddenly discovered she was bored with long hikes and rustic living, and fed up with forever wearing sweaters and anoraks and jeans and muddy boots. She would not particularly care if she never saw another wild animal or bird or flower again in her life. She had had *enough*!

Perhaps it was what they called the *itch*, an awakening of rebellion and restlessness caused by the established patterns of their marriage becoming too settled. Or perhaps it was the realization that if she did not do something different with her life soon then she would never do anything different. The children were growing up. A few more years and Julia would have flown the nest, and Jonathon would not be long to follow. They were not totally dependent upon her any more, and Barry with his infinite love of birds and the countryside could probably manage just as well without her. She was not sure that what she really wanted was freedom, but she did want a change.

Her feelings might simply have lain dormant and passed after some heart-searching and a level-headed balancing of the emotional books – but then she had met Simon Lancing.

The occasion had been one of Brian's parties. Princess Publishing were launching a new series of children's books, all of them written around Britain's woodland animals by a naturalist author. Barry had done the line drawings for the first book on squirrels, and so they had automatically been invited to the launching. Valerie had not been impressed by the author, a figure in grey tweeds and whiskers with whom Barry had spent most of the evening exchanging anecdotes of nature lore. But she had been impressed by Simon Lancing.

Simon was an advertising executive, young, fashion-conscious, and very, very trendy. He had been called in to breathe life into the campaign to promote the new series, and he was clearly a very bright young man, destined for early stardom in the advertising world. He was tall and good-looking, perfectly at ease in any company, smiled often, and had a smooth, accomplished line in conversation which had the circle around him constantly laughing. And he didn't talk about squirrels, rabbits or birds! His topics were art, the cinema, the theatre, nightclubs, people and places. By night he was a self-confessed city playboy, and by day a whizz-kid success in an exciting business. He was, in short, everything her jeans-and-sweater, outdoor husband was not.

She had thoroughly enjoyed the evening, and it might have ended there if she hadn't bumped into him by chance in Oxford Street a week later in the middle of a shopping expedition. They had stopped to exchange hellos. She was just about ready to stop for a coffee and it was that time of the afternoon for him too. He knew just the right place, and so it was perfectly natural for them to have coffee together. That was the beginning.

At least every other weekend Valerie was in the habit of going up to London to spend a few hours with her mother, who lived in Greenwich. Barry had always opted out, and now that the children were finding their own interests they too were less keen to see their grandmother. Julia spent all her spare time at the stables in the village, and Jonathon hated to be dragged away from the woods and the company of his father. So more and more often Valerie had taken to going on her own. Visits to her mother became the perfect cover for stolen afternoons and evenings with Simon Lancing.

Now she could see that her secret affair might be severely interrupted, if not terminated altogether. She wished that Barry had not sold his idea for his precious book; but she also knew she could not be too adamant in her opposition in case Barry became suspicious. She did not want to burn her bridges yet, and Barry was far from being a fool. She would have to go along for the time being. Barry had involved the children completely in his plans, and if they went she would have no excuse for not going with them.

She was jerked out of her brooding by a squeal of excitement from Jonathon; the children were unwrapping the gift parcels with the Harrods labels. There were four parcels, one for each of them, and it was soon obvious that each contained a brand new, warm-lined anorak. Jonathan's was bright blue; Julia's was red, and Barry's was green.

'Your's is yellow,' Barry told her, because she was slow in undoing the parcel. 'We'll need warm clothes, and when we walk along the cliffs in these we'll look like a rainbow.'

The children laughed, and Valerie forced a smile.

After they had tried on the new jackets they returned to the map, and Barry found the spot again. Even on this, the largest-scale map he had been able to buy, it was only just visible to the north-east of the main group of the Shetland Isles. He marked it again with his finger.

'Lairg Island,' he declared, 'we are coming to see you, and we can hardly wait.'

Galina had no suspicions about her remaining plant until she returned home one evening and found that she had inadvertently left the door of her canary's cage open. There was no sign of the bird, and the windows were closed, so there was no way in which it could have escaped from the apartment. She glared accusingly at Misha, but the white kitten was curled up peacefully on a chair and there were no tell-tale traces of feathers in his fur. When she spoke to him he opened sleepy green eyes and stretched his paws, looking all innocence.

Galina frowned and made another search of the apartment, looking under the bed and in all the corners, feeling sure there must be some explanation. Finally she double-checked the windows, and it was on the kitchen windowsill that she found the crushed body of the canary. The little feathered corpse was caught in the coils of the blue-flowered plant, and its blood had dripped on to the velvety green leaves and into the peaty compost packed around the roots. The plant was much bigger than when she had left it that morning.

Barry did not know it, but if his finger had slipped an inch to the north he would have touched the exact spot where the *Yenisei* was then fishing in the North Sea. The trawler had completed her repairs in Riga and sailed down through the Baltic and out through the Skagerrak Straits to reach the fishing grounds two days before. Her nets were out, and for the moment the weather was fine and the prospects for a large catch were good.

Aleksandr Savenkova had rejoined his ship, and with him he had brought the little blue-flowered plant, his parting gift from his sister. He had changed his mind about leaving it with his parents, because he had re-

FLOWERS OF EVIL

membered that Galina visited them regularly and might be offended if she saw it there. So, feeling slightly foolish, he had carried it on board the *Yenisei*. No one had passed comment, and fortunately his rank entitled him to a small cabin of his own. The plant pot was now standing on a small bedside shelf between portraits of his parents and his latest girl friend. He had to admit that it looked quite pleasing.

It was not until his second night at sea that he began to take a different view of the strange new plant. He had just completed the midnight watch on the trawler's bridge and turned thankfully into his bunk. Time ashore was too rare and precious to waste on sleep, and so after a leave he was always tired for the first few days. He slipped quickly into the deep, dreamless sleep of those to whom sleep was always well-earned, lulled by the gentle motion of the ship and the slight creaking of her steel joints. He should have slept soundly until dawn, but less than two hours later he was struggling reluctantly awake, his brain still dulled and wondering vaguely what was wrong.

After a minute he had established the source of his discomfort. It came from the index finger of his left hand. He could see nothing as he lay there in the darkness, but he could feel a definite, constricting pain in his finger. He tried to pull his hand away, but something pulled back and restricted the movement. Aleksandr felt a moment of panic and groped with his unfettered right hand for the light switch beside his bunk.

The light clicked on, blinding him and making him blink for a moment. He turned his head to the left, away from the bulkhead, and then he saw that in his sleep his outflung left hand had come to rest on the bedside shelf. The fine green tendrils which interspersed the leafy green branches growing from the stem of the little blue-flowered plant had reached down to curl around his finger. They had tightened their grip and were cutting painfully into the flesh with all the tenacity of strong elastic.

Aleksandr sat upright in alarm. His first impulse was to smash the plant against the bulkhead, pot and all, but that might have hurt his trapped finger even more. Cursing softly and muttering his disbelief, he finally used the fingers of his right hand to unwind the tendrils from the one finger on his left hand, and freed himself with some difficulty.

He stared down at the throbbing red grooves cut into his finger, and then looked wonderingly at the plant. In his father's vegetable garden he had seen runner and dwarf beans use similar tendrils to draw themselves up to the sun, but never had he seen anything like this. He would never have believed that their grip could be so strong. Then he blinked at another phenomenon. The plant was vibrating as though in a rage, its leaves quivering and tendrils flailing in the air before they withdrew.

He jumped up and moved to the porthole. For a moment he considered hurling the sinister little plant out into the night sea. But he hesitated. Even if the plant did possess unusual appetites, he had to concede that it was nowhere near big enough to harm him. While he hesitated the pain in his finger receded, and he became slightly ashamed of himself. A six-foot man afraid of a three-inch plant! It was ridiculous. He felt he *ought* to laugh at himself, but at the same time he did not feel much like laughing.

Finally he decided that he would keep the plant for a little while longer, just out of curiosity, to see how it behaved. However, before he went back to sleep he pushed the plant pot away from his bunk to the far end of the shelf, where the tendrils could not possibly reach him.

CHAPTER FOUR

At Babushskaya the villagers had noticed a group of peculiar new plants which had appeared at the edge of their village. They were growing by the side of the road leading out to the Khyshtym wasteland, screened from the nearest timber-built house by a small stand of birch trees. Anywhere else they might have escaped comment, but in Babushskaya life was so dull and uneventful that anything even slightly out of the ordinary was worthy of discussion.

So a few of the villagers went to look, and pondered. They were close to the soil, it was their work and their life, it all but broke their backs and in return gave grudgingly just enough sustenance to enable them to survive. They knew everything which could possibly grow on their soil, or so they thought. Yet this was something completely different.

They wondered if the matter should be reported. The Second Secretary of the Regional Party Committee paid them a passing visit on average every six months, and he had always impressed upon them the fact that everything noteworthy should be passed on to him. The state authorities must have constant up-to-date information on everyone and everything. No event must go unreported. It was the only way in which the state could function efficiently for the benefit of them all. The Second Secretary always stressed firmly that this was their first duty as good Soviet citizens.

That was the official Soviet state requirement and as such, best adhered to. On the other hand, the Second Secretary was a powerful man, concerned mainly with Party doctrine, and capable of causing a lot of trouble.

He could become most annoyed if he was bothered for no adequate reason. Those who had gone to him with trifling complaints or requests for help had soon found that out to their cost.

So the final summing-up of the placid village debate was to follow the golden rule of a remote rural community under communism: to mind their own business and say nothing which might involve them in any face-to-face contact with their local commissar.

After the first flicker of interest the plants were forgotten and left to their own devices behind the screen of birch trees.

In Moscow Galina Savenkova faced a similar dilemma, except that her fears and feelings revolving around the problem of whether to tell or not to tell were much more acute. She knew that the proper course of action was to go direct to Shumilov and tell him everything that had happened, but it was not an easy thing to do. Shumilov could be kind to her sometimes – usually when there was no one else of authority within hearing – but she knew he would be very angry over this. She had been sworn to secrecy over the Khyshtym expedition, and yet she had deliberately removed a mutated plant form from the forbidden zone without seeking his permission. It had seemed an innocent enough act when the plant itself had seemed innocent, but now she knew it was unforgivable. The least she could expect was a severe reprimand, and at the worst she might lose her job.

In the end she chose to say nothing. She removed the dead canary and shed a few tears as she threw it out with the kitchen rubbish. She was tempted to throw the plant out too, but if someone else discovered it and reported it she could still be in trouble, so she held back. A few anguished days passed and then she tried to convince herself that perhaps it was the kitten which had killed the canary after all. Misha could have tossed the bird up on to the windowsill with a scoop of his paw after he had finished playing with it. Perhaps, by pure chance, the little corpse had landed in the plant pot. Perhaps also it was just a coincidence that the plant had grown. It was now six inches high, at least double its former size.

Two days after she had disposed of the canary, she took the cage down from the wall and threw that out as well, and from that point on she tried to forget the whole business. But it was impossible. Shumilov did not have more than two or three hours' secretarial work for her each day, and so she filled in the rest of her time helping him out in various simple ways in his laboratory. It was her job each day to water, feed and measure a whole variety of flower, vegetable and cereal plants, most of them cross-breeding experiments which had begun long before the Khyshtym expedition. Now that the routine care of the Khyshtym plants was also her responsibility, she found herself forced to tend the revolting little blue-flower plants as well.

The laboratory specimens were still no more than three inches high. Shumilov had ordered different mixtures of plant food for the individual plants and had tried various stimulants to growth without success. Plainly they were tenacious little plants, or else they would never have survived at all in their original barren environment; but Shumilov had formed a cautious first opinion that three inches was the limit of their growth. Galina could have informed him better, but could not pluck up the courage.

While Galina was absent, the kitten was free to roam her apartment as he pleased. Most of the time he slept, for he was still very young, only just old enough to take milk and be removed from his mother. Sometimes he curled up on Galina's bed, but mostly he favoured one of the kitchen chairs. The sunlight from the kitchen window fell directly on to the chair and he was able to bask comfortably in its warmth.

When it rained and the sun went in, the kitten sat on its chair, puzzled, looking up at the window where the raindrops pattered and broke into rivulets on the outside of the panes. He mewed plaintively, a lonely sound in the empty apartment.

The kitten stood up and stretched on the chair. Then it jumped on to the table top and padded across the table toward the window. There was a longer gap between the far edge of the table and the worktop beside the kitchen sink. The kitten hesitated doubtfully, but then bunched his tiny muscles for a spring and made the crossing with only inches to spare. A quick clawing and he had his balance again. A final short jump took him on to the windowsill where he knocked over one of the cacti plants. He pushed through the remaining plant pots until his twitching nose was close to the window pane. His whiskers shivered as he stared at the fascinating patterns of the raindrops on the glass.

It was not exactly curiosity which killed the cat; but it did lead indirectly to its demise. A thin green tendril snaked around Misha's hind leg. It remained unfelt and unseen until it tightened its grip – but by then it was too late. The kitten mewed in sudden fear, turning toward the plant, and a second tendril curled around its neck. Misha began to howl, miaowing frantically as he struggled, but the remaining tendrils had his body in their grip: there was no escape. Slowly the tiny white kitten was hauled into the clutches of the deathseed plant, and slowly the last breath was crushed out of its body. When the kitten became still the plant continued to exert all the pressure it could bring to bear, until under the white fur the skin split and the blood began to drip.

While the unfortunate kitten was in its death throes, Valerie Gordon was sitting in the lounge bar of a London pub with Simon Lancing. As usual Barry had misjudged the growth rate of his own children, and the blue anorak he had bought for Jonathon was a size too small. Valerie had volunteered to take it back to Harrods and exchange it, thus providing herself with an opportunity to get into the city at lunch time. As soon as she was out of the house she had telephoned Simon and persuaded him to meet her.

They sat over gin and tonics while Simon listened gravely to her news. He wore a smart, made-to-measure light grey business suit complete with waistcoat, and an expensive wine-red silk tie. A matching handkerchief fluffed not too ostentatiously from his top pocket and there were ruby cuff links at his wrists. He was clean-shaven with a smooth, strong jawline and smelled deliciously of after-shave. His dark, wavy hair was perfectly groomed, not greasy, she knew, but just the right texture for running her fingers through.

'Damn it, Val,' he said when she had finished, 'it's more than any man has a right to expect – marooning you on a bloody rock in the North Sea while he watches some stupid flock of birds. Surely you don't *have* to go with him?'

'The children are going,' she said bitterly. 'They're mad keen for the great adventure. They always are. Barry can talk them into anything. If they didn't want to go I could argue my way out of it and let him go alone. But if Julia and Jonathon go, then I have to go too. Someone has to look after them while he writes his book.'

FLOWERS OF EVIL

'But can't you work on the kids? You must be able to persuade them it isn't such a good idea?'

'You don't know Barry. He has a way with them. They adore him and believe everything he tells them. Jonathon is convinced he is going to find the wrecks of Viking longships in the sand. And Julia can see herself feeding seal pups from a baby bottle, surrounded by puffins.'

'There must be some argument you can use. How about their schooling? Surely you can't just take them away from school without anything being said?'

Valerie sighed gloomily. 'Julia sat for her O levels at the end of last term. She's staying on to try and get some A levels but her compulsory schooling is finished. She can be more flexible now – and anyway, she's taking a pile of her books with her to study on the island. Jonathon hasn't started swotting for his O levels yet, so he'll be doing the same. Barry went to see both their headmasters and convinced them that this is a working trip, the same as an engineer going out to Saudi Arabia on a short contract or something, and naturally he wants the family with him. It means I also have to be their bloody school-teacher for the next six weeks.'

'What a rotten shame.' Simon's hand covered hers and gave a sympathetic squeeze. 'It really does look as though you're stuck, old girl.' He paused. 'I'm going to miss seeing you terribly.'

She looked into his eyes, feeling weak and wretched. There was an almost schoolgirlish lump in her throat. 'Simon, darling, I'm going to miss seeing you too.'

'Tell you what,' he offered. 'If you can make it on Saturday, let's have dinner together. Champagne and candlelight. Then back to my place.' His eyes suggested the rest, softly reminding her of other times. 'If it's going to be our last time together we'd better make it good.'

She wanted it desperately – wanted to share his bed

again, to feel his touch and his kisses, to feel his young, naked body close beside her, his hardness inside her, thrusting and exploding in sweet agony. She wanted it so much the need was a hurt. But it couldn't be.

'I can't,' she said miserably. 'We're leaving for Scotland first thing Saturday morning. It's all arranged.'

'I'm sorry,' Simon said gently, still squeezing her hand.

'But there'll be other times, won't there? When I come back?' She looked at him desperately, realizing what he had said: 'Our last time together' was taking on a new, possibly sinister meaning in her mind. She couldn't bear for it to be over.

'Of course,' he nodded, 'when you come back. Six weeks isn't such a long time. We'll survive it.' He raised his glass and made a toast. 'To when you come back.'

Valerie drank with tears in her eyes.

Simon kissed her and then ordered more drinks. A few minutes later he glanced at the heavy gold digital watch on his left wrist.

'Val, darling, I feel awful about this, but I really must dash. I've got an urgent appointment this afternoon and there's a £40,000 contract in the balance – a whole new advertising campaign. I'm sorry, but I have to leave you.'

Valerie understood, and said so as she stood up to be kissed. Simon held her tight, oblivious to the other customers in the bar. When he finally released her it was with obvious reluctance.

'Thanks for telling me,' he said. 'I hope your trip won't be as awful as it sounds. You will ring me as soon as you get back?'

'Yes,' Valerie nodded, holding back more tears.

He kissed her again, quickly, and then left.

Valerie sat down again slowly and stared after him toward the door. He had been nice, understanding and gentle, but she knew this time it was really goodbye. She had lost him. With so many smart young women flocking round him, he would have far too many temptations to wait six weeks for her.

She finished her gin and tonic and ordered another. She didn't know whether she wanted to get drunk or cry. Perhaps she would do both. Suddenly she hated Barry.

When Galina returned to her apartment that evening she was humming a little tune. Ilya was coming round to see her later, and when Ilya was due all the problems of the day seemed to vanish miraculously. She put her shopping bag on the table and hung up her coat briskly, because she was in a hurry to get washed and changed before Ilya arrived. Tonight he was taking her out to a restaurant, so at least she didn't have to cook. Quickly she unpacked her shopping bag: the two tins of cat food reminded her of Misha, and she paused to call his name.

There was no answering miaow. The apartment was silent. Galina looked under the table, but there was no white kitten on the chairs. She went into the bedroom, but there was no white kitten on the bed. Frowning, she returned to the kitchen, trying to avoid looking at the windowsill. Even before she saw what had happened she instinctively knew. She shrieked, but had the good sense to bite the scream off before it reached full volume. She covered her mouth with her hand and backed away, feeling suddenly sick.

There was only one way to turn. She fled down the hallway to the communal telephone and dialled Ilya's number. When he answered she begged him not to wait but to come round immediately. Ilya was naturally curious, probing for an explanation, but with rapidly-rising hysteria Galina could only repeat her pleas for him to come as quickly as possible. Finally he promised to be there within ten minutes and she put the phone down, terrified that someone might overhear and notice her distress.

Slowly she went back to her apartment, and stood trembling outside the door. She was afraid to go back inside, and afraid to wait outside in case someone came along and wondered what she was doing on the landing. Voices from the stairway at the end of the hall made up her mind for her. She went in, almost running through the kitchen and slamming the bedroom door behind her with a shudder. She sat on the bed, biting her lip and hugging her breasts, and waited for Ilya to come.

When she heard his knock she ran to the door, collapsing into his arms. For a few moments he was unable to extract any coherent words from her, and all she could do was point. Ilya followed the direction of her shaking finger and saw the white kitten lying dead in the coils of the deathseed plant.

The kitten was so completely entangled in the tendrils and greenery that Ilya had to go closer to be sure of what he was seeing. Misha's struggles had tipped the plant and its pot over on to one side, but most of its squeezed-out blood had splashed on to the leaves, which had absorbed the moisture, leaving only dark brown stains like bruises on the velvety green. And the plant had increased even further in size. Ilya calculated that if it had been standing upright it would now reach to twelve or fourteen inches. The roots were bursting from the pot.

'It killed the canary,' Galina managed to sob at last. 'And now it's killed poor Misha. I tried to believe it was Misha who killed the canary, but I was wrong. That horrible thing strangled them both!'

'It's unbelievable!' Ilya's jaw had dropped in amazement, and he could hardly manage to speak. 'And the plant has grown so fast! It's twice as big as when I last saw it – and that was only two days ago.'

'It grew bigger after it killed the canary,' Galina told

him. 'Now it's even bigger than it was this morning. Every time it kills something it grows bigger. Oh, Ilya,' her voice became a wail. 'What are we going to do?'

'We should report it at once,' Ilya said doubtfully. 'You must go straight to Shumilov and tell him everything. I will come with you.'

'I daren't.' Galina clutched at the lapels of his coat as though to restrain him. 'Shumilov will be furious, I'll lose my job. Perhaps they'll even send me to prison for endangering state secrets.'

Ilya frowned and scratched the side of his head. 'Perhaps you're right,' he admitted. 'You told me Shumilov has laboratory specimens of these plants. No doubt he'll find out what they can do soon enough.' He paused, his mouth drying up a little at the thought of defying the authorities, of deviating from the correct procedures. 'The only other way is for us to kill the plant and get rid of it.'

'How?'

'There's a rubbish incinerator in the basement of this building. We could take the plant and the kitten down there and burn them. Once they're incinerated no one need ever know.'

Galina felt relieved now that Ilya was here to think and act for her. Then she remembered the plant she had given to her brother.

'Ilya, Alexsandr has one of these plants! It's in the ship with him.'

Ilya scratched his head again, seeking some reassurance. 'Aleksandr won't have canaries and kittens roaming loose in his cabin,' he said at last. 'The plant will have nothing to attack so it won't be able to grow. You must write Aleksandr a letter and tell him to throw the plant overboard as soon as possible.'

Galina nodded, feeling far from happy, but realizing there was nothing more they could do.

Ilya took off his coat, deciding it was best to get the job over and done with. 'Find me a knife,' he ordered. 'I'll cut the kitten free and chop the beastly thing up.'

Galina hunted in the drawer where she kept her kitchen tools and produced a large pair of scissors. 'These are sharp,' she offered. 'Will they be better?'

Ilya nodded and took them from her. She found him a pair of rubber kitchen gloves as well, not wanting the hands which would later caress her to come into contact with the plant or its victim. Ilya pulled on the gloves and advanced toward the windowsill, determined for Galina's sake to be quick and efficient. He reached for the plant pot and lifted it down on to the table. Then he picked up the scissors.

He had snipped through two of the tendrils holding the kitten before the plant realized it was threatened. Then it began to writhe furiously in his hands. Ilya had heard of plants silently screaming, and although there was no sound except the leafy thrashing of its branches he knew this plant was screaming in agony. The tendrils lashed at him like whips and sought to curl around his wrists. One of them succeeded, and he was surprised and alarmed by the immediate, painful strangling pressure it was able to exert.

Galina watched in horror, uttering little breath-catching yelps of anguish. For the first time ever, Ilya swore in her presence and cut off the tendril that had trapped his wrist with a fierce snap of the scissors. The plant continued to grope for another hold as he hacked at it viciously with the scissors. Severed leaves, tendrils and branches rained down on the table top, and soon the struggle was over. The smell of the watery pink sap was thick, sweet and repellant.

They found a plastic carrier bag, and while Galina held it open Ilya swept into it the remains of the dead kitten, the broken pot and all the debris of the chopped-up plant. He quickly scrubbed down the table and washed it clean, and then they took the carrier bag down to the basement.

They encountered no one on the stairway, and on the ground floor the caretaker was engrossed in a magazine in her cubicle near the main doorway and did not bother to look up as they passed. Thinking themselves lucky to avoid being seen, they hurried down the last flight of stone steps. If the caretaker had spotted them she would be sure to have stopped them and asked questions – partly because it was her job to know and report everything which went on in the building, and partly because by nature she was a nosey old busybody.

The door into the basement was not locked – another piece of luck – and there was a fire blazing in the incinerator. Ilya opened the furnace door and thrust the plastic carrier bag and its contents inside. He found a long-handled rake to push the bag right into the heart of the fire, and when he had withdrawn the rake he closed the iron door with a solid bang, shutting off the escaping heat and the nauseating smell which came from the burning remains of the kitten and the plant.

'That's the end of that,' he told Galina, putting his arm around her and holding her tight. 'Now all you have to do is to write that letter to your brother.'

Galina believed him, and felt her peace of mind begin to return.

Neither of them had any cause to glance up at the ventilator grating which was set high in the basement wall, just below the level of the ceiling. Outside the grating, in a border of shaded earth which had been given over to a small flower bed, were two more of the hardy little blue-flowered plants. They had been seeded by spores drifting down from Galina's open windowsill four floors above. Hidden by larger clumps of golden, late-summer marigolds, so far they had escaped notice.

Both plants detected the scent of the watery pink sap bled by their dismembered parent, and their tendrils reached vainly toward the grating in a frantic rustling of cannibalistic agitation.

CHAPTER FIVE

The *Yenisei* had been at sea for just over a week when a violent storm on the North Sea brought her fishing activities to a temporary halt. The ship's radio was picking up warnings of gales of up to force fourteen on the Beaufort scale and hurricane force winds. Lesser vessels fled the fishing grounds in search of cover, but the *Yenisei* was a sturdy, modern ship, one of the largest trawlers in the Soviet fleet, and she was considered well able to withstand the onslaught. Besides, she was far from her home port. Her trawl nets were winched on board, her hatches battened down, and her bows turned into the wind to meet whatever the angry seas had in store.

Aleksandr Savenkova had the duty watch on the bridge, but the ship's captain, a weather-hardened old seaman from Riga, chose to stay by him. The skies darkened and icy seas towered over them on all sides. The wind was whipping white spray from the hoary wave tops and flinging vicious squalls of racing rain at the windows of the wheelhouse. The storm broke upon them with all the howling fury the most hostile waters in the world could muster, and for the next twenty-four hours Aleksandr Savenkova had no time at all to think of his sister's little blue-flowered plant.

Before the storm he had been both fascinated and disturbed every time he entered his cabin, for it seemed that every time the plant had grown just a little larger. He had never seen a plant grow so fast and could only assume that it was thriving in the sea air. Already it needed re-potting and he had considered transferring it to a bucket in order to see how large it would grow. Only a reluctance to go within reach of the lengthening tendrils held him back.

The truth was that he was embarrassed by the plant, and still undecided as to the best way of dealing with it. He would be a laughing stock if he asked one of his shipmates to stand by in case the plant attacked him, and yet he hesitated to approach it alone. Consequently the decision of whether to re-pot the plant or throw it out was continually postponed. The storm postponed it even further.

Unfortunately, there were two facts of which Aleksandr was unaware. One was that sea water possessed many similar constituents to the basically salty mixture of human and animal blood. The most abundant metal in blood plasma is sodium and the most abundant acid hydrochloric, together forming sodium chloride – which also comprises the largest element of salt in the ocean. Other substances like calcium and magnesium are also present in both fluids.

Even if Aleksandr had known of these similarities they would not have been meaningful to him in any way. But the second fact of which he was unaware would undoubtedly have prompted him to action, for he would not have wanted to see his cabin and his belongings flooded. By mistake he had left his porthole open, and with every pitch and roll of the *Yenisei*, sea water was cascading inside. The third wave knocked the deathseed plant from its position on his bedside shelf and the pot shattered as it hit the deck. There the plant lay as the salt water continued to pour over it.

Barry had driven his family as far north as Aberdeen, and there they had spent the night in a hotel before boarding the P & O car ferry *St Clair*. The ferry carried them out over the North Sea on the hundred-mile voyage to Lerwick, the capital town of Mainland, the largest of the Shetland Isles.

For Valerie it was a bad trip. The skies were grey and sullen, the seas huge and heavy, and she spent most of her time confined to her cabin with sea-sickness. However her condition at least served to mask her deeper, hidden misery, and she was almost glad to be laid low. Barry and the children seemed unaffected by the weather and the constant rolling motion of the ship, and apart from dutiful checks to show their concern for her they stayed in the lounge, Barry drinking beer and the children drinking cokes, playing cards and discussing their plans. After maintaining a strained show of normality on the long car journey up through England and Scotland, Valerie was not sorry to have an excuse to avoid their company.

In Lerwick Barry had booked two rooms for an overnight stop at the Queens Hotel, but in the event their stay was prolonged to three days. The gales which were battering the *Yenisei* further north were sparing nothing within a radius of fifty square miles, and the Shetlands were receiving their fair share. Barry and his family had made the crossing only just in time, for the *St Clair*'s journey to Aberdeen was delayed. The small mailboat which plied between the outlying islands, calling only once a fortnight at Lairg, stayed in port with all the other tight-packed steamers, ferries and fishing boats, her departure postponed indefinitely.

On solid ground Valerie's stomach quickly improved, although her mood remained as bleak as the weather. It all proved her point; the Shetlands were nothing but lumps of freezing, gale-lashed rock where no man in his right senses would willingly strand his family. But Barry promptly retorted that the seventeen-thousand-strong permanent population of the Shetlands seemed to find the main islands perfectly habitable. Besides, they were now seeing the weather at its worst; after this, it could only get better. He went on to launch into another discourse on the unspoilt magnificence of the scenery, the wonders of the bird life, and the romantic Viking heritage, which again left Valerie silently fuming.

Simon had never made her angry. He had always been polite and charming, always ready to listen to her views, and almost always in agreement with them. Barry, on the other hand, sailed carelessly through life on the full tide of his own viewpoint and opinions. For Simon, a worthwhile experience would be something beautiful, sensuous or satisfying; a painting, a piece of music, or a party surrounded by sophisticated and talented people. Barry's only notion of a worthwhile experience seemed to consist of being stranded by a bloody hurricane.

As they dressed to go down to dinner on their first evening, Valerie watched her husband pulling on yet another of his heavy-knit, roll-neck sweaters, and inwardly groaned. She knew it was no use asking him to wear a collar and tie; he only owned two neckties and he hadn't bothered to bring either of them. When Simon asked her out to dine he always dressed for the occasion, usually in a dinner jacket with a frilled white shirtfront and a bow tie of red, black, or maroon silk. Simon had always made her feel like a lady. She was wearing the same evening dress tonight, but thanks to Barry's casual attire she felt like a fishwife.

Barry whistled as he combed his hair in the mirror, trimming his beard with a pair of scissors. Once Valerie had loved the beard for its connotations of virile masculinity, but now she longed for a smooth cheek and the scent of after-shave.

She realized she was making comparisons between Barry and Simon Lancing, and that Barry was comparing unfavourably not only in the way he looked and dressed, but in everything he said and did. Compared to

Simon's high gloss polish, her husband was a very rough diamond. In fact, she thought unkindly, if they could both be likened to diamonds then Barry was more like a lump of coal.

Julia could sense her mother's moods, but attributed them entirely to the inclement weather. Therefore she was doubly glad when after two days the storms broke up, the wind dropped and the black downpours of rain dwindled to scattered, gusty showers. She remembered other field trips when her mother had been as lively and enthusiastic as the rest of them, and so assumed, logically enough, that the reappearance of sunny skies would improve her mother's frame of mind.

In the meantime mother's moods were a bit of a strain, and Jonathon was his usual pestering self. All of which meant that Julia was glad to get out of the hotel as soon as the weather allowed. She put on a warm jumper and her new red anorak and went out to see what Lerwick had to offer.

The old town was grey and grim in the wet aftermath of the storms, but it was built right up to the sea, and some of the old merchants' houses still had their own loading piers jutting into the harbour. Set back from the sea were steep, narrow lanes between the rising backcloth of grey stone buildings. But Julia's interest focused on the harbour and the fishing boats. They formed a tossing armada of bumping hulls and swaying wheelhouse cabins, festooned with brown nets and strung with bright orange floats, all beneath a massed phalanx of masts that heeled back and forth across the sullen sky like the uplifted spears of a vast, wavering army. Above the masts the gulls swooped and screamed on soaring white wings, hungry for food now that the wind had abated enough for them to take to the air again.

But most awe-inspiring of all was the sea itself. Even

here in the sheltered harbour the wave crests were running high, their white spume flying in the wind before they crashed into the solid grey gable ends of the shoreline buildings. Julia could taste the salt of the blown spray and with it came all the smells of the fishing fleet. After two days cooped up in the stuffy hotel the taste and the smells were good, and she inhaled deeply.

She walked slowly, her anorak zipped up tight against the wind and her hands thrust into the pockets. The damp wind buffeted her and played havoc with her hair, but she did not care. She found her way to the small boat harbour and was drawn to the sight of the huge waves dashing themselves to destruction against the solid stone arm of the harbour wall. In the shelter of the encircling arm was a large flock of sailing boats, small yachts and launches, all smartly painted with blue and white, green and white, and red and white hulls.

Julia walked out on to the harbour wall, thrilling to the boom and crash of the white-jawed breakers on the wild side. Spray burst over her, drenching her hair, and she took a quick step back.

'Hey there!'

The voice in her ear startled her. She hadn't seen its owner approach. A hand gripped her upper arm and drew her back another step.

'You'd best not get too close, lass. It's rough today. A big wave could pick you right off the arm and carry you out to sea.'

'Oh,' Julia said. Her heart was jumping with the sudden fright, but she turned and smiled.

The voice and the hand had both seemed firm enough to belong to a man, but when she faced her protector she saw the youthful face of a boy who could only have been a year or two older than herself. He had brilliant blue eyes beneath a shock of wild but attractive black curls. His face was strong and tanned, although the jaw had yet to feel the first touch of a razor. He was a few inches taller than Julia and wore seaboots and a bright yellow oilskin over a fisherman's jersey.

'My name's Alistair Mckenna.' He smiled back at her and became momentarily self-conscious as he released her arm. 'I saw you going out on to the wall; I wouldn't have like to see you swept away without a warning.'

'Thank you,' Julia said. 'I'm Julia Gordon.'

'A visitor?' Julia nodded. 'Are you on holiday then?'

'Not exactly. My father's here to write a book. Although I suppose you could say that it's a holiday for me. We're going out to an island called Lairg. Do you know it?'

'Aye, I know Lairg.' He smiled again, as though amused that she should suppose he might not know it. 'But you'll not see Lairg Island from here. It's away out to sea. The land you can see across the sound is Bressay.'

'Oh,' Julia said, a little uncomfortably. She knew it wasn't a very intelligent response, but for the moment she could think of nothing else to say. Instead she stared out at the low hills across the sound, hills that seemed to be flattened by the swollen rain clouds pressing down upon them.

'Lairg is to the north,' Alistair told her. 'Beyond Whalsay and the Skerries. But there's nothing there. What sort of a book would a man write about Lairg?'

'A book about bird migration,' Julia answered promptly, glad of the opportunity to air some knowledge. 'Lairg's one of the main landfalls for seabirds as they move down from the Arctic Circle. My father has a commission to write the book. A publishing company in London paid him an advance.'

'Aye,' Alistair nodded. 'Lairg is marvellous for the birds. But there's Fair Isle to the south. There's an observatory built there and good accommodation. That's where most of the bird watchers go.'

'My father doesn't want to be rubbing shoulders with other ornithologists all the time. He wants somewhere completely unspoilt, an island where there's nothing but the lonely grandeur of the sky, the sea and the birds.' She was quoting her father now and the words had a confident ring.

Alistair chuckled. 'Lairg is all of that, right enough, and a wee bit more – when the gales blow.' He leaned back on his heels and tilted his head back to face the sky, a knowledge-airing gesture of his own. 'But you'll not be going out to Lairg today. Tomorrow perhaps, if there's no more storms.'

'Oh,' Julia said again, and immediately wished she had not. She had said 'Oh' three times now and it sounded so very schoolgirlish. It was suddenly important to appear grown up, and she was acutely aware that with her wet hair in a mess she looked anything but.

Alistair did not seem to notice her discomfiture. He was pointing across the small boat harbour to a larger steamer, some sixty feet long with a white-painted superstructure and a pale-blue hull, moored against the far pier.

'There's the mailboat that serves the outer islands. She'll not sail until the weather clears, and even then you'll have a lively voyage.' He paused and added proudly: 'I'm one of her crew. I'm only a deckhand now, but one day I'll be her captain.'

Julia looked at him, afraid he was boasting because he thought she was just a child who could be impressed with a story or two. 'You're not old enough.'

'I am that!' Alistair was indignant. 'I left school this summer, and I've been sailing with the mailboat these past six weeks.'

Julia was suitably rebuked. 'It must be exciting,' she said lamely. 'I mean, to go to sea.'

'I've been at sea all my life. I'm a Shetlander – there's

salt in my blood. All the men in my family are fishermen. My father is first mate on one of the drifters – you probably saw her in the main harbour, she's called the *Margaret*.' He smiled and took her arm again. 'We own a sailing boat too. Come, and I'll show you. You're quite safe with me.'

He pulled at her arm and, doubtfully, Julia allowed herself to be drawn out along the harbour wall. The big waves roared up against the barrier and spray flew over them with every explosion of heaving grey water, but Alistair seemed unconcerned. He kept close to the inner side of the wall, and halfway out to where the bar turned across the harbour mouth he stopped and pointed down.

'That's our boat – the *Brave Viking*, she's called.' He indicated a green and white-painted craft bobbing below them. The boat was some eighteen feet long, slim and rakish, with a small cabin and tall mast. 'We take her out for rod or hand-line fishing, or just sailing around the islands for fun. I've been sailing with my father ever since I could walk.' His voice swelled with pride again. 'And now I'm allowed to take her out on my own. She's a fine, bonny boat.'

'You're lucky.' Julia felt a twinge of envy.

'Would you like to go aboard? I'll show you round.'

His voice was hopeful, but Julia pulled back. Even on the sheltered side of the harbour wall the water was choppy and the boats were rolling back and forth. Also there was no way down to the *Brave Viking*'s deck that she could see except for a slippery iron ladder bolted vertically to the harbour wall.

'No, thank you,' she said decisively. 'I can see it quite well enough from here.'

Alistair was disappointed. They stood for a moment looking down at the boats with the gulls crying overhead. Then a squall of rain blew over them and Julia turned and walked back to the quay. Alistair followed her.

'There's a bonxie,' he said suddenly, pointing upward as a great skua flashed low overhead, diving in pursuit of a herring gull fluttering upward with a scrap of fish in its beak. The powerful, brown-winged predator snatched the morsel of silver in mid-flight, knocking the herring gull off course as it soared up and away. The brief aerial drama was enacted in seconds, leaving the deprived herring gull shrieking its helpless fury.

'The bonxies always rob the other gulls,' Alistair told Julia. 'Sometimes they'll even kill the smaller gulls, if they're hungry and there's no scraps for them to steal.'

'Nature can be as cruel as she is beautiful.' Julia was quoting her father again. She did her best to sound matter-of-fact and knowledgeable, but inside the thought of a skua killing a gull made her shiver.

They stood in silence for a minute, watching the gulls and waiting for another drama. The rain began to fall more steadily, stinging their faces and bouncing off the hard concrete of the quay. Hesitantly they looked at each other.

Alistair had not had much to do with girls yet, but he felt an immediate strong attraction to this pretty stranger. The blonde hair plastered wetly to the side of her face made her look vulnerable, and aroused his protective instinct. She seemed so ignorant of the power of the sea. Her eyes had a soft, bruised look, half enquiring and half knowing as they met his own. He searched desperately for something else to say.

Julia spoke first. 'I must be going. Thank you for showing me your boat.'

'There's more things I could show you. Lerwick's an old town. I could show you where the smuggling went on – the old houses with the caves and the secret passages.'

'But it's pouring with rain. It's silly to stay out and get soaking wet.' Julia tossed her head, a sure sign that her mind was made up. 'Besides, my parents will worry. It's time I went back to the hotel.'

'To the Lerwick?'

'No, we're staying at the Queens.'

'I know it. I'll walk there with you,' he offered. 'I'll see you back.'

Julia was beginning to find Alistair interesting. However, he was just a little too boastful for her liking – and a bit too fast and forward. She shied off and said quickly:

'There's no need. I found my way here. I can find my way back. Thank you very much.'

'It's no bother,' Alistair persisted.

Julia panicked. She had a sudden fear of Jonathon seeing her return with a boyfriend, and she knew her young brother's taunts and teasing would be merciless. She felt her cheeks blushing red at the thought.

'Then don't bother.' Crushing him curtly, she ran away.

After a dozen strides she regretted the impulse. It was so *schoolgirlish*. She stopped and turned round, and raised one hand in an uncertain wave.

'Good-bye,' she called. And in an effort to apologize, she added: 'Perhaps I'll see you tomorrow – on the mailboat.'

Alistair nodded without speaking. He had pushed his hands into the pockets of his oilskin jacket and kept them there.

Julia turned and hurried on her way, head down against the now heavy rain. When she was almost out of sight she glanced back once more and saw him still standing on the quay. From this distance, he was a small, lonely figure with the white gulls circling and crying above his head. He was still watching her.

The rain found its way down the back of her neck in

an icy trickle and she broke into a run back to the dry warmth of the hotel. Her mind buzzed with secret thoughts and her stomach was awhirl with a whole range of strange new emotions. She felt embarrassed by brash young Alistair Mckenna with his blue eyes and bonny black curls, and yet at the same time she was secretly pleased and flattered by his attentions.

A hundred miles out into the North Sea the *Yenisei* had ridden out the first storm, and after twenty-four hours of ceaseless battering there came the first calm. The terrible raging seas that had tried to drown the trawler, smothering her in their all-enveloping onslaught, drew back and became merely mountainous. Through the curtain of rain the crew could now see the bows again, and miraculously, except for a torn hatch canvas and a broken gap in the deck railing, the whole forward part of the ship seemed undamaged.

Technically Aleksandr Savenkova should have been relieved twice, but knowing that sleep would have been impossible in the nightmare they had just survived, he had chosen to remain on the trawler's bridge with the captain. Now both of them were raw-eyed and bone weary, aching in every muscle from the tensions of the storm, the constant fight to keep their balance on the pitching deck, and from the long hours without sleep.

The trawler's first officer had been ordered below six hours before to ensure that there was one fully refreshed officer to whom the captain could hand over command when he felt able to relinquish his own position on the bridge. The weather forecast showed that the calm would be only a lull between two storms, but it promised a respite for a few hours. The first officer was called back to the bridge, and a change of helmsman and lookouts was ordered.

The captain clapped Aleksandr on the shoulder.

'Sleep for you, Comrade Savenkova. This time it's an order. I will sleep too. Grigori will keep the watch on the bridge.' He paused and looked at his first officer. 'But you are to call me when the weather worsens.'

The first officer nodded. He was a large man of few words, but a shrewd and able sailor. The captain knew his ship was in safe hands.

They left the bridge together and parted to go to their separate cabins. The captain's accommodation was immediately behind the bridge, but the second officer's cabin was much further back. The ship was still rolling heavily and Aleksandr found it necessary to keep a firm grip on the safety rail. He reached his cabin and ducked inside quickly with the wind and rain pounding hammerblows on his shoulders. Thankfully he slammed the door shut behind him.

It was dark inside the cabin, but Aleksandr did not bother to switch on the light. He knew where to find his bunk and collapsed on it in a state near to exhaustion. He closed his eyes and allowed his whole body to go limp, and within a very few minutes he would have been asleep, had he not heard the slopping of water on the cabin floor.

With an effort he opened his eyes again, and swore bitterly as he realized what had happened. His bunk was wet, and as his eyes became accustomed to the gloom he could just distinguish the fact that the cabin porthole was open.

Still cursing, he pushed himself to his feet and stumbled forward to close the port. As he did so he heard a rustle of leaves and tendrils, and out of the blackness a tendril half as thick as his wrist rose into the faint disc of light from the open porthole, and curled towards him.

CHAPTER SIX

Dawn the next morning saw a complete transformation. The gales had blown over and the sky and the sea mirrored each other in pure duck-egg blue. Lerwick dried out rapidly in the hot, bright sunshine, and across the calm waters of the sound the low hills of Bressay showed a rich new green. The *St Clair* sailed before breakfast, and Julia and Jonathon hurried down to the pier to watch the big, yellow-funnel car ferry make her stately departure. They did some quick fact-finding and returned with good news; the mailboat for the outer islands would be sailing at her scheduled time a few hours later.

Barry was full of cheerful enthusiasm. He ate a hearty breakfast and set to work on re-packing the cases and making final arrangements. The car had to be left at the hotel, for there were no roads on Lairg. Barry had promised Julia that if time permitted on their stop-overs in Lerwick they would drive around Mainland to look for Shetland ponies – his only reason for bringing the car over from Aberdeen.

Valerie made an effort to stir herself out of her gloom. She was here and there was no escape, so there was nothing to do but resign herself to their stay on the island. For the sake of the children she had to put on a brave face and keep smiling.

But when they boarded the mailboat her new sense of determination almost deserted her. The *Island Pride* was tiny, not even a quarter the size of the *St Clair*, and when she remembered her suffering aboard the larger vessel she had a mad urge to run back down the gangway to the shore and refuse point blank to go any further. However, the blue waters of the sound had an inviting sparkle, and the voyage would only be a short one. She stepped down on to the steamer's deck and stayed.

Barry dumped his rucksack and suitcases and then went to check that the boxes of stores and foodstuffs he had ordered had been put on board. When he was satisfied he came back to join Valerie and the children at the ship's rail. They were all wearing sweaters and their new anoraks, which made a bright splash of colour as they stood together in a family group. Julia and Jonathon were trying to identify the multitudes of seabirds wheeling above the harbour and the sound, and Barry was quick to come to their aid. He reeled out the list of names with easy confidence: black-backed gulls, herring gulls, common gulls, skuas, black guillemots, kittiwakes, shags and terns.

Julia made a mental note to refrain from calling the great skuas *bonxies*, just in case either of her parents became curious and asked where she had learned the island name.

Valerie watched them gesturing and pointing, listening to their eager voices and feeling a pang of odd-woman-out annoyance. If Simon was to ever take her on board a boat, she would make sure it would be nothing less than a cruise ship, with every comfort, entertainment and dancing, romantic ports of call and first-class cuisine. With Barry it was always sandwiches and seasickness, and his eternal bloody birds.

Julia had not failed to notice that Alistair Mckenna was on board, although with Jonathon at her heels she avoided any signs of acknowledgement and tried hard not to look in his direction. She saw him in the bows, hauling in the mooring line after it had been cast off from the heavy iron bollard on shore, and was relieved that he had not been fibbing after all. If only the boat was bigger, so she could get out of sight of her family. And if only Jonathon would disappear!

They left Lerwick behind them, steering north between Mainland and Bressay, and as Valerie feared, the sea became less smooth as soon as they were out of sight of the harbour. When they cleared the sound and the bows butted into the open sea the waves became white-capped, surging from north to south in a lazy swell, and the *Island Pride* developed an easy pitch and roll.

Barry's binoculars were trained constantly on the great flocks of nesting birds on the rugged Mainland cliffs. Valerie had a second pair of binoculars which she yielded to the children. Usually they argued incessantly about whose turn it was, but today Julia seemed content to let Jonathon hog them. After a while Julia murmured something about stretching her legs, and moved away to stroll aimlessly around the deck.

Valerie watched her daughter anxiously for a moment. Barry would never have noticed in a million years, but Valerie was aware that Julia was behaving strangely. At first she wondered what was wrong, then she suffered a twinge of guilt: Julia was probably reacting to her own moods. That was the trouble with daughters: they were too close and sensed too much. And Julia was growing up fast, becoming a woman in her own right. For a moment she was tempted to go after her, to try and talk to her; but there was nothing she could talk about, nothing she dared bring out into the open, so she was forced to let her go. Julia would have to work out her own moods.

Julia circled the limited deck space twice, slowly, pausing often to stare out over the sea or back to the land. When she finally came to a stop it was by the rail on the opposite side of the ship to the rest of her family, screened from their view by the wheelhouse and cabins. Her parents or Jonathon could come round the corner at any moment, but she hoped they would remain absorbed in the receding cliffs to landward. She folded her arms and leaned on the rail, staring out to where the sea met the sky, half hoping and half afraid.

After five minutes Alistair Mckenna came and stood at the rail beside her, his elbow almost touching hers.

'It's a bonny sight, lass – the sea on a good day. It makes you feel grand to be alive. I'll never know how other folk can spend all their days in an office or a factory. I'd die in one of those places.'

Julia straightened up and turned to face him. He was smiling and his black curls danced in the light breeze. All her carefully rehearsed responses went tumbling from her mind, and all she could say was an awkward hello.

'I've seen the sea on its good days, and I've seen it bad—' He was trying hard to impress her. 'But there's nowhere else I'd rather be.' He pointed to where a flock of gulls were noisily circling another boat out on the horizon. 'You see that fishing boat? She's a drifter, like my father's. She'll lay out as much as a mile of nets to catch the mackerel and herring. Now that's a real job. Maybe when there's a place I'll go to sea on a fishing boat. Cruising round the islands on the *Pride* is fine enough, but a real man's work is on the fishing.'

'You said you were going to be captain of this boat,' Julia reminded him.

'I did, and perhaps I will,' he shrugged carelessly. 'Or perhaps I'll take up the fishing. There's time yet to make up my mind.'

'I've never been fishing,' Julia said thoughtfully. 'Not sea fishing. I've been fishing for trout in the rivers in Scotland. I went last year with my father.'

'There's fine trout fishing in the lochs on Mainland, but there's nae comparison with rod fishing at sea.' He hesitated, remembering the rebuff of yesterday, and then decided to have a second try. 'I could take you if you wanted. I take *Brave Viking* out most weekends when the weather's good. It's a fair long run to Lairg, but it's nothing to me. I've been further. I could pick you up for a couple of hours' fishing.'

Julia was tempted. She might even have said yes, but in that moment she saw Jonathon coming round the corner of the wheelhouse. Her heart sank and she groaned inwardly. She tried to pretend that she wasn't talking to Alistair and stared rigidly out to sea, saying nothing.

Jonathon came up jauntily and pushed his tousled head between them, twisting his neck to stare from one to the other. His cheeky face began to brighten as he realized that here was a prime opportunity for mischief.

'What are you looking at?' he demanded, with the arrogance only a younger brother can command.

Julia scowled at him and pointed silently to the distant fishing boat. She knew there was no point in telling him to clear off, because the more she made it plain that he was unwanted the more determined he would be to stay.

'There's more to see on the other side,' Jonathon enthused. 'We've already seen cormorants and puffins. We've seen them right close up through the binoculars. The puffins really do have big red, blue and yellow beaks.' He changed his subject abruptly and regarded Alistair with a critical eye. 'Who's he?'

'He's one of the crew,' Julia said briefly.

'I see. Is he your new boyfriend?'

'Of course not.'

'You were talking to him.'

'That doesn't mean he's my boyfriend,' Julia said in exasperation, feeling the blood rising hot in her cheeks.

'Then why are you going red?' Jonathon demanded, smugly triumphant.

'You pest,' Julia hissed at him. 'Go away!'

'I don't know which is redder,' Jonathon said as though it was a matter for careful academic study, 'your face or your anorak.'

Thus goaded, Julia aimed a swipe at him which he dodged with a nimble ease borne of past experience. Jonathon knew he was winning, and Julia knew she had lost. Staying just out of reach, Jonathon aimed his next remark at Alistair.

'Do you really fancy my ugly sister?'

'More so than you,' Alistair told him stoutly, and aimed a cuff that was meant to miss. He had to remember that the boy was a passenger and he was crew.

But it was too late to retrieve the situation. Julia knew that Jonathon would not be scared off, and already she had begun to walk away. Jonathon gave Alistair his most cheeky grin and then strolled after his sister, whistling.

For the rest of the voyage Julia stayed close to her mother, fuming, but knowing that Jonathon would refrain from teasing so long as their parents could overhear. Jonathon's sneaking presence made any further conversation with Alistair Mckenna completely impossible. She could have cheerfully drowned him.

When they first saw Lairg it was from the low south side, where a small cove with a white-pebbled beach, flanked by steep black rocks on either side, formed a small natural harbour. The island rose out of the sea, sloping back in green and brown folds towards steep cliffs and wind- and sea-eroded stacks on the north side. White breakers pounded the cliffs and shores, and the seabirds whirled in vast snowfalls of white wings in the blue skies. Barry had never seen so many different varieties of gulls and terns, shearwaters and skuas; there must have been millions of them. In the first minute he knew that Lairg was going to suit his purpose to perfection.

FLOWERS OF EVIL

The steamer nosed slowly into the cove, to where a crude harbour wall had been hacked out of the grey rock on the west side. The captain reversed the engines briefly to bring the slowly drifting hull to a stop and one of her crewmen jumped to the shore. Alistair Mckenna threw him the mooring line, which he quickly made fast. The gangplank was pushed out and their stores carried ashore.

The captain of the *Island Pride* came down on to the deck to talk to Barry while the stores were being unloaded. Looking landward there were two square grey chimneys visible, indicating the positions of the only two cottages on the island, hidden behind the fold of the first hill. They were half a mile apart, one to the west and one to the east. The captain pointed out the one to the right.

'There's your cottage, Mr Gordon. You'll have the key, I take it?'

Barry nodded. 'I collected it from the agent in Lerwick this morning.'

'Good. You should find peat stacked for the fire, and oil for the lamps. It's not your modern council house, you understand, but it's snug and dry enough. It's rented out from time to time to other bird watchers like yourself.'

Barry smiled. 'I'm sure it's going to be just fine.'

'Aye, but if you have any needs you'll find the Mathesons at the next cottage. Ross Matheson tends the sheep, and he also keeps an eye on your cottage. They're friendly folk, they'll help you all they can. On the islands folk have to help each other.'

'We'll call on them as soon as we can,' Barry promised. 'We'll want to meet our only neighbours.'

'Aye.' The captain searched the island with a keen eye and frowned slightly. 'I canna think why Matheson hasn't come to meet us. Perhaps there's a sheep in trouble. Aye, that'll be it, nae doubt. There's cliffs and gulleys where a sheep can get trapped or hurt itself, only a sheep would keep Ross Matheson from being here when the boat's due.' He turned back to Barry. 'I've some mail for them, and a box of stores. Will you take it?'

'Of course.' Barry took the small handful of letters and pushed them inside his anorak. 'I'll see they get delivered.'

'We'll be off, then.' The captain offered a leathery hand. 'We'll call again in two weeks' time. If you make a list of anything you need we'll bring it on the next trip out. That's weather permitting, mind. We'll try not to leave you for too long, but you saw how the weather was yesterday.'

Barry grinned as he shook hands. 'If it's blowing a gale we won't expect you. But don't worry – we'll manage.'

'Good luck to you. And you, Mrs Gordon.' He turned to Valerie and touched his cap.

Jonathon was already ashore, impatient to explore and determined to be first. Barry went next down the gangplank, turning to steady Julia; and finally Valerie. They stayed there to watch as the steamer was cast off and began to back out of the cove.

Once clear of the rocks, the boat began to turn her bows to the sea and begin the return journey. Her crew waved briefly and the Gordons waved back.

Julia saw Alistair against the rail and she knew that his wave was especially for her. She felt a little pang of sadness as she waved back. If only Alistair could have been living on the island, then the next six weeks might have been real fun.

Valerie watched the stretch of blue water widening between herself and her only link with civilization and heaved a silent but bitter sigh. She could only hope that the next few weeks would pass quickly. A few seconds later a passing tern added insult to injury by depositing a large brown and white dropping on the sleeve of her yellow anorak. The sharp, wet-smacking sound made her jump, and Jonathon let out a peal of delighted laughter.

'Hey, dad, mum's been christened.'

They all laughed, and ruefully Valerie found herself smiling too. Despite Simon Lancing the old family ties were still binding.

Barry looked down at the piles of suitcases, rucksacks and boxes strewn around their feet and said cheerfully: 'Right, kids, let's get organized and move all this stuff up to the cottage.'

CHAPTER SEVEN

On board the *Yenisei* the horror in Aleksandr Savenkova's cabin had been discovered some twenty-four hours before the Gordons made their delayed voyage to Lairg. At that time the storms were still raging and the trawler's first officer had held the bridge for eight hours. He had allowed the captain and second officer to rest undisturbed for as long as possible, but it looked as if the first and last of this particular run of storms were going to be the big ones, and when the wind force rose up to hurricane level again he knew it was time to hand over the watch. A seaman was despatched to recall the captain.

The master of the *Yenisei* responded promptly, appearing on the bridge in a matter of minutes. His oilskins and his greying beard were wet from his short dash through the blinding rain still lashing the heeling decks, and a blast of icy wind accompanied him into the wheelhouse. He had to slam the door hard to close it behind him.

The two officers exchanged formal greetings and then moved to the chart table, where the first officer explained their present position. They were approximately fifty miles due north of the Shetlands, which meant that despite full power from the engines with the bows pushed into the teeth of the storms, the ship had in fact been forced backward over some five or six miles of sea space during the previous eight hours. The captain frowned slightly and studied the chart, the frown easing once he had satisfied himself that they still had plenty of searoom and were in no danger of being driven on to any coastline.

He straightened up from the chart table and looked

directly at his first officer, noting the man's red-rimmed eyes and haggard lines of strain. 'You should have called me sooner, Grigori,' he reproved gently.

'There was no need,' the first officer smiled wearily. 'I'm tired, but there was no danger and we've both stayed awake for longer periods than this. I can feel another big blow coming, but I can't guess how long it'll last. So I've saved it for you.'

The captain returned the smile. 'You're too generous. Go now, Grigori. Sleep. I'll relieve you.'

The first officer left the bridge, briefly letting in the roar of the storm and more howls of wind and rain before he succeeded in hauling the door shut behind him. The captain exchanged a few words with the three seamen on duty, two lookouts and the helmsman, checking when they were due for relief. There were more sailors to rotate than officers, so the crew had been sticking strictly to the duty watches. These men were comparatively fresh and still had two hours before their replacements would arrive.

Silence settled within the wheelhouse. The captain did not encourage idle conversation on duty, and the seamen simply stared out through the streaming windows at the storm. The captain prowled softly for a few minutes, checking the compass bearing, engine speed and wind direction. He picked up and read the latest radio weather reports. The forecast gave no let-up in the foul weather for at least another eighteen hours. The captain silently cursed. Two days' fishing already lost, and another day at least before they could cast a net.

Dropping the depressing message slips back on the table, the captain moved forward to stare through the forward window, keeping company with his men as they watched the grey-black mountains of sea crashing over the labouring bows of the *Yenisei*. Outside the glass was an insane world of raging water; water pouring down vertically in black curtains from the cloud-swamped sky, cross-streams of wind-whipped rain and spray hurled horizontally across the decks, and on all sides the huge, angry waves looming in monstrous proportions.

The storm was rapidly building up to a new peak. After a few moments of thoughtful consideration, the captain reached a decision. He would allow Second Officer Savenkova to take over the bridge. His junior officer was showing promise and needed only time and a little more learning to fit him for promotion. The coming hours would provide valuable experience. Savenkova could give the orders and make the decisions, all under the watchful eye of the captain, of course.

'Comrade Kotov,' he addressed one of the two lookouts. 'Go to the second officer's cabin. Give my compliments to Comrade Savenkova and ask him to attend on the bridge.'

Kotov had spent two hours alternately gazing out of the windows at the storm and down at the small radar screen in front of him. Boredom had set in; but at least it was dry in the wheelhouse. He made a gruff acknowledgement and turned up the hood of his oilskin jacket before plunging reluctantly out into the flailing rain.

The captain moved a pace sideways to keep one eye on the radar screen until Kotov returned. The illuminated radial line was making clean sweeps of the softly glowing green screen, indicating that the *Yenisei* was alone on this particular patch of ocean. There was no other ship in the vicinity to cause a possible collision, and no near land mass. The trawler was rolling heavily and taking a savage pounding from the storm, but she was in no danger.

The captain relaxed, feet apart, arms folded, letting his body sway with the motion of the ship. His most pressing thought at that moment, and the last complacent thought that would ever occupy his mind, was to send Kotov back to the galley for hot coffee as soon as he reappeared.

Kotov had given vent to a spate of cursing as soon as he was out of earshot of the wheelhouse, which meant as soon as he had closed the door behind him. The wind whipped the useless words from his grumbling lips and chased them out into the roaring darkness. Kotov swallowed a mouthful of rain and wisely decided to keep his mouth shut from now on. He hung on to the handrail and groped his way back along the slippery deck, knowing he could very easily be swept overboard if he did not take care.

He reached the cabin and knocked on the closed door. There was no response. Impatiently he hammered again, bruising his knuckles and cursing the noise of the storm. Finally he pulled open the door and poked his head inside, shouting Savenkova's name.

Technically it was dawn, but the black thunderclouds and the sheeting rain blotted out all but a faint filtering of grey, which was the only indication that the earth had completed another rotation and the sun was actually higher than the eastern horizon. Beneath the swirling mass of rain clouds the sun could not penetrate and it was almost as dark as night. Inside the cabin, the darkness was total.

Kotov mumbled his own scathing views on the ancestry and intelligence of deaf, thick-headed officers who could sleep like the dead, and groped around the inside bulkhead for a light switch. His fingers found it and the light clicked on.

Kotov blinked, his unshaven jaw dropped and his mouth hung open. Then fear and nausea surged up from his stomach as though powered by an express elevator, and exploded in a scream of strangled terror from his throat.

The scream was heard very faintly in the wheelhouse,

but was none the less audible even over the nightmare roaring of the storm. Captain and helmsman looked at each other doubtfully, wondered what they had heard, or even *if* they had heard it. Storm sounds, they both knew, could be deceiving. The captain turned his back on the rain-smeared view of the plunging bows to look at the door. In the same second the door burst open and Kotov stumbled inside, almost sprawling headlong on the deck in his haste.

Kotov had taken two minutes to make his cautious outward journey, but only ten fear-crazed seconds to make his desperate flight back. His face was drained white and his arms waved in panic-driven frenzy as he babbled incoherently about the *Thing!* in Savenkova's cabin.

The master of the *Yenisei* grabbed the luckless sailor by the shoulders and shook him, but the shaking served no useful purpose. With the wheelhouse door left banging open and the storm noise driving inside with all the ferocity of a passing locomotive, it was impossible to make any sense out of Kotov's ravings. Obviously the man was in a state of shock. Impatiently the captain pushed him aside, called on the second duty seaman on the bridge to follow him, and hurried off to investigate for himself.

The door to the second officer's cabin was also swinging open, hurled to and fro by the wind, which threatened to tear it bodily from its shrieking hinges. The captain grabbed the door to hold it open and stared inside the cabin. The seaman who had followed him blundered into him from behind as he stopped short, and gaped over his shoulder.

The cabin light had been left on and both men experienced the same shock of horror and revulsion that had caused Kotov to scream. The old sea-dog from Riga was made of sterner stuff, and would not have been captain if he had not been able to keep a cool head and remain calm in a crisis; but even his face turned a sick and blotchy grey behind his beard. The seaman behind him made a gagging noise and pulled away.

The scene inside was like an alien jungle. The death-seed plant, gorged on blood and grown to monstrous proportions, now filled more than half the cabin with its dense mass of huge, velvety-green leaves and thick, writhing tendrils. Its roots were curled firmly round the bunk supports and the legs of a small table bolted to the floor. The petals of the little blue flowers, the camouflage which had made it so attractive when small, had been discarded in the early stages of growth, and now it was a purely malevolent and monstrous freak of nature which swayed and rustled with unmistakable menace. Caught in the tangle of its coils, held as though in a grotesque and obscene lover's embrace, was the crushed corpse of Aleksandr Savenkova. With every roll of the ship the dead man's face lolled towards the cabin door, eyeballs bulging, the lips peeled back from grinning teeth in a mouth wide open in distorted agony. Every last drop of blood had been drained from the waxy, grey-white skin.

'Holy mother of God,' the captain breathed at last. As a good communist he was not supposed to have any religious faith, but he was a sailor first, a Russian second, and only then a communist. As a sailor he lived close to the sea and the power of the elements, and like most sailors he was a God-fearing man. He stared at the abomination which had somehow invaded his ship, and finished weakly: 'What in God's name is that?'

There was only the seaman at his shoulder to answer, but the man could only shake his head dumbly. He was trembling and biting his lip.

All around them the storm raged, and the decks heaved under their feet, but for the moment the storm was forgotten. It was as though the whole torrential universe had shrunk away to nothing, leaving only the nightmare scene in the cabin before them. Every stark and dreadful detail was etched upon their consciousness. The plant flicked the tip of its tendrils in an enticing, curling movement, as though sensing they were out of range and willing them to come closer.

The horror was *waiting* for them, the captain realized. It was still *hungry*. Somehow it had been feeding upon the poor mangled corpse of Savenkova; perhaps it still was. The thought was one the captain could not tolerate. He had no way of knowing what this vile miscreation might be, or where it could have come from, but he would not stand idly by while it continued calmly to make a meal of one of his officers.

He turned to the seaman behind him and said hoarsely, 'Go below. Fetch the bo'sun. I want three men up here, all armed with axes. And bring one axe for me! We must kill this thing and retrieve Comrade Savenkova's remains.'

The man nodded and hurried away, needing no further prompting, while the captain remained in the cabin doorway, watching the giant plant and trying to judge the length of its tendrils. He guessed the longest of the snaking green arms to be up to eight foot from its arm-thick base to its hair-fine tip, and he was careful to stay out of reach. He had no intention of getting to grips with the thing until he had some suitably sharp weapon in his hand.

Savenkova was still dressed in his yellow oilskins, but before dying his frantic struggles had been sufficiently violent to tear open the thick, coarse material in a dozen places. Through the rents, especially where the coils had tightened, the captain could see that the dead man's clothing was stained dark brown with dried blood, as though the flesh beneath had burst open under pressure.

There were also dark brown rivulets trailing from the corners of Savenkova's mouth. The captain realized that the plant must have crushed his second officer the way a strong man might crush a lemon, squeezing out the juices until the flesh was dry.

How loud had Savenkova screamed behind the closed door of the cabin, his screams unheard due to the tumult of the storm? And how long had he fought before he had died so horribly?

The captain's morbid reflections were cut short by a clatter of movement behind him. He turned and saw three men scrambling up the steel companionway from the deck below, their progress hampered by the almost solid downpour of rain and by the howling winds that sought to pluck them off the ship and hurl them bodily into the sea. The *Yenisei* rolled violently to starboard and the captain was reminded that his ship was still fighting a hurricane.

But, the grisly business in the cabin would not wait. The captain was determined to finish it quickly. The first man to reach him was the ship's bo'sun, a big, burly man who ruled the lower decks with an iron fist. Clinging to the handrails with one hand, in the other he gripped the hafts of two long fire-axes. The captain took the spare axe from the bo'sun's hand and pointed with it inside the lighted cabin.

'In there,' he said grimly. 'I don't know what kind of evil this thing is, but we're going to attack it, cut it to pieces and destroy it. I intend to recover the second officer's body for a decent burial.'

The bo'sun looked stunned, but swallowed hard and nodded. His big knuckles whitened as he took a firm grip on his axe. Of the two sailors who accompanied the bo'sun, one was the on-duty seaman from the bridge who had been sent below with the message. He had seen the horror before and hung back. The second sailor turned pale and his eyes rolled wide open in disbelief.

The captain advanced cautiously into the cabin. The bo'sun moved up beside him. Very reluctantly the two sailors brought up the rear. The plant became agitated, its leaves rustling and the tendrils beginning to wave threateningly in the air. The captain was poised to rush in and strike a blow with his axe when a huge wave hit the *Yenisei* on the port bow. The trawler made another steep, lurching roll to starboard, and all four men were caught off balance and thrown sideways into a sliding heap. One of the plant's longest tendrils lashed out with lightning speed and fastened on the bo'sun's arm.

In that same moment, although he did not know it yet, the captain had lost another member of his crew. The sailor Kotov had stayed in the wheelhouse, where the mystified helmsman had continued to try and coax out of him a sensible account of what he had seen. For several minutes Kotov could only splutter helplessly, unable to describe the hideous scene in Savenkova's cabin. It was, he insisted, some kind of man-eating plant which had killed the second officer, snaring him like a human fly in a hideous green web. To the helmsman the story sounded incredible, but to Kotov the memory was only too stark and real. Recalling the horrific details he felt a sudden urge to vomit, and in his anguish he stumbled out of the wheelhouse and back into the storm. Almost losing his footing on the slippery deck, he reeled towards the bridge handrail and held on with both hands as he retched. It was at that moment the big wave hit, the rising angle of the deck tilting Kotov towards the sea. The wind tore him loose from the rail and in a split-second he was lost, swallowed up by the darkness and the icy black seas.

The helmsman was left alone in the wheelhouse, unable to leave his post, yelling vainly for Kotov to come back, and wondering desperately what was happening behind him. Kotov had left the door banging open again and faintly, above the clamour of the storm, the helmsman heard another distant scream, which only added to his concern and confusion.

In fact Kotov had been swept away with vomit in his throat, rendering him soundless as well as helpless. Instead, the scream had come from the second officer's cabin, where the four men with axes were now engaged in a desperate battle with the outsize deathseed plant.

The captain had been quick to strike the first blow, hacking off the tendril which had seized the bo'sun while it lay close to the deck. However, it was only one lucky cut, and it proved to be less easy to use the axes with good effect when there was nothing solid behind the writhing tentacles to take the impact of the blade. All the time the plant was shaking in defensive fury, swishing its thick leaves and branches to and fro and deflecting many of the wildly swung axe blows. The flailing tendrils had the consistency of thick rubber, and if the cutting edge of the axe did not bite at the correct angle the flat of the blade would bounce or slide harmlessly away. The efforts of the four assailants were also restricted by the confined space, and by the captain's instructions to refrain from chopping at the dead body of Savenkova.

The inevitable happened. One of the sailors made a desperate, ill-judged lunge. The axe blade was deflected and continued on a wild, uncontrolled swing around the cabin, finishing up embedded deep in the bo'sun's thigh. It was his shriek of agony which was heard in the wheelhouse by the helmsman. The axe blade jerked free and the luckless bo'sun staggered to the bulkhead, where the blood gushed in a red wave from the gaping wound.

As the sweet, thick smell of blood filled the cabin the plant exploded into a tendril-thrashing frenzy. A lashing blow that failed to get a hold knocked the captain sprawling, and another tendril fastened round the neck of the nearest seaman. Instantly the man was hauled into the plant's embrace and more tendrils locked around him. The sailor screamed in a blood-curdling blend of pain and mortal terror.

On the bridge the helmsman was biting his lip, leaning back from the wheel and twisting round to peer into the rain-filled blackness beyond the open door. Straining his ears, he picked up the storm-muffled sound of more screaming, and could bear the suspense no longer. The racing winds and the hurricane seas had been bearing down consistently from north-north-west and for the past hour his task had been simply to hold the wheel in one position, keeping the vessel's bows into the teeth of the wind with no variation of heading. Now he took a fateful risk. Taking a length of thick cord from his pocket, he set about lashing the wheel in place.

He stepped back, his hands free at last, and waited a moment to ensure that the lashing would hold. The wheel creaked and groaned, but did not move. Turning, the helmsman hurried out of the wheelhouse to find out for himself what was happening. He knew he was committing a cardinal sin in leaving the wheel unattended, but he had to know, and he did not anticipate being absent for more than a few seconds.

There was no sign of Kotov, but the helmsman had no time to ponder on the fate of the missing man. Guided by the screams, he raced to the second officer's cabin – and all his questions were answered. The hellish spectacle which met his gaze proved that all of Kotov's incredible babblings had been true. Except that now the picture was even more horrific. In addition to the dead corpse of Savenkova, the nightmare plant now had one of the struggling sailors enmeshed firmly in its coils. Another tendril had curled around the bo'sun's injured leg and was dragging the screaming man across the deck, leaving a slick of wet blood behind him. The captain was still endeavouring to wield his axe without striking the bodies of his entangled crew, but he was the only one still fighting. The fourth man in the cabin had backed off and was pressing his shoulders hard into a corner of the bulkheads, his eyes glazed and his whole body paralysed with fear.

The helmsman picked up a fire-axe dropped by one of the sailors, but paused before joining battle with the killer plant. Instead, he chose what seemed to be a better course of action. He ran back along the deck to the captain's cabin, burst his way inside, and launched an immediate axe attack on the locked cabinet on the bulkhead where the captain was permitted by the Soviet marine authorities to keep two revolvers for emergencies. The wooden panels splintered under the biting steel blade and he levered them frantically out of the way. Throwing down the axe, he snatched up one of the revolvers, but then hesitated. Was it loaded? If not, how were you supposed to load it? He fumbled for a way to break open the bullet chamber, but it was a problem he was fated never to resolve.

The wind had shifted, veering suddenly to blow from due north-west, and the huge seas began to pile up on the *Yenisei*'s port bow. As each succeeding wave sought to push her head over, the strain on the thin cord holding the wheel became too much. It snapped, and the wheel spun free. Immediately the *Yenisei*'s bows began to yaw round to starboard, bringing the ship's hull broadside-on to the storm.

Given another few minutes the ship's captain might have won his desperate battle with the deathseed plant. The tendrils had now released the dry corpse of Savenkova and were fully occupied with holding on to their new prey. Both the bo'sun and the half-strangled sailor were still struggling for their lives, and with the tendrils straining to keep a hold on them, the captain found he was able to move into close quarters, where there was no other axe in play and swing his own axe to better effect. He had changed his tactics and was now chopping at the roots anchoring the plant to the bunk and table, where there was something solid for the axe to bite on. Each time a root was severed, the movements of the tendrils became less powerful. Like a python, the plant needed an anchorage before it could exert its full crushing strength.

Unfortunately the captain had learned how to fight the plant too late. He felt the movement of the ship as the head slewed round and the deck canted beneath his feet. He was thrown back to the doorway and lowered his axe, realizing that his entire ship was now in deadly danger.

The bo'sun read his mind and screamed at him, pleading, but it was to no avail. Instinctively the ship's master knew where his first duty lay. He felt a deep sense of anguish, but no hesitation. He threw his axe within reach of the bo'sun's hand, giving the man a last chance to save himself, and then turned and raced with new desperation for the bridge.

When he had felt the movement of the ship, the helmsman too had recognized its terrible portent and his own unforgivable mistake. He dropped the revolver he had intended to use against the plant and ran to regain his post. He collided with the captain as he came out of the other's cabin, and in that moment both of them almost lost their footing and narrowly avoided being swept over the side.

They untangled themselves and the captain ran on to the bridge. Right now there was no time for cursing and reprimands. He crashed into the wheelhouse, saw the wheel still spinning and made a grab for it, but as he did so, one of the heavy wooden spokes cracked into his wrist and snapped the bone. He yelled with the pain but his other arm succeeded in checking the wheel. Then the helmsman was beside him, and with three hands they struggled to bring the trawler's bows back into the storm.

The ship's first officer had dropped into a heavy sleep and had remained blissfully unaware throughout the preceding drama. But no true sailor could sleep as his ship lurched and rolled towards oblivion. The first officer woke and his instinct brought him hurrying back to the bridge. Though his brain was still fuddled and he could not even guess at how this situation had come about, he could see the first necessary course of action. He threw his weight on to the wheel with the others, and all three fought to avert disaster.

Their combined weight was too much. A rudder cable snapped under the strain and abruptly the three men were flung sideways to the deck, leaving the wheel to spin loose. The ship wallowed helplessly. Their destiny was no longer theirs to command.

The *Yenisei* was rolled like a toy in a bathtub, the great waves smashing into her exposed flank. As her starboard deck rails went under, a towering freak wave reared up and crashed down in a thundering avalanche of water on her port side. Under that onslaught, broadside-on in the trough of the wave, the *Yenisei* floundered helplessly, and the bridge went under. The wheelhouse windows shattered and the sea poured in. Now she was bows down and sliding forward, still turning like a corkscrew, her propeller blades thrashing for a few seconds but meeting nothing but spray and rain. Finally she was gone. The sea buried her, cleanly and without trace.

The final act of the drama had unfolded so swiftly that there had been no time even to think of launching a lifeboat. On her short, sharp voyage to the ocean floor, the *Yenisei* took down every man on board. There were no survivors – except for a few tiny spores of the death-seed plant, now travelling fast on the wet, racing winds, due south towards the lonely rocky outpost of Lairg Island.

CHAPTER EIGHT

Lairg Island was a wind-battered, sea-indented oval, roughly a mile in length from the south headland to the north cliffs. From east to west at its widest point it was a bare three-quarters of a mile across. The south headland was a bald shoulder rising a hundred feet above sea level, and from there the land sloped down before rising again in a series of steep grassy hills. There were steep cliffs on the north-east and west sides of the island, but nothing to match the awesome splendour of the sheer five- and six-hundred-foot drops to the pounding sea at the north end. Here three spectacular stacks rose in mighty pinnacles of wind and sea-carved rock, like stone sentries waiting to take the first brunt of the furious Arctic gales.

A rough path led from the landing cove to the grey, stone-built cottage in the hollow, beyond the brow of the first hill. It was the best part of a quarter-mile haul for the Gordons and their stores and luggage, and because they had to make three trips it turned out to be a tiresome business. Whoever had built the cottage had preferred to have a small amount of shelter from the winds than proximity to the landing stage.

The cottage was thatched, giving it a crude and shaggy look at first approach. The chimney stack built on to the gable end was short, stubby and solid – anything slender or elegant would have been blown away by the winter storms – and even in warm sunlight the building had a hunched, scared look. *Primitive*, was Valerie's heart-sinking first thought. She had the feeling they had stepped back over a hundred years.

Barry unlocked the heavy wooden door and let them in. There were two large rooms at ground level, a living room and a kitchen. Both were white-washed with low, black-beamed ceilings. There was a large open fireplace in the living room with a heavy oak mantelpiece. The furniture was all hand-made; in the kitchen a solid pine-wood dresser with a matching table and four wooden chairs; in the living room, another wooden table and wooden armchairs, the latter upholstered only by cushions. All of it looked as though it might have been shaped from driftwood washed up on the island's beaches. There were no wall-to-wall carpets, but plenty of thick pile rugs to cover the bare flagstones.

'It's like Robinson Crusoe's house,' Jonathon declared, with ten-year-old authority and approval.

'It's a lovely old place,' Barry agreed. 'Hang up some fancy horse brasses, a few framed prints, fit a bar, and we'd have ourselves a smashing *Olde Englishe* pub.'

'It's bloody primitive,' Valerie muttered to herself inaudibly, and she knew Simon Lancing would have agreed with her.

The children explored ahead of them, running up the wooden staircase and dashing from bedroom to bedroom, Jonathon's voice shouting the loudest as he made each new discovery. There were three white-washed bedrooms, whose ceiling beams were even lower than on the ground floor. Barry had to duck his head to enter each room. The beds were flat wooden boxes containing mattresses – like the cabin bunks of an old ship, as Jonathon was quick to observe – and each bed was covered with a brightly-coloured hand-knitted patchwork quilt. They had brought their own sheets, but piles of thick grey blankets were stored in the bedroom cupboards.

The two smaller bedrooms looked out north and south on to bare grass slopes, but the large main bedroom had an end window which looked west to another small cove and the sea, only a few hundred yards away. Barry gazed out, exulting in the fact that he could watch the sunsets and the seabirds in flight without even getting out of bed.

They went downstairs again, back to the living room. Julia was fascinated by the large brass oil-lamp hanging over the fireplace, and by the big copper kettle and the straw basket filled with cut and dried peat turves which stood by the hearth. Jonathon seized upon the mantelshelf ornaments – a carved whalebone, a ram's horn, and a matchstick ship in a whisky bottle, his excitement mounting with each find.

'Some of this stuff would fetch a damned good price in an antique shop,' Barry said cheerfully. 'Look at that old spinning-wheel in the corner!'

Valerie could have told her husband that she had no desire to live in an antique shop, but the children's eyes were shining and she refrained from spoiling their fun. Instead, she returned to the kitchen. Christ! Was she really expected to *cook* on that stove? She went in search of what other basic amenities the cottage had to offer, and found them in a more recent extension built on to the north wall beneath a roof of grey slates. Here there was a long tin bathtub and a large enamelled sink for washing clothes, both of which obviously had to be filled and emptied by hand. Four tin buckets of fresh water stood on a stone bench, no doubt drawn as a goodwill gesture by the neighbouring shepherd. Through the small window she could see the outside well pump which appeared to be the only source of water. Behind a door, in a separate corner of the extension, she found an elsan-type camping toilet.

Barry met her as she came back into the house. He was carrying a blackened metal kettle from the hob which he thrust automatically into her unresisting hand.

'Found the water, Val? Good girl! Put the kettle on and make a cup of tea while we unpack. Then we'll have a couple of sandwiches and take a walk across the island to say hello to our neighbours. We ought at least to give the chap his mail as soon as possible.'

He flashed her a smile and disappeared back to the children. Valerie leaned against the stone wall, holding the kettle, and briefly closed her eyes. Simon's voice echoed in her memory, charming and courteous – '*A sherry, Val? Or a martini? Gin and tonic maybe, if it's not too early?*' But that was Simon. With Barry, it was just put the kettle on and make the tea.

An hour later they were walking across the island, following the hollow between the hills and guided by the grey chimney just visible behind the bend. Jonathon scrambled enthusiastically up the hill slopes on either side, running between the clumps of thick, wiry heather and shouting back reports from each vantage point. There were no trees on the island, but wild flowers made tiny splashes of white and yellow, and soon they began to encounter the odd sheep grazing placidly on the patches of lush green grass.

Above their heads the raucous gulls made white-winged kaleidoscope patterns in the blue sky, and Barry was quick to note a small flock of redshanks, two curlews with their distinctive long, curved bills, some lapwings in flight, and a diminutive brown bird almost hidden in the heather which he was sure could only be a Shetland wren. He was carrying the box of stores the mailboat had left for the Mathesons on his shoulder, and had to resist the temptation to drop it every few seconds in order to grab the binoculars or camera hanging against his chest.

When the Mathesons' cottage came into view they saw that it was of grey stone and thatch, exactly like their own. The only outward difference was in the spiral of smoke curling up from the chimney, suggesting warmth and comfort inside. The two cottages were a little less than half a mile apart and beyond the Matheson cottage the sea was immediately visible again.

Their first sight of Ross Matheson was heralded by the excited barking of a dog, and inevitably it was Jonathon, patrolling ahead on the brow of the hill, who made the first contact. Barry looked up to see his son run forward to meet a large black and white collie which came bounding over the hilltop. A moment later Jonathon was staggering backward under the animal's weight, its forepaws bearing down on his shoulders and he pushed back its head and patted its neck.

'Good boy, good boy,' Jonathon shouted. His voice delighted and unafraid. 'Good dog. Down boy.'

'Be careful,' Barry called quickly, realizing that the dog would be unaccustomed to strangers. 'Back off him, Jon. He might bite.'

The shepherd appeared from behind the hill. He was a solidly built man of average height, wearing a grey check jacket with leather patches sewn at the cuffs and elbows. Beneath the jacket he wore a heavy wool rollneck jersey and hard-wearing corduroy trousers. The trousers were tucked into black wellington boots and on his head he wore a flat, grey check cap. To Barry he looked surprisingly like a young country squire.

'It's all right, lad, Robbie'll not harm you.' His voice was as slow and calm as his smile. 'I've seen him nip a sheep just enough to turn her in the right direction, but I've never known him to hurt another living thing. At heart he's as gentle as the lambs.'

'He's smashing,' Jonathon enthused. 'I wish I had a dog like him.' He allowed the collie to lick his hand, tickling its ear and laughing. 'Robbie, hey Robbie, I've had one wash already this morning!'

Matheson's smile broadened and he pushed the dog down, giving its head a good-natured ruffle. Then they came down the hill together, the dog racing ahead to sniff around the rest of the new arrivals.

'Thanks for bringing these over,' Matheson said, after they had introduced themselves, pocketing his letters. 'Normally, I'd meet the mailboat myself, but this morning I had to rescue a sheep with its foot trapped in some heather roots up near the east cliffs. That's the trouble with sheep – they've no sense. If there's a way for an animal to get itself stuck, a sheep'll find it.'

'The captain guessed right,' Barry observed. 'He said only a sheep in trouble would keep you from meeting the boat.'

'Aye, he knows me well enough. Luckily for this sheep Robbie heard her bleating, so he came to fetch me. It was just before the boat was due.' He patted the collie's neck with affection. 'He's a good dog with the sheep, is Robbie.'

'What about your wife?' Valerie asked curiously. She couldn't understand how a woman could live this isolated life and not be desperate to see any passing human faces.

'It'll be the sickness, I expect,' Matheson said, in the placid, matter-of-fact tone which on the surface seemed to sum up his whole character and attitude to life. 'She wasn't too well when I left this morning. Come on to the house and you'll meet her.'

He turned and led the way to the cottage, picking up the box of stores, which Barry had lowered in order to shake hands. Barry walked with him, chatting sociably, while Jonathon cemented his friendship with the dog, and Valerie brought up the rear with Julia, her heart sinking again. Barry had been too polite to pick up on Matheson's casual reference to his wife's sickness, but Valerie knew it would be just her luck to be stranded on an island whose only other female inhabitant was already stricken by the galloping plague or some highly contagious disease.

In the event, Valerie's fears were unfounded. Janet Matheson had watched them approach from a window and came to the cottage door to meet them. She was in her mid-twenties, neither pretty nor plain, but giving out the softly radiant glow of a woman well content with fulfilling her natural role. Matheson's reference to her sickness was immediately explained by her distended waistline. Janet Matheson was heavily pregnant – at least eight months so, by Valerie's experienced eye. Her premature animosity quickly vanished in a surge of fellow-feeling.

The introductions were made again. Barry rejected 'Mister Gordon' as far too formal and insisted the island couple use their christian names.

Matheson smiled his easy-natured smile. 'If that's to be, then we're Ross and Janet.'

They were invited in for tea and spent a pleasant hour getting to know their new neighbours. The interior of the Mathesons' cottage was much the same as their own, but had a more cosy, lived-in- appearance. There were wedding and family photographs on the mantelshelf, framed pictures on the walls, and shelves full of books; a wide range of novels and poetry, and big illustrated books on household crafts and natural history. There was no TV set, since there was no electricity, but pride of place on the handsome polished sideboard was given to a large, battery-powered radio and cassette-player. Janet was almost childishly pleased to discover that among the stores the Gordons had brought over were a supply of new batteries and three new cassettes she had ordered.

The Mathesons were a much younger couple than they had expected, and Jonathon remarked on it. 'I thought you were going to be an old man,' he told Ross Matheson, 'with a white beard and a crooked stick, like in the Bible.'

FLOWERS OF EVIL

Ross smiled. 'Then you should have come four years ago. The man you're looking for was my father. He was alive then – a grand old man, he was, with a white beard. And he knew his Bible too. He didn't carry a crooked stick, though.'

'What happened to him?'

'Jonathon,' Valerie reproved. 'You shouldn't ask so many questions.'

'It's all right,' Ross said. 'He died, that's all. The gales and the rain and the winds finally got him. Bronchial pneumonia, the doctor said it was.'

'Is that when you came here?' Julia asked.

'I was born here,' said Ross. 'In the house across the island where you're staying now. That was my father's house. I left to go to Mainland when I was a young lad. There was nothing here for me, so I lived and worked in Lerwick for a while. It was there I met Janet. A year or so before my father died he found he was getting too old to scramble over the north rocks after the sheep, so I came back to help him out. This house had been standing empty then for several years, so after he died I stayed on to tend the sheep. Now I'm the shepherd.'

'Will you stay here for the rest of your life?' Jonathon asked.

'Perhaps one day we'll leave,' Ross said wistfully. But the dream, if such it was, was faint and uncertain. He had made one youthful break from the island, but it was obvious that deep down he was firmly rooted to his lonely life.

'What about you?' Valerie asked Janet. 'Don't you ever want to go back to Lerwick? Don't you miss the shops and the people?'

'Aye, I miss the shops sometimes. I worked in a shop before we were married. But my place is with Ross now. Where he's happy, I'm happy.'

'But surely you'll go back to Mainland to have your

baby?' Valerie knew she was doing exactly what she had told Jonathon not to do, but she was genuinely concerned over the young woman's condition. 'You can't have it here, alone. You'll have to go to hospital, surely?'

'Oh, I dare say Ross would manage well enough if he had to. He delivers the lambs when the mothers get into difficulty.' Janet laughed. 'But no – I'll go back to Lerwick the next time the mailboat calls. The baby's not due for another month, so the next trip will be soon enough. I don't want to leave Ross for any longer than I have to. He'll find it lonely here without me.'

'Well, if you do need any help before the mailboat comes, be sure to call me. I've had two of my own so I know a little bit about it.'

'That's very kind of you, but there shouldn't be any need to bother you. We wouldn't want to spoil your holiday.'

'It'll be no bother – and you won't spoil anything,' Valerie assured her. She turned to Ross. 'You know where to find me. If she needs any help, make sure you come and fetch me. Promise?'

Ross smiled. 'I promise. And thank you. As Janet says, the mailboat should be back well before the baby's due, but it's good to have another woman on the island all the same.'

As they spoke, Barry was pleased to discover that Ross was a mine of information on the island's bird life. Other ornithologists had rented the empty cottage for short periods since the older Matheson had died, and so bird talk was a familiar topic for him.

Julia also found something to excite her. She noticed an old violin, worn and polished by use, resting in the corner, and Janet told her it was a family heirloom which Ross played passably well. Following immediately after horses and ponies, Julia's second current passion was music. She had played the recorder in school concerts and was learning to play the clarinet. Ross told her to call round any evening and he would 'Fiddle her a reel'.

When they left it was with a standing invitation for any of them to call round at any time. Ross accompanied them to the door, talking for a few more minutes as he pointed out the low stone walls built to protect his cabbage and potato patches, and the long, part-walled and part-fenced corral, where the sheep sheltered from the worst of the winter gales.

'Most of the time the sheep fend for themselves,' Ross told them. 'But when it's really bad the winds would blow them clean off the island. That's the only time they come into the corral. If they're near enough to see it, they make their own way. If not, Robbie and I round up the strays.'

Barry proposed that instead of taking the short, direct route back to their own cottage they should take a longer walk round the perimeter of the island. Ross made his apologies for not acting as guide, but he had been up since dawn and was overdue for his midday meal. However, he smiled his slow smile and assured them that Lairg was hardly big enough to get lost in. He found them a walking stick each to deflect any dive-bombing tactics by the great skuas on the north cliffs, and warned them against the fulmars, which were liable to spit an evil-smelling fluid at anyone who disturbed their nest.

They waved him good-bye and began their walk, with Robbie bounding along beside them for the first ten minutes, much to Jonathon's delight. The sea, a glittering, magnetic blue in the afternoon sun, drew them down to the nearest cove on the east side of the island, where they found a long, narrow, crescent-curved beach of white pebbles and sand, sprinkled with small pools among the rocks and rounded boulders at either end. Scores of oyster-catchers were in evidence, large black and white birds probing the rocks and pools for shellfish with their long, coral-red beaks. Less distinctive but equally numerous were the smaller sandpipers and waders. In less than a minute Barry had counted a dozen different species of ducks, gulls and terns.

When they resumed their walk, they followed the coastline to the north, passing two more small rocky coves before the cliffs began to rise steeply in height. Inland were green pastures where the sheep grazed in small groups between tangles of heather and rocks, but as they climbed higher toward the northern tip of the island the terrain became rougher. In places they passed strips of bare black earth, and Barry guessed that it was here Ross came to cut his peat turves for the fire.

On the seaward side, the cliffs became more stark and dramatic with every twist and turn of the coastline, with a continually lengthening drop down to the sea, which crashed in white breakers and sparkling spray-curtains on the jagged black rocks below. The fantastic bird population also became more crowded and varied, with nests wedged into every crack and cranny, piled along the multitude of ledges, and seemingly plastered on to the sheer face of the rock. There were colonies of razorbills, guillemots, shags, auks, gulls and gannets, noisy and bustling, thronging the cliffs in thousands. Plainly they were the dominant life species of the island.

Jonathon was as ecstatic as Barry, and had to be physically restrained from rushing too close to every new, fascinating and precipitous drop. Julia was appreciative too, and even Valerie began to thaw a little inside and concede that the island did have a wild and spectacular beauty. If she couldn't escape the bird-watchers, she might as well join them – after all, this had to be the ultimate ornithological experience.

On the north-east cliffs they found great flocks of kittiwakes, so Barry promptly named them the kittiwake cliffs.

They turned here toward the north cliffs, the highest point of the island, and saw the first of the three great stacks, rising like some colossal, crudely-hacked monument from the pounding sea.

'Gosh,' Jonathon said, in awe. 'It's as big as the post office tower in London.'

'Nearly as big,' Barry said. 'And look at the birds.'

The stack was alive with seabirds, swarming all over it and filling the sky above and on all sides with fluttering white wings, like great snow flakes and silver streamers whirling around some splendid natural maypole.

The remaining two stacks were smaller but equally impressive, and again they formed the home of thousands of seabirds nesting on every ledge and crevice. The great skuas ruled the bleak heights, gulls occupied the middle levels, and guillemots and razorbills inhabited the wave-drenched caves and caverns at sea level.

They turned back along the west side of the island, the cliffs descending in height and finally giving way to a series of small coves with sand or pebble beaches. Here, on a series of grassy slopes, Julia found her dream come true. Several hundred pairs of puffins had made their homes in burrows in the soft earth.

The last of the small west-side coves was the one they had first seen from the bedroom window of their cottage, and they lingered there to watch the sun set behind ragged banks of purple, crimson and gold-laced cloud. For a few moments the sun was suspended between the cloud and the horizon, making a broad highway of molten bronze across the heaving sea. Then it was gone, and the seabirds were black, homecoming shadows in the deepening dusk.

They returned to the cottage, lit the oil-lamps, and busied themselves with preparations for the evening meal. Jonathon and Julia chattered together, for once agreeing instead of arguing as they recounted the delights of the island. Barry too was in a fine mood. Their first taste of Lairg had lived up to all his expectations.

'I'm going to enjoy writing this book,' he told Valerie. 'And you should be able to enjoy a nice, restful holiday.'

Valerie agreed, but doubtfully. She was still reserving judgement on that.

Barry smiled at her and went back to the living room and the children. In that moment, Valerie had a sharp flash of intuition and glanced up quickly from the frying pan full of bacon, sausages and eggs to stare at his retreating back. It suddenly seemed to her that Barry was more than pleased with their total isolation, and that his smile had been somehow *knowing*. Was it possible that Barry knew about her and Simon?

She found herself once again comparing her lover and her husband, wondering how each of them would deal with an unfaithful woman. Simon might slap her face and make a splendid scene, or walk majestically out of her life, or give her a masterful spanking and tell her not to do it again. With Barry she was not so sure. But she knew it would not be beyond her husband to have deliberately marooned her here, just to keep her out of her lover's reach.

CHAPTER NINE

The first lung-tearing screech carried clearly up to the fourth floor, penetrating the closed window and the drawn curtains of Galina's bedroom. The time was midmorning, and enough sunlight had filtered through to fill the room with soft shadows. Galina was dozing, luxuriating in the cosy, shared warmth of her bed, and the simple pleasure of being lazy and lying in late. It was her day off. She opened her eyes with a start, staring up at the blank ceiling. Her body stiffened and her fists clenched tight as she gripped the bedclothes. From somewhere outside and below, there came the sound of hysterical screaming. And it went on, and on, and on.

Ilya sat up beside her and for a moment they stared at each other, wide-eyed and uncertain. Then Ilya threw back the bedclothes and jumped out, naked, to hurry to the window. He jerked the curtains back and pressed his face to the glass. Unable to see clearly, he unhooked the catch and pushed open the window.

Galina joined him, and they both shivered as the cool, outside air breezed in to touch their bare bodies. They pushed their heads out as far as they dared, and looked down.

Almost immediately below them was the source of the screaming; a small, elderly woman in a dark brown, faded coat. Brown coats were common in Moscow, since it was rarely possible to buy anything that was not drab-coloured, but Galina recognized the wearer by her stature and her black widow's hat. It was the old lady from an apartment on the floor below. In common with millions of Russian women, she had lost her husband in the war many years before, and now in her final years her only friend and companion was the small, brown-and-white, mongrel dog which she walked twice daily around the block.

Two passing workmen had already reached the old woman, and more people were hurrying to the scene. The two men were trying to calm her, but the old woman was completely distraught. She was screaming and shaking her head, hands pressed to her face as though trying to shut out something she could not bear to see. As Galina and Ilya watched, the black hat fell off to reveal thinning strands of grey-white hair. There was no sign of the dog, but the cause of her distress was something hidden in the corner of the building, out of sight of the two observers at the fourth-floor window.

Galina drew back and began a frantic hunt for her clothes.

'It's poor old Katya,' she said, feeling a deep surge of compassion for the frail old woman who, without her hat, had suddenly seemed so vulnerable. 'I must go down and see what's wrong.'

Ilya nodded, and he too scrambled into his clothes. As soon as they were both dressed they hurried out of the apartment and down through the building.

By the time they emerged from the main doors, a small knot of curious and excited people had gathered around the old widow. The woman's hysteria and the piercing volume of her screams had abated, and now she was making a pitiful wailing sound, partially muffled as she hung half-collapsed in the arms of the two workmen.

Galina and Ilya pushed forward, circling the edge of the small crowd. The root of the disturbance, indicated by pointing fingers and shocked stares, was in the small flower bed in the corner of the main building walls. The summer marigolds were fading now and many of the yellow petals had already fallen, but behind them was something else, something with familiar velvety-green leaves obscuring a white and brown form.

As Galina had raced downstairs she had experienced a moment of foreboding, a deep, dark knot of suspicion in the pit of her stomach. Now that premonition was realized. Her hand flew to her mouth and her stomach heaved as she recognized another deathseed plant. It was identical to the one she had grown on her windowsill, the plant which Ilya had cut up and destroyed, except that this one was even bigger. It stood over two feet tall. And dead, but still warm in its clutches, was Katya's little brown and white mongrel. The first tendril had whipped around the unfortunate animal's throat and strangled it before it could even bark. The dog was crushed and still bleeding, each fresh drip of blood being quickly soaked up by the plant's hungry leaves, or by the brown-stained earth at its roots. Also entangled in the plant's coils were several small birds; a few sparrows, a linnet and a mistle thrush, all squeezed into scraps of bone and feathers, drained and dried, and several days old.

'Oh *no*,' Galina groaned in horror. 'It's another one.'

She turned away and clung to Ilya. For a moment he stared down over her shoulder, unable to tear his gaze away from the plant and its prey. Then, suddenly alarmed by the curious looks they were receiving, he tried to move away, to escape back into the building or at least blend in with the crowd.

He was too late. The busybody caretaker of the apartment block was there beside them and her sharp eyes and ears missed nothing.

'What do you mean, *another* one? What do you know of this?' she demanded.

'Nothing,' Galina protested unconvincingly. 'I don't know anything.'

'Oh yes, you do,' the bossy old harridan persisted. 'You said it's another one! That means you must know something we don't. What is this thing?'

'I don't know. I swear I don't know,' Galina wailed. But by now Katya had swooned, and all eyes were upon her and Ilya. The circle of previously hesitant faces had hardened with menace. All the eyes were full of suspicion.

'You all heard.' The caretaker turned to face the little crowd, appealing loudly for support, her strident, overbearing voice commanding their attention. 'She said, *it's another one*! They must know something about it.'

The faces nodded sombre agreement.

'It's no good going on at her,' Ilya snapped defensively. 'It's not her fault.'

'But you know something. We want to know what it is. Tell us!'

'No,' Ilya said firmly, much more firmly than he was actually feeling inside. He was realizing that things had got out of hand, and although his heart quailed at the thought, he knew what he had to do. It was what he should have done right at the start. 'Please,' he tried to push a way through the circle of bodies. 'I must make a telephone call.'

'Oh no.' The caretaker knew her duty too. 'If there are to be any telephone calls I'm the one who'll make them. I'll telephone the authorities. I'll call the police! Then maybe we'll see what this is all about.'

'It isn't a police matter.'

'*Everything is a police matter*,' the caretaker retorted with total conviction. She turned to the two workmen, who had now lowered Katya into a chair hastily brought out by another occupant of the building. 'Watch these two,' she ordered. 'They must wait here until the police arrive.' With that she marched off to make her telephone call, confident that she would be obeyed.

Ilya bit his lip and looked at the faces of the two workmen. They looked back uncomfortably but determinedly. Galina was trembling against him, and Ilya knew they were both in serious trouble. He tried to keep a bold face.

'I must use the telephone,' he told the two men. 'There are other state authorities who must be informed. I won't object if you come to the telephone with me.'

The two men looked at each other doubtfully, but Ilya had placed heavy stress upon the words "state authorities". One of the men finally nodded.

Ilya pulled at Galina's arm and all four of them followed the caretaker into the building. As they passed through the entrance doors Ilya said urgently, 'Galina, what's the number of Professor Shumilov's laboratory?'

The police arrived within ten minutes in the form of two grim-jowled, heavily-built men in dark overcoats and hats driving a large black car. For perhaps a further minute they stared down at the strange plant and the dead dog, masking their bafflement behind blank expressions. The caretaker reported her story, loud enough to impress everyone within hearing, and finished by giving herself a self-righteous, verbal pat on the back for correctly interpreting her duty as a citizen. She was somewhat peeved when the two policemen unceremoniously brushed her aside in order to concentrate on the two prime suspects.

Ilya and Galina were interrogated in the caretaker's ground-floor cubicle – after the aggrieved woman had been locked out – and here Galina promptly broke down and confessed the whole story. Ilya also confessed to his role in the affair, but added a strong protest to the effect that neither of them had actually done anything wrong. No crime had been committed, or intended.

Their defence created no noticeable impression on the two policemen, who only scowled more severely and asked more questions. One of the men stared at their identity cards, which had been demanded at the outset

FLOWERS OF EVIL

with a curt snap of the fingers, and which he obviously had no immediate intention of returning. The other wrote laboriously in a thick black notebook. Both men had intimidation down to a fine art.

When every last scrap of information had been wrung out of the two unfortunate young people, the notebook closed with a snap. But they knew it was too much to hope that it would end there. Dog-eating plants were not encountered every day on the streets of Moscow, and police procedures were rigid and inflexible. Comrades Kachenko and Savenkova were informed brusquely that they were required to accompany the two police officers to headquarters to assist with further enquiries.

Galina wept. Ilya protested. But the police were adamant, and the hapless pair were marched out to the black car.

Mercifully, Shumilov appeared in the nick of time. His car pulled up behind the police car and he hurried out to intercept the small procession as it crossed the pavement.

The policemen growled warily at his interference and instantly demanded his identity card.

Shumilov produced it. 'I am Professor Leonid Shumilov, senior professor of botany at the Soviet Academy of Scientists.' He delivered each word in ringing tones and drew himself up to his full height as he spoke. Unfortunately he proved to be several inches shorter than the two policemen, but to dare to stand up to the massive law and order machine of the state was something in itself. The men in dark coats read the card, rubbed their jowls doubtfully, and accorded him a grudging respect.

'This girl is my secretary,' Shumilov continued. 'She has been very foolish and I am very cross with her.' He gave Galina a glare which boded ill for later. 'But now you must release her into my custody. I will take full responsibility for her.'

'They must both come to headquarters,' the senior of the two insisted stolidly.

'Fools,' Shumilov snapped, to the gasping, unbelieving delight of the small crowd of spectators. 'What earthly good would it do for these young people to be further questioned by the police? No civil or state crime has been committed. And what possible use would you make of her information anyway?'

'It is still a police matter,' the senior man said stubbornly.

'Nonsense. It is a matter for science.' Shumilov was becoming exasperated, but he was still intrigued and excited by what Ilya had been able to tell him over the telephone. Suddenly, he could wait no longer: 'Where is the plant – and the dog it is supposed to have killed?'

'Over there.' Galina pointed.

'Come along, then.'

Shumilov hurried to the scene. Galina hesitated, not wanting to set eyes on the plant again, but Ilya knew it was imperative that they stick close to the professor. He pulled at her arm and they followed. Reluctantly, the policemen came too.

Shumilov was fascinated by the plant. He knelt to examine it from all angles, and then found a short stick with which he tried to dislodge the trapped mongrel from its tendrils. Instantly, a tendril curled round the stick and snapped it with a brittle crack.

'Incredible,' Shumilov murmured, his eyes shining bright with the joy of discovery. 'Incredible, absolutely incredible.'

He straightened up and turned to the two policemen standing immovable but silent behind him.

'It cannot remain here. It must be dug up, carefully, and removed to my laboratory for detailed study. I will arrange for some of my own people to come out here and attend to it. As for Miss Savenkova and her friend, I insist that they come back to the laboratory with me. There is much they must tell me. You will report this incident to your superiors, of course, and if there should be anything more you require, you will find us all at the laboratory. Make sure you guard this plant well until my staff arrive to collect it.'

The two men exchanged sullen glances. They were not sure of Shumilov's authority and were not accustomed to taking orders from anyone but their own superiors. Finally, one of them shrugged and they both stepped aside.

Galina's relief was short-lived. Shumilov drove them straight back to his laboratory and questioned her over and over again until she was hoarse. Though less brutal, he was far more exacting than the police, demanding that she dredge her memory for every last, minute detail of the plant's growth and development. Eventually she almost began to wish that he had not rescued her from their clutches.

Kaznovetsky arrived in time for the first experiment. Shumilov had telephoned his colleague partly out of courtesy, because Kaznovetsky had been the leader of their Khyshtym expedition; partly because he realized he might have need of Kaznovetsky's superior scientific weight if the police enquiries continued to prove difficult; but mostly because in his excitement he needed to communicate with another mind on his own intellectual level.

Ilya was left to wait outside in Shumilov's office, while Galina accompanied the two scientists into the laboratory. The large plant from outside her apartment had not yet arrived, but the small three-inch samples which Shumilov had brought back from Khyshtym were neatly arranged in a series of glass trays. Most of them were still

FLOWERS OF EVIL

decorated with the tiny bright blue flowers. Galina shuddered as she looked at them.

'Some of these were transplanted direct from Khyshtym,' Shumilov explained to Kaznovetsky. 'The others I have grown from seed spores taken from the originals. They are growing in different soils and have been fed on different foods, but none of them have developed beyond the size you see here. They appear harmless. But now watch.'

He had sent for three white mice which had been delivered in a small cage. Carefully he opened the cage and reached inside to grasp one of the mice between finger and thumb. The mouse squeaked in alarm and wriggled helplessly as it was drawn out. Shumilov now selected one of the glass trays and set the mouse down on the moist earth, just out of reach of the nearest blue-flowered plant. Kaznovetsky leaned closer to observe. Galina shut her eyes and looked away.

For perhaps ten seconds the mouse did not move. Then it began to explore. It scuttled to the edge of the glass tray, sniffed the barrier for a moment, and then turned back. With its whiskers still twitching, it made a run for the other side of the tray. The plant's leaves rustled. Suddenly a tendril snatched. The mouse squeaked in terror as it was seized and drawn instantly into the plant's embrace. More tendrils bound it and tightened. A minute later the mouse had stopped shrieking and struggling. It was dead, and its blood was beginning to drip.

'You see,' Shumilov exulted, with the pure delight of a scientist solving a riddle. 'It feeds on blood. From what I have seen and from what Galina has told me, it will take any form of bird or animal life it can snare and crush in its tendrils. Then it absorbs the dripping blood through its leaves and through its roots. It must be a mutation of some kind, shaped by the radioactive explosion at Khyshtym and prevented from developing when the explosion killed all animal and bird life in the area.

'Fascinating,' Kaznovetsky murmured. Although this was not his speciality, he could appreciate any major scientific discovery. 'But if it is a mutation, Leonid – then a mutation of what? What kind of plant was the original?'

'I don't really know,' Shumilov admitted. 'I've never encountered any plant quite like this in the whole of my career as a botanist. There are climbing plants which use tendrils to pull themselves up to find sunlight, but a plant which uses tendrils to trap and crush prey is unique.'

'Then you think this is a mutation of a climbing plant?'

'No,' Shumilov said doubtfully. 'I think –' he paused, frowning. Then he said slowly, 'I have a theory. Do you remember that in 1908 a giant meteor crashed in the Tunguska River area of Siberia? It was calculated to have had an effect equivalent to a huge H-bomb explosion, and the flash fire obliterated an area of over one and a half thousand square miles.'

Kaznovetsky nodded. 'I remember. The area was so remote that no one knew very much about the event at the time. The only investigations were made many years later.'

'Yes, and when the most recent investigations were made it was found that the area has now been covered with a huge coniferous forest. Once the natural flora established itself, the growth rate was phenomenal. Many mutations were recorded. There are also said to be strange plants growing there which are *unknown* to botanical science.'

Kaznovetsky nodded again, not yet sure where Shumilov was leading.

'So consider this.' Shumilov was becoming excited. 'When the meteor crashed more than seventy years ago it brought with it seed spores from an alien environment. The seeds of *this*!' He pointed to one of the little blue-flowered plants. 'Perhaps in their original form this was the limit of their growth; the tendrils might have been designed to catch nothing bigger than flies and insects. After all, we do have native insect-eating plants on this planet.'

Kaznovetsky began to understand. 'You think these plants originated in the Tunguska area of Siberia, and were somehow transferred to Khyshtym and underwent further mutation when the nuclear accident occurred there?'

'Precisely. The Khyshtym release of radiation created the genetic changes which now allow them to seize bigger prey and grow. As yet we cannot know the full possible extent of their development.'

'So the original came from another world?'

'It's a possible explanation. To find out, we must take another expedition, this time to Siberia where the meteor crashed. We must search this strange new forest for the original of the plant as it existed before the Khyshtym mutation.'

Kaznovetsky smiled at the eagerness of his friend. 'Expeditions cost money,' he warned.

'Yes, but there's a scientific mystery here which *must* be solved. Also, if these plants are capable of spreading they could be very dangerous.'

Kaznovetsky looked again at the crushed mouse and did not argue. Instead, he made a decision. 'The question of an expedition must wait. In the meantime we must make sure that all the plants growing here are kept under strict supervision – and we must be certain there are no more growing wild in Moscow.'

Shumilov agreed, and turned to Galina again, repeating the same questions and receiving the same answers back. She still had not dared to mention the second plant

FLOWERS OF EVIL

which she had given to Aleksandr, praying that by now he had received her letter and thrown it into the sea. Instead, she insisted that she had only brought from Khyshtym the one plant, which Ilya had finally chopped up.

The plant which had strangled Katya's dog was brought in while they talked, together with a second plant which had been found beside it, and Shumilov was assured that a thorough search of the lawns and flowerbeds around the apartment had revealed no more of its kind.

Shumilov and Kaznovetsky were finally both satisfied that all the deathseed plants outside Khyshtym were now safely locked up in Shumilov's laboratory.

But they were wrong. At Babushskaya the plants were flowering, seeding and spreading, and growing swiftly larger on a diet of small rodents, birds and rabbits.

From time to time the forest wolves came down at night from the dark Ural Mountains, hunting around the edges of the small rural villages, always hoping to snap up a stray dog – their favourite meal. They were lean, hungry and savage, hunting always in packs, killers of the forest, masters of the long winter nights. They roamed at will, unchallenged except by the occasional hunter with a rifle, until they came to Babushskaya.

Like dark shadows they flitted through the trees, circling the sleeping village, but they found nothing to appease their appetite this time. The dogs had all been locked up for the night. Silently the wolves came closer, searching and scenting the air. With tongues lolling, eyes burning in the darkness, they prowled the perimeter of the small huddle of wooden houses.

This was the limit of their territory. They would go no closer to the dead land of the forbidden zone, but circled on the Khyshtym side of the village, padding silently over the crumbling track to nowhere. The danger there was something no wolf had ever experienced before. It came suddenly, without warning, as leaves rustled and a tendril lashed out in the night.

The snared wolf howled and fought. With its powerful muscles and sharp jaws it might have freed itself, but a wolf trapped was a wolf doomed. These were among the most vicious animals in the world, and the law of the pack was wolf eat wolf. Seeing one of their number struggling, the others turned on it and began ripping it to pieces. Wolves and plants tangled together and a second lean grey shape was caught in the hungry tendrils. In the howling pandemonium the wolves attacked each other and more flesh and fur was torn open by the foaming, slashing jaws. The cruel wounds bled freely and the deathseed plants feasted and grew strong in the bestial orgy of spilled blood.

CHAPTER TEN

On Lairg Island the Gordons quickly settled into the new routine. Barry spent his time moving slowly about the island with binoculars, notebooks and camera, especially eager to witness the spectacular flushed dawns and sunsets; in the evenings he busily typed or sketched, watching his book slowly take shape. He was mainly using a telephoto lens on his camera, and with the island so rich in birdlife he was confident he would be able to illustrate the entire text with his own colour photographs.

Sometimes Julia or Jonathon would accompany him, particularly when he walked along the dangerous north cliffs, where Jonathon had been forbidden to play alone. At other times the two children explored the rest of the island together. They became firm friends with the Mathesons, helping Ross to keep count of his sheep, cut peat, and haul water from the island's only well. Jonathon and the sheepdog Robbie became virtually inseparable.

As always, Valerie found herself cooking and cleaning and making half-hearted attempts to get the children to buckle down to the school-books they had brought with them. To break the routine she made daily visits to the Matheson cottage to check up on Janet, who was so big now that she looked due to go into labour at any moment. Valerie was convinced she should already be in hospital, but Janet merely laughed cheerfully and said that being an island baby it would be sure to have the patience to wait for the next boat.

Valerie was the only one who was bored. When she could walk over to the Matheson cottage, or walk up by the cliffs to watch the sea boiling in rage over the black rocks and headlands far below, life was just about bearable. At other times, in other moods, she might have enjoyed the wild, rugged beauty, with the taste of the sea in her lungs and the fierce salt wind in her hair, but on this trip there was too much frustration simmering inside her. Lairg was not where she wanted to be, and it was a far cry from the gay social whirl she had only recently tasted.

It was the nights which were worst, or more precisely the long evenings between sunset and bedtime. After they had eaten and cleared up after the meal there was nothing to do except listen to the radio or read a book. Barry was usually occupied with his writing or sketching, and if he talked at all his only topic was the list of birds he had spotted during the day. The children amused themselves with board games, painting or jigsaws, and although in the past Valerie would willingly have joined them for a round of monopoly or scrabble, now the very idea made her want to scream. She had brought *War and Peace* and half a dozen other classics she had never read before because of their daunting size, but she was unaccustomed to the poor lamplight and soon found any sustained reading to be a strain on her eyes. So her feeling of grievance slowly came to the boil.

The explosion came on their first Saturday on the island. On Saturday afternoons she could usually find a valid excuse to slip off to London and spend a few hours of blissful dalliance with Simon – perhaps it would be the theatre, or a concert, or straight to his flat for an immediate orgy of sinful new sex. The very wickedness of what she was doing always made it far more exciting than the stale old marital routines.

All through the day the thoughts of what she might have been doing stayed uppermost in her mind. She felt cheated, sick to death of the island, and more and more angry with Barry for bringing her here. When darkness fell she felt more claustrophobic and shut off than ever. There was nothing that suited her on the radio and the particular chapter of Tolstoy she was trying to read seemed dry as dust. The children played backgammon for a while, but they had spent an energetic day hiking the length and breadth of the island and soon went to bed. Barry remained at his typewriter, hammering away as though she did not even exist.

'I'm going to bed,' she decided aloud, no longer trying to hide the bitterness in her voice. She got up and went into the kitchen to put on the kettle and heat the water for a wash, a chore she had already come to hate.

Barry stopped typing and stared after her. For a moment he was undecided, but then he rose to his feet and followed her. He came up behind her, letting one hand touch her shoulder, the other caressing the curve of her bottom. He felt her go rigid as he kissed the side of her neck.

'Good idea, love,' he said calmly. 'I'll come too.'

'Please don't bother,' Valerie snapped tartly.

'Why not? You're still my wife – or are you?'

She turned on him, the words exploding. 'For God's sake! I'm still *married* to you, that's all. The only wife you'd be interested in would have to be a rare passage migrant with a bloody beak and feathers.'

'That's not true, Val.' His voice was still steady, but there was a hard stare in his eyes and a slightly twisted set to his jaw: the danger signs which always warned her when his slowly wound-up temper was ready to uncoil.

'I haven't lost interest in you, Val. You know that. If anything, I'd say it's the other way round. For the past month you haven't shown any real interest in me. Your tired nights and headaches are beginning to wear a bit thin.'

'Well, what do you expect when you bring me to a God-forsaken place like this? You might as well have dumped me at the North Pole. Why did you have to bring me along anyway? It wasn't really necessary to drag me up here, or the kids. You can write your rotten, stupid book on your own. You don't need any of us.'

'I would have thought it was obvious,' Barry said grimly.

'*What* was obvious?' Valerie had become so heated she had lost track of her own argument.

'Why I brought you here.'

It was spilling out into the open. She could see in his eyes now that he *knew*. But it had to come right out. It had to be ripped out in words, bare and hurtful.

'Why, Barry? Why *did* you bring me here?'

'Because I was damned if I was going to leave you behind, just to screw your time away uninterrupted with mister Simon-fancyarse-bloody-Lancing.'

'You mean you *knew*!' Somehow that seemed to make it more shocking. It meant he had marooned her here deliberately.

'Of course I knew. I knew a month ago that something was wrong. You changed virtually overnight. And then all those trips to see your mother. Such a bloody sanctimonious and dutiful daughter all of a sudden. Of course, I knew there was another man. Until a week ago I just didn't know who.'

'Who told you?' Valerie demanded fiercely. She felt betrayed, angry and sufficiently vengeful to want to claw out the eyes of the unknown spy.

'Brian,' Barry said shortly.

'Brian Prince? Your pansy bloody publisher! What business is it of his anyway?'

'Brian is no pansy, but he is a good friend – to both of us. He didn't want to see me lose my wife. And he didn't want to see you make a complete and utter fool of yourself.'

'That's for me to worry about. And anyway, I'm not making a fool of myself.'

'Aren't you? How well do you know your sweet friend Simon's reputation with women?'

She glared at him and said icily. 'Exactly what do you mean?'

'I mean that to Simon it's all a game. He's tried them all; blondes, brunettes, redheads; black girls, brown girls – for all I know he can even tell you the truth about the Chinese. Now he's stealing older women from their husbands because it's a new kick. And do you know why young men like older women? Because they don't yell, they don't tell, and they're grateful as hell!'

'You bastard!' Valerie let go of all her carefully retained dignity and slapped him hard across the face.

Before she realized what he intended, Barry spun her round, hauled up the seat of her skirt with one hand, and with the other dealt her a violent, stinging smack across the seat of her panties. Her blow had lost its impact against the cushion of his beard, but his brought tears of pain and humiliation springing to her eyes.

Barry swung her back again and gripped her forearms hard, holding her fast before she could lash out again.

'I don't want to fight,' he told her harshly, 'for the sake of the kids. I don't want a big, tearing bust-up that's going to hurt Julia and Jonathon more than it'll hurt us. That's why I brought you away from him, out here. But I'll promise you one thing – if this doesn't work, if you go back to Lancing after we leave Lairg, then I'll bring you his balls on a bloody plate. You can have them for earrings and be damned to you.'

Valerie stared at him and burst into tears. He let her go and she ran sobbing to the bedroom.

Barry didn't follow her upstairs. To continue the quarrel up there would mean that the children would almost certainly overhear, and that he didn't want. He went slowly back to the living room and stood there, his fists clenched, looking down at them and wishing there was something he could hit. He wondered whether he had said too much or not enough, too soon or too late. Either way, he and Valerie still had to live together for the next ten days. There was no way out for either of them until the boat came back.

After the first spell of bright sunshine, the weather on Lairg became unsettled, sometimes stormy and sometimes fine, and they began to experience the island in all its moods. Unless it was too wet and windy to move out of doors, there was always something to see. The patterns of light and cloud were never the same, and even the blackest thunderclouds rolling over the angry sea made ever-changing seascapes of stark drama. When the weather was rough the great seas crashed more violently against the cliffs and rocks, and the spray boomed higher. The great autumn migrations from the north had not yet begun, but there were plenty of resident birds for Barry to watch, and he was glad to have the time to study these before the real spectacle began.

Outwardly, for the benefit of the children, Barry made a show of being totally absorbed in his work. Valerie became withdrawn and sulked, and not a private word passed between them. When they spoke in front of the children it was in carefully polite tones, each word weighed and measured to ensure that it was strictly practical, unemotional and above all, necessary.

The children knew their parents had had a row, but Julia threatened to twist Jonathon's ear off if he dared to ask embarrassing questions. Julia knew that all married people had rows, and her mother and father were no exception. Usually the bad atmosphere lasted only a couple of days and then blew over. This one seemed a lot worse than most, but still she hoped that sooner or later it would disappear.

In the meantime it was difficult to talk to either Mum or Dad, because she loved them both and did not want to appear to be taking sides. After the first few days of exploring, she had also tired of Jonathon's company. His schoolboy games were a bit *too* childish. So, with all the wisdom of a soon-to-be-fifteen-year-old, Julia decided that now was as good a time as any to practise her clarinet. When the weather was bad she stayed in her room, and when it was fine she took her music with her in search of solitude.

Jonathon was left more and more to his own devices, but he did not really mind. He had a lively imagination and he had a splendid new friend in Robbie. A dog was much more fun than a sister any day of the week, and if she didn't want to play, then that was her loss. Like his father he had an all-consuming interest in nature and her mysteries and miracles – and also he had invented some smashing games. One day he would be Blood-Axe the Viking, leading his desperate band of sea raiders ashore to burn and plunder. Other times he would be Black Patch the Pirate, scouring the island in search of buried treasure, or Hook-hand the Smuggler, outwitting the devious excise men as his gallant crew landed casks of illicit brandy in the coves.

On the day he discovered the first of the strange new plants, his imagination had jumped forward a few centuries to the Second World War. Today he was Captain Killer, Ace Commando, leading his small task-force of hand-picked men up the slope of the south headland to storm the outcrop of grey rocks which had become a vital German radar installation. The hand-picked task-force was silently wiping out a German machinegun post on his left (*i.e.* Robbie had found something interesting to sniff at in a sandy hollow) and fearless Captain Killer was crawling up the heather-tangled slope on his belly. A black-headed gull standing on one of the nearer rocks unwittingly played the role of a German sentry, and when the bird turned its head and stared with one sharp, black eye down the hill, Captain Killer was sent diving for cover. He wriggled behind a clump of heather and pressed his body close to the ground, his face touching the grass. When he judged it safe to move he raised his head an inch and opened his eyes. The plant was no more than three inches from his left eyeball.

Jonathon regarded it with interest. It was no more than a seedling and he could have enclosed it in his hand. But the bright, emerald-green leaves were already distinctive, and this close he could see the almost invisible tendrils, finer than a cat's whiskers.

'That's what it is,' he told himself. 'It's a cat-whisker plant.' And he was pleased to have invented an appropriate name for it.

He stared at the plant for a few moments, his game temporarily forgotten. It was not as nice as the profusion of sea pinks and wild yellow irises which dotted other parts of the island, but all the same it was something different. His brows furrowed as he tried to recall every page of his father's well-thumbed field guide to the wild plants and flowers of the British Isles, but he couldn't remember anything quite like this. He had always dreamed of discovering something rare or new in nature which his father had never seen or did not know about, and he had the exciting feeling that this might be it.

Barry was down by the first of the west-side coves, just below the headland, watching a pair of golden plover and waiting to get a precise camera study. But when Jonathon called him over, he came reluctantly and showed only a momentary flicker of interest in his son's find.

'We'll look it up tonight in the field guide,' he promised. 'It's bound to be in there somewhere.'

The last remark left Jonathon's hopes deflated. It was always the same. Anything he found always turned out to be somewhere in the field guides. Like the eagle that had proved to be a buzzard, nothing ever quite came up to expectations.

Suddenly Barry spotted a movement in a thick clump of heather twenty yards away. As he levelled his binoculars he felt a surge of real excitement. He was looking at a small brown and reddish bird the size of a robin, with a definite red-centred blue bib under its throat.

'Look, Jon,' he said softly, handing his son his binoculars and showing him where to point them. 'It's a bluethroat. They breed in Russia and Scandinavia, so this one must be a migrant. Now that *is* something you've never seen before.'

The next morning Jonathon was playing alone on the south headland when he discovered a small clump of no less than four of the strange new plants. These were a little further developed and had sprouted tiny bright-blue flowers. Jonathon squatted on his haunches and studied them thoughtfully.

Yesterday Barry had spotted several more personal first sightings: a lapland bunting, a small flock of snow buntings, storm petrels in flight, and the undisputed highlight of his day – a rare sparrowhawk resting on a rock before making the last leg of its flight to one of the larger islands. After that he had given no more thought to Jonathon's plant – and neither had Jonathon.

But now the boy's curiosity was aroused again. More cat-whisker plants. He was sure, because of the rich green colour and shape and the velvety texture of the leaves, and because once again he could see the little cat-whisker tendrils. But the blue flowers were new; he was sure there

FLOWERS OF EVIL

was nothing like them in the book. He wished now that he had found the book last night and looked.

He would have challenged Barry again and put his conviction that this was an original discovery to the test, but Barry was up on the other end of the island, overlooking the kittiwake cliffs. It didn't matter anyway, Jonathon thought gloomily. His father was only interested in birds – plants were nothing. Maybe if he could discover a new bird – something like a white-tailed eagle that hadn't bred on these islands since the middle of the last century – then Dad would have to take notice.

He looked up hopefully at the bright blue sky, but saw only the same old gulls and terns and the dark brown sickle wings of the manx shearwaters. There was no sign of a white-tailed eagle.

With a sigh Jonathon rose to his feet, about to continue his latest game – but then he remembered Mum. His mother was depressed about something, he knew that much, and for a couple of days now he had been trying to think of something to cheer her up. There were no shops on the island where he could spend his pocket money on a box of chocolates or a small present, but he had considered collecting up a posy of wild flowers. The trouble was that flowers were such a sissyish present when you were ten. On the other hand, he had often brought his mother flowers when he was only a little boy and she had always been delighted.

He looked down at the pretty blue flowers at his feet and his desire to do something nice for Mum wrestled with his new feelings of manliness. The blue flowers were tiny and there were not many of them, but mixed in with some sea pinks and a few other varieties they would make a nice bouquet. Finally the memory of his mother's sad face won and peering round to make sure no one was looking, he knelt self-consciously to pick the flowers.

With finger and thumbnail he severed the stem supporting the tiny, daisy-like blossom of sky-blue petals. And as he did so, with the speed of a striking snake-tongue, a tendril curled around his wrist.

Jonathon was startled and frightened. Another tendril whipped around his fingers tight enough to hurt him. He jerked his hand back and tore the tendrils out of the parent plant by the roots. The long green cat-whiskers went limp and he shook his hand violently until they fell away. He backed away staring down at the plants and rubbing his smarting wrist. They had tried to catch him, he realized, and suddenly he was angry – angry with the tiny blue plants, and angry with the silly thumping of his own trembling heart. He stamped down on the little blue-flowered plants with his boots until he had crushed them to nothing and ground them into the grassy earth. Satisfied, he then walked away, failing to notice that there were more of the little cat-whisker plants lurking in the heather.

For the next couple of days, storms and bad weather kept them all indoors, except for Barry who went out stubbornly in oilskins with his binoculars. Most of the time the heavy rain grounded the seabirds, but in the brief clear intervals the hungry colonies would swirl into flight to hunt for food.

Barry claimed he had to be out in all weathers, ready to observe, but both he and Valerie knew he was deliberately avoiding her whenever possible, and that the atmosphere was better on the rain-lashed, wind-swept cliff tops than it was in the cottage.

Having examined every corner of the island and listed its residents, Barry was now spending most of his time on the north cliffs watching for the migrants. Soon, he knew, the great winged skyway which passed directly over the island would be filled with the vast autumn movement of birds coming down from the Arctic and Scandinavia. The high north end of Lairg, with its steep cliffs and stacks and magnificent, swarming, squabbling bird-cities, promised to make a magnificent vantage point from which to view the migration.

So the south headland was left unvisited until the weather cleared, and here the first deathseed plants had taken root among the heather. They thrived in the salt-tanged air and began to snare the smaller birds, and then the larger birds. Very swiftly they began to grow.

CHAPTER ELEVEN

Ivan Kitkev was a grizzled, grey-bearded old man of nearly seventy. He had lived a hard life and what was visible of his face beneath his beard and fur-lined hat was deeply wrinkled. His eyes were rheumy, flecked with yellow, and the purple veins stood out like cords on his gnarled hands. He carried a long-barrelled rifle of World War Two vintage, but as he grew older he used it more and more as a crutch to help him over rough terrain. Everyone for miles around shook their heads and observed sadly that one day poor old Ivan would accidentally shoot himself. He lived alone in a village not far from Babushskaya, and for most of his life he had eked out a meagre living as a professional wolf-hunter. When the villagers of Babushskaya sent for him in their hour of need he came, slowly, but as fast as he was able, in answer to their call.

At Babushskaya there had been no sleep that night. Every soul in the village had been kept awake by the frenzied howling of the wolves. Of course, they had heard wolf howls before, but never anything as close and as terrifying as this. When at last daylight came and there was silence, they emerged cautiously from their houses and conferred in a nervous huddle in the centre of the village. They were all agreed: the sounds had not been the normal yelps and snarls of a wolf pack running down some luckless dog or a rabbit. They had been ghoulish, blood-curdling and terror-stricken, as if the wolves were under attack by something even more ravenous and ferocious than themselves.

No one had the courage to venture out on to the Khyshtym road where the sounds had come from. Instead, they voted unanimously to send for Ivan. Via the only telephone in Babushskaya, a vintage instrument located in the one shop and post office, they contacted the old wolf-hunter.

Ivan arrived at mid-morning, having walked the three miles between the two villages. The peasants of Babushskaya had still not dared to move beyond the village boundary, and when Ivan heard their story he was not particularly keen to investigate either. The people had obviously been petrified out of their wits during the night, and their fear communicated itself to him all too easily.

However, the old wolf-hunter had a job to do, and a reputation to maintain. Also, if he wanted his daily ration of vodka and tobacco, he had to earn some money. The state paid him a small salary for his services, but those few roubles barely kept him alive. To get the little luxuries which made life worth living, he had to kill wolves, show their pelts – and claim his bounty.

No one wanted to accompany him. They simply pointed to the Khyshtym road and told him where the diabolical howling had come from. Ivan scowled and called them cowards, but they remained unmoved. Finally, he turned his back on them. It was his normal practice now to use his rifle as a walking aid until he was actually on to fresh wolf tracks, but today he levered back the bolt and cocked it, ready to fire. The villagers watched him as he walked slowly off, disappearing from sight through the silver screen of birch trees.

It was very quiet. There was no breeze, and everything was perfectly still. Sunlight filtering through the trees dappled the crumbling road at Ivan's feet. He stopped, and looked up with blinking eyes at the light tracery of yellowing leaves and silver-grey branches. There were no birds, he noticed, which was unusual. In fact, there was no sight or sound of any form of wild life.

As he approached the édge of the forbidden zone, he remembered that terrible day all those many years ago when the sky had burned and the forests had been consumed in great, roaring blasts of fire. Perhaps it was going to happen again. Perhaps the birds knew and had all flown away. Perhaps the wolves had sensed it too, and had fled in howling panic. Ivan shivered at his thoughts but forced himself to move on. He was an old man, and if he could not do his job then he was no use to anybody. He would be a living corpse, just waiting for a grave. It was better to go on, to find the tracks and hunt the wolves.

As he emerged from the stand of birch trees, almost immediately a smell assailed his nostrils. It was a familiar smell – he had killed and skinned too many wolves not to recognize it. He took a tighter grip on his rifle and followed the scent.

Half a minute later, he was staring pop-eyed at the profusion of strange and monstrous new plants. They were as tall as he was himself, with thick, very bright green leaves, and a most unusual feature: tangles of long, spiralling green tendrils, like the tentacles of sea creatures he had once seen in a school picture book. He wondered if he was looking at some form of vegetable squid or octopus. The surrounding grass and undergrowth and many of the leaves and fronds of the plants themselves, were mangled, trampled and broken, and thickly smeared with streaks of blood. And caught up in three of the larger plants were the mutilated, fang-ripped corpses of three large wolves, the bodies further crushed and distorted by the merciless grip of the green coils.

Ivan Kitkev was bewildered and amazed, but he made an effort to read the signs and piece together what had happened. The nature and power of the plants was beyond his understanding, but it seemed clear that the wolves had killed each other by fighting among themselves. He knew it was not unusual for the rest of the pack to turn on a crippled or injured member. He peered closer and nodded to himself, confirming that most of the gaping wounds on the bodies of the dead wolves had been caused by the powerful, snapping jaws of their fellows.

Elation crept over him slowly. Here were three dead wolves, more than he would normally shoot in a month, and they were free for the taking. If he could only retrieve the skins, or even the heads, he could claim his bounty – and the authorities would have no way of knowing he had not shot them himself. He counted up the extra bounty money and converted it into vodka, and a slow smile spread over his whiskery face.

He edged closer. The peculiar plants made him feel slightly uneasy, and he moved cautiously. Holding his rifle with both hands near the butt, he used the long reach of the muzzle to try and push the tendrils off the nearest wolf carcass.

But he failed to allow for the exceptionally long reach of the tendrils. Neither was he prepared for their lightning speed. With all the blinding suddenness of a Bombay strangler, the plant struck, and the tip of an outflung tendril curled twice around his neck. And tightened.

Ivan squawked – everything had happened too quickly for him to scream, and the sound was a cut-off gagging, deep in his throat. A fierce tug yanked him in toward the parent plant and a second tendril slapped around his waist. The third secured his right leg just below the knee. Crazy with terror, the old man struggled to pull back his rifle to a firing position, and squeezed the trigger. The noise of the shot rang out above the blood pounding in his ears, and the bullet ripped holes through half a dozen of the thick, fleshy leaves. He worked the bolt and fired again, and then again, but to no avail. The life was being compressed out of him and darkness was pouring over his brain in a hot, black, roaring curtain. A tendril plucked the rifle from his nerveless fingers and a minute later he was dead, from the combined effects of suffocation and a massive heart attack.

In Babushskaya, they heard the shots and assumed that the old hunter was shooting at the wolves. Whatever had happened during the night, some of the animals must have been left injured and Ivan was finishing them off. That was the final consensus of opinion, though some of the younger men began to look at each other shamefacedly. They knew they should not have allowed the old greybeard to go alone. At last, two of the boldest of them volunteered to go and help the old man skin his prizes.

What they saw brought them hurtling back within two minutes in a state of babbling shock. The death of Ivan Kitkev outweighed their reluctance to be questioned by the dreaded Second Secretary of the Regional Party Committee, and at last the district authorities were informed.

Shumilov and Kaznovetsky arrived with the second wave of officials late in the afternoon, and with them came a very reluctant Galina. She had begged to be allowed to remain behind in Moscow, but Shumilov had insisted that he could not manage without a secretary. With inexorable party logic, he had pointed out that this whole business was still an important state secret and that she was already deeply involved, so by accompanying him she could help to avoid involving outsiders. Galina had hardly dared to protest. So far her boss had been so excited by the discoveries stemming from her actions that the reprimands he had given had only been a curt formality; but he had not forgotten that earlier she had committed the unpardonable sin of disobeying his instructions.

When they went to view the new crop of advanced

plants, which were still feeding on the bled and drained corpse of Ivan Kitkev, Galina felt extremely sick. Shumilov looked at her with some impatience at first, but then relented a little, and told her she could wait in the car which had brought them out from the regional capital.

The local officials had wisely cordoned off the area, using stakes and thick ropes to encircle the plants and keep onlookers safely out of reach of the tendrils. No attempt had yet been made to retrieve the body of the old wolf-hunter.

'I feared they could be dangerous,' Kaznovetsky said, as they stood by the rope and observed. 'But I never expected them to start eating people – or to grow to such a size as this.'

'And even this may not be their ultimate potential,' Shumilov speculated, his eyes shining. 'We have yet to see how big they can grow. My friend, what we are witnessing is the most sensational botanical discovery of all time – perhaps the most unique phenomenon in the natural world.'

'But I thought we agreed that they weren't created by nature alone,' Kaznovetsky reminded him. 'They must be a mutation.'

They continued their debate as they walked slowly round the outside of the ropes, viewing the plants from every angle. They had been given all the known details on their way here, and had been told about the trapped corpses of the wolves, which were now mostly smothered under the green vegetation.

'What do you want to do with them?' Kaznovetsky asked at last, when they came back to their starting point.

'Watch them,' Shumilov said promptly. 'I could never let them grow to this size in the laboratory, but here we can set up a field study to determine their full development. Fortunately, we're a long way from any large centre of population, and if necessary this village can be evacuated.'

Kaznovetsky nodded approval. He could see the importance of a detailed study. 'But what about the body of the old man?' he asked. 'How do we get it back?'

'We don't,' Shumilov said simply. 'It would be too dangerous to try and remove it from a living plant. And of course, we don't want to damage the plant.'

Kaznovetsky looked doubtful. 'I hope his relatives don't complain.'

'Their objections must be ignored. This is a vital scientific experiment. The plants can keep the old man, and we'll feed them regularly with fresh meat, perhaps even live meat. Maybe we could introduce a goat or cow into the enclosure. We must have a film record of how these things actually catch and devour their prey.'

Shumilov was rubbing his hands together as he talked, and Kaznovetsky continued to nod cautious agreement at each point. Meanwhile Galina, who could hear them from the car, was forced to open the door and vomit yet again.

On Lairg, the ever-changing winds brought fine weather, and piles of white cloud raced fast and high over the brilliant blue skies. The island was a constantly moving patchwork of bright sunlight and shadows, and the seabirds were aloft and screaming in flight with the first red blush of dawn.

The bird cries woke Barry early, and within minutes he was up and dressed. He ate a hasty but hearty breakfast, then shouldered his small rucksack and hurried off to the north cliffs. The brilliant sunlight piercing the clouds was perfect for camera work, and Barry could not bear to miss a moment of it.

The children were up almost as quickly, clattering down the stairs and arguing furiously over who should have first use of the primitive bathroom. Julia swore in exasperation when Jonathon beat her as usual by giving her a rude, sideways push just as they arrived neck and neck at the door. Valerie had allowed Barry to go off on his own, but now she reluctantly stirred and went downstairs to supervise the children's breakfast and act as referee in their eternal, bickering squabbles.

For once there was no real animosity in their sparring voices: today they had planned to do something together. After breakfast they put on warm sweaters and anoraks, zipped up tight, and went out into the keen, bracing breeze.

They were banned from the high cliffs, so for them the most exciting parts of the island after a bout of rough weather were the small beaches and coves. Anything might have been washed up or uncovered by the surging seas, and so every rock-pool and hollow, and every curve of pebbled sand, had to be re-explored.

They ran down to the nearest of the west coves and scrambled over the rocks, sending up flocks of indignant gulls and waders into disturbed, complaining flight. There they played happily for the rest of the morning, beachcombing from cove to cove and turning over every piece of driftwood and seaweed.

Jonathon was determined to find signs of a shipwreck; either some modern vessel driven on to the cliffs during the wild hours of darkness, or the silt-clogged remains of some Viking longboat which had rested for centuries on the sea bottom. How fantastic it would be if he could find something that had belonged to the Vikings – perhaps a horned helmet, or a great broadsword, or even a mighty, double-bladed axe! Perhaps there really had been a Viking called Blood-Axe – a heroic warrior who had conquered all the islands in the North Sea, a giant of a man unbeatable in battle, who finally perished in some terrible storm just off the coast of this very island. Jonathon thrilled at the thought and his eager eyes scoured the rocks for a glint of Viking gold or weapons.

Julia, meanwhile, was searching for a seal pup. Soon after they had arrived, she had stood on the south headland and watched a group of grey seals gambolling in the blue-green waters far below. The sleek, arrowing bodies had rolled and dived with sporting ease in their natural element, and she had stood enthralled until their pursuit of fish took them round the headland and out to sea.

Maybe one of the smaller pups could have been hurled up on the beach by the storm waves of the last two days. If she found one, she could take it home and care for it until it was well enough to be returned to the sea. Or she might come across an injured bird. If there was no seal pup she would be just as happy to look after a puffin. She adored their over-large heads and rainbow bills.

As the morning wore on their more romantic hopes faded, but there was still plenty to interest them. They collected seashells, Jonathon diving for the big spiral ones he could hold to his ear, and Julia filling her anorak pocket with pretty little ones for making necklaces. Jonathon chased crabs and poked starfish, and Julia turned over the polished, multi-coloured pebbles. If she could find one that was the right size, something quartzy or translucent, she might try to make a brooch.

Their questing kept them on the beaches and away from the south headland.

Valerie finished the washing up and sat down at the table to drink a final cup of coffee. She was fed up with being confined to the cottage and was briefly tempted to go out and join the children. At the same time her nerves were on edge. The stresses and strains of her mixed-up private feelings were tearing her apart. She didn't know whether or not she wanted to divorce Barry. But one thing she did know was that for the time being she could not bear to face any of the family for any longer than was absolutely necessary. The only other thing she knew was that if she stayed cooped up in the cottage for much longer she'd go crazy.

Her options were pretty limited. Eventually she decided to take a walk over the island and visit the Mathesons. In the two days since she had last seen Janet, the poor woman might even have had her baby. In any case, Ross would probably be out checking on his sheep now that the weather had let up, so at least she would have another woman to talk to alone for the next couple of hours.

She put on her anorak, pulled the hood forward and began the half-mile walk down the gentle valley between the two low hills. The wind was cold and buffeting despite the strong sunshine, and she walked with her shoulders hunched and her hands thrust deep in her pockets.

Halfway to the cottage she passed a jumble of rocks and heather where a deathseed plant was waiting.

Although she passed very nearly in range the plant made no move, its leaves remaining still. It was as though it could sense that its prey must come closer, and was not prepared to betray itself until it was certain of making a successful strike.

Instead it waited motionless for her to make the return journey.

CHAPTER TWELVE

Barry had headed for the north-east corner of the island overlooking the jagged kittiwake cliffs. He walked briskly as he left the cottage, but once over the brow of the first hill his pace slowed as he climbed the steepening slopes. His gaze searched the skies, always alert for a bird that was rare or unusual among the flapping wings of the resident gulls, or for the warning scream and dive-bombing attack of a great skua. Most of the skua dives were a dramatic bluff, aimed at steering an intruder away from a nest, but all the same a passing clout could be painful and even a near miss could be frightening. It was one of the reasons why he had barred Jonathon from the high cliffs. Apart from his son's natural recklessness, there was always the risk that a fierce swoop by a skua could startle the boy and cause him to tumble over the cliffs.

As he walked, his thoughts were very much on his deteriorating relationship with Val. Their marriage was on a cliff-edge as stark, dizzy and deadly as any of the awesome precipices around the north end of Lairg – and he did not know yet whether she was going to step back or plunge them both over. He did not want his marriage to end, but the choice had to be hers. He would take her back this once. But there was no way on earth he was going to share her, either with Simon Lancing or anyone else.

They had barely exchanged a word since their quarrel. Several times he had been tempted to re-open the subject, to suggest they talk it over, but each time he had held back. He had told her bluntly where he stood, and now it was her move, her decision. Thus far he had acted with more restraint than she had any right to expect; he had not thrashed her, or chucked her out, or rushed to beat up her lover. But enough was enough. He was not prepared to go on being conciliatory forever. A man's pride could only take so much. Now it was up to her to come back to him.

One thought frustrated him above all others: perhaps she had already made her decision. If she *was* planning to leave him she would probably avoid unpleasantness as far as possible simply by not telling him until the boat was due. Then she could spare them both the long, soul-searching debates and just walk out on him with a quick good-bye to the children.

And yet he could not bring himself to believe that she would really do it. They had shared so many good times together. But right now she was hating him and the island, and their enforced stay was probably doing more harm than good. Maybe bringing Val here had not been such a good idea after all. It might have given Lancing time to cool off and find another bedmate, always assuming that Brian's assessment of Lancing's reputation as a womanizer was correct. But a prolonged stay would only make Val more bitter, and perhaps force her into making a decision she would later regret.

It was all a stupid bloody mess, he told himself miserably. And it was all Val's fault for getting them into it. He felt the bottled anger rising again, and wished for the umpteenth time that instead of slapping her backside once he had given her the full, red-blooded spanking she really deserved.

He reached the kittiwake cliffs and tried to push his personal problems aside for a moment as he scanned the noisy, overcrowded ledges of the bird colonies with his binoculars. As usual there were thousands upon thousands of kittiwakes, fulmars, razorbills and other auks, but no strangers. He lowered the glasses and scowled in a rare moment of frustration and impatience.

His work on the book was going well, and he had already gathered most of what he needed in the way of background material and photographic studies of the island. All that remained now was to witness the autumn migration flocks and prepare the photographs and text for the final chapters. After that he could take the family home to Surrey and finish compiling the book in the comfort of his own study. He would have preferred to do most of the writing here, with more bird-watching breaks in between bouts at the typewriter, but it wasn't absolutely necessary. He had to finish the book, of course – he had already spent more than half of the advance – but the first priority was to get Val away from the island as quickly as possible. He searched the north horizon, where the blue-grey seas heaved slow waves to blur with the lighter blue of the sky, and wished the migration would hurry up and begin.

After a while he began to follow the cliff tops around the north end of the island, nearing the spot where the great pinnacle stacks had been cut away from the mainland. Here, on the dizzy heights, he settled down to watch the gannets diving into the surging waves far below. His perch was a large, smooth boulder, just the right height for sitting on. With his elbows supported on his knees, he held the binoculars to his eyes.

The boulder was one of a small cluster half-buried in the soft earth on the very edge of the cliff top. The rest were partially covered in a close-matted carpet of wiry grass and thick clumps of red and purple flowering heather. So solidly were Barry's boots planted in the heather that he failed to notice the green tendril which suddenly flicked out and curled around the toe of his left boot.

All his attention was on the gannets planing gracefully through the air currents below. They were large, handsome birds with snow-white plummage and black wingtips. Each bird had a deep yellow neck and head with delicate black eye markings, and was armed with a long, fish-snapping beak. They were falling from the sky like gold-tipped, feathered missiles, closing their wings to plummet deep through the surface of the sea. Most came up immediately, and sometimes a wriggling blur of silver was visible in the long beak before it was greedily gulped down. Others stayed under longer. They were fast underwater swimmers and if they missed on the first lunge they would chase the luckless fish spotted from above until at last it was gobbled up. Barry watched them fascinated. He especially liked to see half a dozen or more take the plunge together, zooming down like an aerial combat team to split the waves and snatch their meal.

The tendril which had curled around his boot belonged to a foot-high deathseed plant growing in a heather-masked crevice between two of the larger rocks. It tightened its grip and made an effort to crush the unyielding leather. Barry felt nothing and remained unaware. His heavy-duty boots had reinforced toe-caps, and even the tendril did not have the strength to buckle the thin plate of shaped steel.

The gannets were the biggest and most powerful birds in the sky, but even so they were fair game for the determined bonxie. Barry watched as one of the gannets came up with a fish clasped in its beak, and the smaller, dark-brown skua came streaking up behind it. The sunlight flashed on the white wing patches of the skua as it rammed the flapping wing of the gannet in mid-flight. The gannet tumbled seaward again with the smaller predator still clinging fast to its wing. With a shriek the gannet opened its beak and let fall the fish. Instantly the skua released the gannet and turned to dive on the falling meal. Snatching up the fish before it hit the sea, the triumphant skua soared up again and away.

'Fantastic,' Barry breathed, lowering the binoculars.

He rubbed his aching eyes for a moment, wishing he had brought a movie camera. Still he did not notice the thin green tendril curled around the toe of his boot. The plant had been squeezing in vain for several minutes now, and at last it gave up. The tendril relaxed and uncurled, and silently withdrew into the heather.

Barry was beginning to find the hard surface of his boulder seat uncomfortable. He stood up, shouldered his rucksack, and continued his slow walk along the cliffs.

Truce between Julia and Jonathon was always a short-lived affair, and by the following day they had fallen out again. Jonathon had broken one of Julia's prize seashells and refused to replace it with one of his own. They argued over breakfast until Valerie screamed at them to shut up, and then left to go their separate ways.

As they had exhausted the interest potential of beachcombing until the next bout of rough weather, they did not go back to the coves. It was another fine, sunny day, and Julia chose instead to go walking along the low west cliffs where the puffin colony had their burrows.

Jonathan had more active plans. He had fashioned a broadsword from two pieces of driftwood picked up the day before, so today he was Blood-Axe the Viking again. He had lost his great axe in battle but he had captured the sword from an enemy he had killed with his bare hands. Now his quest was to recover the great axe, the symbol of his power and rule. Before setting out to search the whole island, he first had to gather up his valiant crew. It was three days since he had last played with Robbie.

He hurried over to the Matheson cottage and was just in time to catch Ross before he disappeared over the brow of the hill. The shepherd was heading up the island carrying a straw basket with shoulder straps which he called a *kishie*, to fetch peats for the fires. A couple of times Jonathon had helped him, but peat-carrying was hard, boring work which soon lost its novelty appeal.

'Hey, Mister Matheson, where's Robbie?'

Ross turned and came back down the hill to meet him.

'Hello, laddie. I wouldn't be surprised if Robbie's out looking for you. I let him out this morning and he went running off toward the south headland. That's where you usually play, isn't it?'

Jonathon nodded. 'If I find Robbie can I play with him?'

'Of course you can,' Ross smiled. 'I reckon if you run fast enough you might catch him.'

'Thanks, Mister Matheson.' Jonathon waved and hurried off toward the south headland, drawing his wooden sword as he went. As Ross watched him go, for a moment his smile faded and his eyes clouded with uncertainty. He was remembering the strange new plants he had noticed yesterday, dotted here and there about the island. Two of the plants had small dead birds in their clutches, a stonechat and a redstart. They were only small, but they looked as though they might have somehow killed the wee birds. And that made him ill at ease.

Should he call the boy back? No – he was beginning to think like an old woman. A wee plant couldn't hurt a boy. He would be believing in trolls and ogres next, just like his old grandmother, God rest her soul. He forced a chuckle to drive away his own fears and then turned and continued on his way to the peat bog at the north end of the island.

The rabbit sat in bright sunlight on one of the grassy slopes of the south headland. It was a young rabbit, half-grown, brown in colour with the inevitable fluff of white tail. With its front paws it was busily cleaning its long ears.

The black and white collie was watching the rabbit

from a distance of about thirty yards, belly flat on the grass, nose and tail twitching with excitement. Chasing sheep was just a chore; they were slow and stupid and easy to catch, and he had been trained to be gentle with them. Rabbits were a different matter – they were fast and quick and he was free to abandon all restraint. Chasing a rabbit was an exhilarating, zestful business, and quite definitely Robbie's favourite sport. There were few of them on Lairg, but they could be seen from time to time on the south headland.

There was a strong breeze bending back the grass blades and rustling the heather, and Robbie was downwind of his quarry. The rabbit was in a slight hollow, and the dog came to within twenty yards before the rabbit sensed that it was being stalked. Its paws dropped down, its head shot up, and it looked round in alarm. Robbie charged, and the rabbit bolted.

The chase was fast and furious, and Robbie gave a loud bark of pure joy as the rabbit fled in terror. Quickly the collie overhauled his quarry and was almost within paw's reach when the rabbit made a sudden right turn. Robbie overshot and all but tumbled nose over tail in his efforts to brake and shift on to the new tack. He could not match the rabbit's tight turn, but once he was off again with his long, leaping bounds, the gap soon began to narrow down once more.

For a second time the rabbit eluded the dog by streaking into the heart of a tumble of rocks. Robbie skidded to a stop, barking ferociously, and managed to scare his petrified quarry out of the other side. The dog rushed around the rocks and the chase continued, but again Robbie had lost ground. The pursuit led over the headland and down into a heather-choked gulley where the rabbit sought desperately for refuge. Robbie plunged after it, but in the dense tangle of undergrowth he lost both sight and scent and came to a frustrated stop. He barked his displeasure and then began to cast round in circles as he hunted for the scent.

The rabbit had slipped under the heather tangles and raced to the far end of the gulley towards a bolt hole in the soft earth. It stopped on the edge of the hole, within inches of safety. It knew it had lost the dog and paused for a moment to reassure itself and look back. The sounds of Robbie's sniffing movements were far back along the gulley, and the hole was comfortingly close. The rabbit sat panting, its tiny heart hammering in its trembling breast, and waited a few fateful seconds to catch its breath.

Unknown to the rabbit, the island had spawned a new enemy – an enemy which was to prove far more deadly than the sporting instincts of a playful dog. In a flash, the nearest deathseed plant lashed out a tendril, and the rabbit was caught and dragged squealing away from the edge of the hole. Then more tendrils pulled it close into the plant's merciless embrace.

Robbie had picked up the scent again, and he was forcing his way, nose to the ground, through the heather. Hearing the shrieks of the rabbit, his ears pricked up. Eagerly he bounded forward once more and skidded to another stop when he broke through the barrier of heather and saw his quarry struggling in the green coils.

For a few moments the dog stood still, its head cocked to one side, ears and tail alert, watching. Robbie was puzzled and disappointed. Something else had caught the rabbit – and ruined his sport. The rabbit was still shrieking pitifully. Robbie moved closed to investigate, sniffing warily.

Another tendril flicked out from a second plant, larger than the first. But Robbie was alert, all his senses fully aroused. He jerked back fast and the tendril flailed and missed. The collie's hackles rose, sensing danger. His nostrils flared and he bared his teeth and began to bark angrily.

Jonathon had been trying to catch up with Robbie for the past five minutes. He had been approaching the headland when he had first heard Robbie's excited barks as he started up the rabbit. Led on by the sounds and an occasional glimpse of the chase, Jonathon had trailed behind at a run but had lost Robbie completely when dog and rabbit disappeared into the gulley. Now the fresh outbreak of barking gave him a new guide. He did not realize that the tone of the barks had changed.

He plunged into the gulley at breakneck speed, falling over the heather and picking himself up again. He shouted Robbie's name and used his wooden sword to beat down the heather as he struggled forward. Finally he broke into the clearing where Robbie crouched, and came to a panting stop. He was out of breath and his knees were feeling wobbly after his run.

'Robbie,' he gasped, and stared with sudden uncertainty at the collie.

Robbie's back was toward him, haunches up and shoulders down, as though preparing to spring. His ears and the stiff hairs around his neck stood erect and his eyes were fixed on something dead ahead. He did not look round at the sound of Jonathon's voice, but growled deep and low in his throat. The growl might have been a warning.

The rabbit was not quite dead. It managed to get out another crushed squeak. Jonathon looked up and saw the brown fur and the puffball of white tail wrapped up in the tendrils of the plant. His eyes opened wide and his heart began to thump.

'Gosh,' he breathed hoarsely. 'It's a cat-whisker plant — a big one! And it's caught a rabbit. Come back, Robbie —' He reached tentatively for the dog's collar. 'Back, boy. Don't get too close.'

Robbie growled again, a deep, menacing snarl. Apart from a shivering of muscles beneath his black and white coat, he stayed motionless. The boy and the dog continued to stare at the rabbit, which was now squirming feebly, its last few gasps of life being squeezed out of it. In a very few seconds it would be dead.

Jonathon's mouth was dry and he wet his lips with his tongue. He wanted to help the poor little rabbit, but he didn't know whether he had the courage. His wooden sword was still gripped tight in his right hand and he wondered if he could attack the plant quickly and chop it down. The sword would chop down heather, or bracken and nettles, but he had a sick-tummy feeling that a cat-whisker plant might be made of tougher stuff. He wondered what Blood-Axe the Viking would do. The answer was clear – Blood-Axe was fearless, Blood-Axe would attack.

Jonathon drew a deep breath and raised his sword. In another moment he would have made a quick, slashing, in-an-out attack. The plant holding the rabbit was only about eighteen inches high and he didn't really believe it was big enough to hurt him. But Jonathon had not seen the second, even larger deathseed plant, half-obscured by the tangles of tall, thick heather. A tendril twice as thick as those holding the rabbit came lashing out of the heather as soon as Jonathon moved into range, curling fast and tight around the upraised wrist holding the sword.

Jonathon screamed. He was caught off-balance and tumbled forward. Before he could pull back, another tendril had fastened around his upper thigh and he was drawn inexorably into the plant's embrace. He was not its first victim. The stiff, bedraggled husks of two dead crows, the remains of its last meal, were already entangled, and Jonathon's face was dragged close to the revolting scraps of dried black feathers. The dead, glazed eye and open, agonized beak of the nearest carrion-eater were only inches from Jonathon's nose, and the vile, rotting smell almost choked him. He shrieked in total, uncontrollable hysteria.

Behind him Robbie began barking again, furiously but helplessly.

Julia had walked as far as she dared along the west cliffs, but after half a mile she came to a reluctant stop. She knew Barry would be angry if he caught her going any further. But for a moment she felt a rebellious impulse to go on and look at the magnificent rock stacks. Of course, her father was right to confine *Jonathon* to the south end of the island, because Jonathon always rushed blindly into things and was so stupid he would probably fall over his own feet. But it was a bit unfair to apply the same rule to her. She was sensible enough to stay away from the dangerous edges, and she was not likely to do anything daft or silly like Jonathon. However, her father had made the rule, and although Julia did not agree with it, she obeyed it.

Before she turned back she stood for several minutes, gazing wistfully out to sea toward Mainland, searching the vast expanse of white-flecked, blue-grey waves. There was a drift-trawler far out on the north-west horizon, but it was not the boat she was looking for. The boat she hoped to see would be smaller and under sail, and she knew who would be in it. Alistair Mckenna had offered to come out to Lairg and take her out for a few hours' fishing. She had not said yes, but she had not said no either, and she felt that he might be keen enough to come anyway. She thought of his dark curling hair and his smile, and wished that she had given him a bit more encouragement.

It would be wonderful if he did come. She was fed up with Lairg Island already. It could have been a really nice holiday, but Jonathon was such a pest, and Mother's mysterious black moods and Dad's long bitter silences were spoiling it all. She would not be at all sorry if Alistair appeared in his boat to take her out to sea for the day – even though she was sure she would be sea-sick and secretly did not particularly want to go fishing in the first place. Just to be with Alistair would make it all worthwhile. But there was no sign of another boat.

The wind was cold and blustery at this height, so soon she turned and began to walk back the way she had come, past the puffin slopes, down toward the west coves, and up again where the coast path wound round the south headland. From the top there was another wide view of the sea, sweeping southward this time. Perhaps she would be able to see more boats from there.

As she climbed up the hill, she suddenly heard Robbie's demented barking, and above it a shrill, high-pitched shrieking that made her blood run cold. She was so accustomed to hearing the loud cries of the seabirds that her first thought was that some huge, monster gull must be attacking the dog. She stared in the direction of the sound. The second shock was like an arrow of ice to her heart. The shrieks were human. There were only the Mathesons and her own family on the island, so the simple process of deduction and the shrillness of the shrieks told her they were coming from Jonathon.

Julia broke into a run, spurred on by the blind panic in Jonathon's cries. She reached the top of the headland and still she could see nothing, but the screaming and barking drew her down into the heather-filled gulley. After almost tripping over Robbie who was making short, frantic rushes from side to side, she saw Jonathon. Her brother was held fast in the long tendrils of a grotesque plant some three feet in height. The heather was now trampled flat on all sides by his efforts to escape, but clearly he did not have the strength to break free. His back was arched and he was screaming in pain, as though his whole body was being crushed and broken.

Julia stared in horror, and then rushed forward to try and break the tendrils away with her fingers, but they were like hard rubber and she could not move them. From the corner of her eye she saw Jonathon's makeshift wooden sword lying in the trampled heather and desperately she snatched it up. Wielding it with all her strength, she hacked down at the plant, trying to chop at the base of the tendrils. But despite their flexibility they seemed solid as wood and refused to be knocked down. Her blows broke off the thick foliage of velvety-green leaves and the leaf-bearing branches, but had no effect on the main stems and the deadly tendrils. Jonathon was writhing and thrashing beside her, eyes bulging and mouth hanging open, and his screams were fading. In terror, Julia realized that between them they did not have the strength to save him.

The plant was defending itself. Most of its tendrils were curled around Jonathon, but two were still waving free. One of them lashed low and snatched at Julia's ankle. Now it was her turn to shriek. The new fear for her own safety flooded through her whole being. Feeling sick and weak, she watched as the last tendril hooked around the wooden sword and pulled it from her fingers. Defenceless, she swayed backward and fell with a thump on to her bottom.

For a moment she could only sit there, and from the intense crushing pressure around her ankle she could fully appreciate her brother's agony. Jonathon was almost silent now, making only gasping sobs, and his struggles had weakened. Julia knew that if she did not get him free within the next few minutes he was going to die. Even as she watched, he was being slowly crushed to death.

She wanted to scream desperately for someone to help her, but she knew there was no one. Her father would be up on the north cliffs, her mother was probably sulking in the cottage, and the Mathesons were on the other side of the island. None of them were likely to hear her calls. She had to fight the battle alone. And now she could not even help herself. The tendril around her ankle was pulling her slowly but surely into the parent plant.

She stared at the horror, trying to think of a way to fight it. Their struggles had partially uprooted the plant, yet still it was holding them in a vice-like grip, each tendril lashed round like a python or a boa-constrictor. Suddenly the sight of the half-bared roots reminded her of something she had read at school about snakes which crushed their prey. Pythons and boa-constrictors had to have an anchor point; they had to be able to curl their tails around a rock or a branch before they could exercise the full squeezing power of their long, muscled bodies. Perhaps this plant-thing worked on the same principle.

She pulled herself up and lunged forward. This time she went straight for the heart of the plant, reached down and seized a root, and with all her strength ripped it out of the earth. Without pausing to judge the effect, she grabbed the next root and the next, hauling them up in a desperate frenzy. She broke her nails and bloodied her fingers on the hard stony soil – but still the roots came out. Finally the whole plant came up and Julia fell back with Jonathon and the plant on top of her.

She wriggled free and found that the tendril around her ankle had fallen away. Robbed of its anchorage in the earth the enfeebled plant had lost its grip. Julia tore the limp tendrils away from Jonathon and dragged him away up the gulley. Her brother had fainted, but mercifully he was still breathing. Julia collapsed at last in a heap beside him, sweating and trembling from head to toe, and began to cry uncontrollably. Robbie still rushed around them in circles, barking madly in his agitation.

CHAPTER THIRTEEN

The storm clouds were brewing up again, bringing more of the icy Arctic gales roaring down from the north. By mid-day the weather had changed completely, the overcast sky shutting out the sun, and the sea changing colour to a heavy grey. The winds whipped up and the rain came, first in wet, gusty squalls and then in a solid downpour. The huge waves smashing over the rocks at the base of the north cliffs were terrifying banks of exploding white foam, and the spray boomed as high as the cliff tops. With the seabirds grounded, Barry was finally driven home, soaking wet and chilled to the bone.

Thankfully, he reached the cottage and reassured himself that all the family were here before him with a quick count of the wet anoraks hanging in the lean-to extension. He hung up his own outer clothes, but hesitated before going to join them. The worst aspect of the bad weather was that it forced him into Val's company – a kind of prison sentence he could have done without. He would have preferred solitary confinement.

Bracing himself inwardly, he went into the kitchen for a cup of coffee. He forced himself to whistle as he checked the water level in the kettle and moved it on to the hot hob of the ancient stove. He stooped to feed another peat block on to the fire beneath.

'Barry,' Valerie's voice called him from the main living area. 'Will you come here, please.'

Barry straightened up slowly. The tone of her voice was deathly flat and serious, graver than he had ever heard it before. His mouth tightened, his brain racing to compute its meaning. So she had made her decision, then. Probably the kids had pushed the issue by asking questions and she had felt obliged to give them some sort of answer. Perhaps she had already told Jonathon and Julia, and now she was about to tell him. Well, he thought grimly, it had to come sometime. Today was a ruined day because of the bloody awful weather, so now was as good a time as any. He squared his shoulders and went into the bigger room, where the peat fire glowed hot and cosy in the large hearth.

Julia and Jonathon were sitting on low stools close to the fire and both of them looked pale and subdued. It was an ill omen. Jonathon was hunched into his blue bath-robe, which was unusual for this time of day, but Barry barely noticed. He was looking at his wife's face, which was grey and tense and confirmed his worst fears.

'What do you want?' he asked bleakly.

'We've got something to tell you,' Valerie said in a low voice. She bit her lip then, and hesitated, afraid of sounding ridiculous, but went on: 'Jonathon was nearly killed this morning. A big plant tried to eat him.'

Barry stared at her and blinked. He had been through this scene so many times in his mind, preparing a response to every possible opening, but this one left him speechless. It was so utterly unlike what he expected that for a moment he could not believe his ears.

Valerie had been sitting in a chair close to the children. Now she stood up to face him and took a step forward. Her lip quivered and he realized she was scared.

'It's true, Barry. It happened up on the south headland. Robbie was chasing a rabbit and Jonathon chasing the dog. They went into the heather, and this plant thing grabbed Jonathon and tried to strangle him. If Julia hadn't been close enough to help him, then God knows what would have happened. They're both convinced it would have killed him.'

Barry struggled to make the mental adjustment between what he had anticipated and what she was actually saying. The whole thing was too incredible to believe.

'A man-eating plant?' he said at last. 'That's rich, even coming from Jonathon's fertile imagination. We've had Vikings, and pirates, and sea-monsters. But a man-eating plant here on Lairg? That's stretching it a bit too far.'

'It's the truth, Daddy,' Julia and Jonathon chorused.

Barry stared at them doubtfully.

'*I* believe them,' Valerie said sharply, getting angry and springing to their defence. 'When they came home an hour ago they were both terrified out of their wits. I know Jonathon can exaggerate and imagine wild things, but this time he was really afraid. It was genuine! And Julia saw this thing too. She swears she had to help Jonathon escape from its tentacles, and she grew out of playing childish games long ago.'

'They're bored,' Barry guessed. 'Julia's just teasing us to humour Jonathon. It's all in their imagination.'

'It's not!' Julia wailed, and looked ready to weep.

Barry was still unconvinced, but Valerie wasted no more time with words. She turned to Jonathon, lifted him to his feet and pulled open his bath-robe. Moving behind him, she pulled the robe back off his shoulders.

'Now will you believe me?' she yelled. 'Or are you telling me he imagined all this, for Christ's sake!'

Barry stared at his son. Jonathon stood naked but for his underpants, and around his arms, the upper part of his thigh, and across his chest there were rows of livid welts and dark purple bruises. The boy looked as though he had been crudely trussed with harsh ropes which had cut deep into his flesh. Jonathon was biting his lip and began to whimper.

'My God,' Barry said slowly. He went closer and knelt in front of his son, staring at the bruises. Gently he touched an unmarked shoulder and Jonathon flinched. 'It's all right, Jon,' he murmured softly. 'It's all right. I won't hurt you.'

'I've checked him over,' Valerie said. 'Mercifully there are no broken bones. I bathed the bruises with a cold compress and then gave him a warm bath. I didn't know what else to do.'

'There isn't much else.' Barry took the bath-robe from her and carefully drew it back around Jonathon's shoulders. 'Easy now, Jon. Just sit down and take it easy. It's painful, I know, but the worst will be over in a couple of days. Soon you'll be fighting fit again.' He looked up at Valerie. 'You said it happened on the south headland?'

She nodded. 'About an hour ago. I would have fetched you straight away, but I had to take care of Jonathon first. Then the weather turned so nasty I knew it would bring you home.'

Barry turned to Julia, and saw from her white face that she too needed comfort. He was still holding Jonathon's hand and he put his other arm around his daughter's shoulders.

'Tell me about it,' he urged gently. 'Tell me everything. This time I promise you I'm listening.'

The gales raged for the rest of that day and continued through the wild black night. It was dawn again before the solid downpour eased to a steady drizzle and the winds lost their strength. Jonathon had slept fitfully through the night and awoke stiff and still sore, but gamely volunteered to accompany his father when Barry decided the weather had improved sufficiently for them to go out and investigate.

All four of them went. The children were needed as guides, and Valerie refused to be left behind. If there was something on the island which posed a threat to her children, then she was determined to learn all about it.

They climbed the wet, slippery slope to the south headland in silence, uncomfortable in the drizzle with their anorak hoods up and their backs bent, butting into the wind. When they reached the spot where Julia had finally untangled Jonathon from the deathseed plant, she held up her hand for them to stop. They all stared at the surrounding grass, rocks and heather, but there was nothing else. The large, uprooted plant had vanished.

'It was here,' Julia insisted as she saw her father frown. 'It was right here, where I'm standing.'

'Then where is it now?'

'I don't know.' Julia made a guess. 'Perhaps the wind blew it away.'

The continuous storm winds of the night before had been powerful, it was true. Several times it had seemed as though they would rip the heavy thatched roof right off the cottage, so it was unlikely they would have left a dead plant unmoved on the exposed headland. Even so, it was an incredible story, and without the evidence Barry's doubts returned.

Julia felt frustrated as she watched her father's face, but Jonathon was not so easily defeated. He searched the ground more closely and then called out,

'Here, Dad. Here's one. This is a cat-whisker plant.'

Barry went to look at the tiny plant at Jonathon's feet. It was just past the seedling stage, and its bright green leaves and sky-blue flowers looked no more harmful than a clump of buttercups.

'This?' he demanded sceptically. 'Are you serious, Jon? Is this it?'

'Not this one,' Jonathon said. 'This is just how they start. It's only a baby. The one which grabbed me was fully grown. But look – you can see the little feelers.'

Barry looked more closely, and indeed there were little hair-fine tendrils growing from the stem of the tiny plant. He frowned again, see-sawing between doubt and belief. Then Jonathon remembered how the whole experience had begun, and pulled hard at Barry's arm.

'Come on, Dad. This way. 'I'll show you the rabbit.'

FLOWERS OF EVIL

Barry allowed himself to be led down into the gulley. For once Jonathon was not eager to run ahead and kept a firm hold on his father's hand. Valerie and Julia followed them as they pushed through the wet heather. A minute later they reached the spot. The trampled heather and uprooted earth showed clearly where the deathseed plant had been ripped away. Beside the hole the smaller plant, now nearly two feet high, was still growing. In its tendrils were the crushed remains of a lapwing and the small brown rabbit.

They gazed at it in silence. Julia pressed closer to her mother, and Valerie felt a sick revulsion.

'The one which caught me was bigger,' Jonathon said nervously.

'Well, this one isn't going to get any bigger,' said Barry. Remembering what Julia had told him, he made a lunge for the plant, grabbing the thick stem close to the ground. Instantly, the tendrils closed around his arm, but he gave a fierce heave and tugged the plant out by its roots before it could tighten its grip. Then he threw it away, tendrils squirming feebly, into the heather. He looked round and saw Valerie staring at him with a white face.

'There may be more of them,' Valerie said, giving voice to her fear. 'Barry, what are we going to do?'

'You're going back to the cottage with the children,' he declared after a pause for thought. 'I'm going to talk to Ross Matheson.'

He met Ross while he was still a hundred yards from the other's cottage. The rain was still falling and the shepherd turned back and invited him inside where they could talk out of the wet. Barry said a polite good morning to Janet and then quickly got to the point.

Ross listened gravely without interrupting. At one point he absent-mindedly packed tobacco into the bowl and lit up his pipe, but his eyes never strayed from Barry's face. Barry finished his story and waited for some comment, but Ross was silent for another half-minute. The shepherd was thinking carefully before he spoke.

'I feared something was wrong,' he said at last. 'Janet told me how Robbie came home yesterday in great distress. He howled to be let in and wouldn't go out again – not even to meet me. That's unusual for Robbie.'

The black and white collie was stretched out by the fire and his ears flicked as his name was mentioned. He pulled closer to his master and whined softly. Ross reached down and stroked the dog's ear and the side of its neck, again absently because his thoughts were far away.

'I was worried about your children,' he confessed. 'That's why I was on my way over to see you just now. But you've saved me a walk. I'm glad you came. There are things I have to show you.'

'What things?' Barry asked warily.

'Plants,' Ross said grimly. 'Devil plants, because that's what they are. There's more like the one that attacked your wee laddie.'

With no more to be said, the two men put on their coats again. Janet had said nothing while they talked, but her face betrayed her anxiety. Ross stooped over her chair to kiss her good-bye.

'Don't fret now, love. I'll be back before you know it.'

'Aye,' Janet said, 'but be careful.' She felt helpless and vulnerable, and for the first time she wished briefly that she was not heavy with child.

Barry and Ross moved to the door. Robbie followed them halfway and then stopped, his tail down between his legs and his brown eyes uncertain. Ross looked back at his dog.

'It's all right, Robbie. You can stay with Janet. Stay, boy. Stay.'

FLOWERS OF EVIL

Robbie lowered his head – almost shamefully, Barry thought – and then went back to settle beside Janet's chair.

They stepped out into the rain-laden wind and Ross led the way up the steep slopes in the general direction of the peat bog and the kittiwake cliffs. Another storm was building up and the noise made conversation difficult. Ross did not seem eager to talk anyway, as though mere words would not describe what he wanted Barry to witness. Barry slipped several times on the wet grass and cursed the foul weather, which seemed capable of blowing up a new gale with every hour.

Ten minutes later they were on the inland edge of the peat bog, where there was good grazing for the sheep. They had passed only a few members of the scattered flock, the ones too stupid to make their own way down to the shelter of the corral or the cottage walls. They were huddled in the soaking hollows, and Barry had felt sorry for them. Now he saw there was a worse fate which could befall a luckless sheep on Lairg. Ross stopped and pointed to a huge, five-foot high deathseed plant which had trapped a bedraggled ewe in its clutches. The sheep was dead, and had obviously been so for a day or more. Its white fleece was streaked with red where the blood had drained from its crushed carcass.

'I found it yesterday,' Ross said grimly, forced to raise his voice above the sound of the wind and rain. 'It was after the weather turned bad, and I was on my way home. I've seen a few more of these things – little ones that might have snared a wee bird or two. But the size of this one scares the hell out of me.'

For an instant Barry had a mental image of Jonathon hanging squeezed and bloodless in place of the ewe, and for the first time he fully understood how his children must have felt, fighting for their lives the day before. His stomach seemed to heave and roll over.

'What in God's name is it?' he asked. 'And how did it get here?'

'I don't know what it is, nor where it came from,' Ross said bleakly. 'But one thing I do know. It multiplies quickly, and it grows awful fast. I'll swear on my father's Bible there was nothing growing here a week ago. In fact I'd swear there wasn't a plant like this anywhere on the island. But now I fear there may be a lot more than the few we've seen.'

Barry stared at the deathseed plant, taking care to stay out of range of its tendrils and trying hard to understand it. 'I don't know much about flesh-eating plants,' he admitted. 'But the ones I've read about have all been small-scale. Usually, they catch flies and things by closing up the head of the flower or a bladder of some kind, and then digest them by breaking down the bodies with the chemicals in their own juices.'

'This one's different,' Ross retorted. 'You can see, the body of the sheep hasn't been digested in any way. But it looks all squeezed up and shrunken. This thing doesn't exactly devour its prey, it just pumps it dry and somehow absorbs the blood.'

'You're right.' Barry remembered the rabbit, which he had been able to study more closely. He shuddered, but not from the cold of the rain. 'Have you seen any more big ones like this?'

'No, but I've got a nasty feeling there may be more sheep missing. With the weather so bad I haven't been able to make a proper count, but I've a feeling for them just the same. In time you get to know them. I can run my eye over the flock and know if it's short before I count them up. It's a shepherd's instinct.'

'How many do you think are missing?'

'Perhaps another two or three. It's hard to tell while the rain lasts. They could be huddled under a bit of cover somewhere. Or stuck in a gulley, or fallen over one of the cliffs. Or else –' He looked at the deathseed plant and its latest victim, and shrugged his shoulders.

Barry said slowly but positively, 'Then it's time we started thinking about getting ourselves off this island, or getting some help out here. At the very least we must let the police or the authorities on Mainland know what's happening. We'll go back to your cottage and you can telephone.'

Ross looked at him with a small measure of pity. Another time he might have smiled gently at the visitor's touching faith that the island had all the amenities of modern living – but this was no laughing matter. 'You forget,' he said. 'There's no telephone on Lairg. Most of the time it's just me and Janet; they'd hardly bother to lay an underwater cable just for the two of us.'

'Damn.' Barry snapped his fingers in exasperation. 'Stupid of me. I meant use the radio.' He stopped and stared at Ross in growing alarm. 'You must have some contact with the rest of the world? You must have a radio, surely?'

Sadly Ross shook his head. 'The only radio you've seen in my house is Janet's. It picks up the BBC programmes and it plays back her cassette tapes, but it's not a transmitter. I'm sorry.'

'So am I,' Barry said with feeling. 'I must be naïve, but I always assumed you'd have some kind of emergency contact with Mainland. What happens if you need a doctor in a hurry?'

'I've thought of getting a radio,' Ross said. 'But amateur equipment is expensive and I kept putting it off. Janet and I are both young and healthy. We don't have much need for doctors. In the meantime, there's only the mailboat.'

'Due in four days' time,' Barry calculated quickly. 'Let's hope it gets here on schedule.'

'It will if the weather's good,' Ross said sombrely, 'but

I wouldn't count on it. This time of the year we get a lot of gales, and the forecast for the next few days isn't too good. The weather might change if we're lucky, but on the other hand it's not uncommon for Lairg to be cut off for a month or more at a time.'

CHAPTER FOURTEEN

Valerie spent a worrying two hours waiting for Barry to return. She had locked the cottage door and securely fastened all the windows, but even though she knew she was taking extreme precautions, she still did not feel safe. The rain rattled steadily on the window panes and she kept the children close beside her, all three of them sitting with knees drawn up beneath them on the thick rug by the fire. She threw on more peats to build up the fire but still cold shivers ran up and down her spine.

She made an effort to occupy the children with a game of scrabble, but Jonathon was not interested. He had found their guide to British wild plants and flowers and was searching diligently through its pages for anything resembling a cat-whisker plant. He found nothing and was delighted. In fact, he was so delighted to have discovered something new, that he almost forgot his ordeal.

Julia was sensitive to her mother's mood, but Jonathon kept on and on about his find until Valerie screamed at him to shut up. Then she immediately repented and cuddled him, tears in her eyes. More than ever she wished that they were anywhere but on this accursed island, but for the first time since they had arrived she was not blaming Barry. It was not his fault that Lairg had suddenly become infested with carnivorous plant life. All she could think of was that he was alone outside and might not come back. Yesterday she had hated him. But now she did not want to be left alone, not here. Desperately she wanted him to come back.

When at last he arrived at the door it made her heart jump. The door rattled and then he knocked and called out her name, realizing it was locked. Hugely relieved at the sound of his voice, she hurried to bring down the stout wooden bar and shoot back the bolt.

Barry came in dripping, with raindrops glistening in the curls of his dark beard. There were streaks of black mud smeared down the sleeve and shoulder of his green anorak, and more mud caked thickly on his boots. When he pushed back the hood of his anorak his hair was dishevelled, beneath it Valerie saw a fresh bruise on his temple.

'Barry, what happened?'

He smiled, more than pleased to see the concern in her eyes. 'Easy now, let me shut the door and get my coat off. Then I'll tell you.'

'Daddy, did you find Ross?' asked Julia.

'What about Robbie? Is Robbie all right?' Jonathon shouted.

'One at a time,' Barry insisted. 'I found Ross Matheson, and he and Janet, and the dog, are all okay. Now give me a minute and I'll tell you the rest.'

He went into the extension to shed his top clothes and his boots, and came back with a towel, rubbing his hair. He pulled up a stool and joined them at the fire. Quietly, he outlined the events of his meeting with Ross.

'What happened to your face?' Valerie asked anxiously. 'And how did you get covered in mud?'

'Well, Ross and I decided it was best to get rid of the plant that had killed his sheep, so we went back to the cottage for a couple of the sharp-edged spades. We tackled it together.' He chose to ignore Valerie's look of horror and grinned boyishly at Jonathon. 'I think it must have been bigger than yours, Jon, but I'll grant you they're a handful. We had to go in close, and the brute grabbed hold of Ross and me. I reckon if either of us had been alone we'd have made its next meal, but between us we dug down, sliced through its roots, and then got the spades under it. We heaved it up and threw it over and the fight went out of it. Just to make sure it couldn't take root again, we dragged it to the edge of the island and tossed it over the cliffs.'

'Wow!' Jonathon looked thrilled, and his eyes were shining.

'You fool,' Valerie burst out. 'Why didn't you just leave the damned thing alone? Both of you could have been strangled.'

Barry put a hand on her knee. 'Val, I had to give Ross a hand, otherwise he would have tackled it alone. We may have the sense to look out for these things and keep away from them now we know they're out there, but he has to think of his sheep.'

'Oh.' Valerie was subdued. She had forgotten about the sheep.

'And there's another thing,' Barry told her. 'We don't know how big these things can grow. They certainly seem to be prolific and they like the sea air. We thought it best to get rid of this one before it got any bigger. We mustn't let them get out of hand.'

'We?' Valerie protested. 'Barry, it just isn't our business. We have got to get away from this place. Ross and Janet will go too, if they've got an ounce of sense.'

'It may not be as simple as that.' Barry broke the bad news about there being no radio, and the ominous weather signs which made the return of the mailboat unpredictable. 'We could be here for a week or more, and we've already seen that these things can grow at a rapid rate. They're dangerous – and the only way we can safeguard ourselves is to keep pulling them up before they get to an unmanageable size.'

'Is that what you plan to do?'

Barry nodded. 'Ross and I have talked it over. As soon as the weather breaks a bit, I'll take you and the children over to the Matheson cottage. You can all stay with Janet and keep each other company. Ross and I will take a couple of spades and scour the island. We have to hunt these things down and destroy them before they get big enough to destroy us.'

Valerie bit her lip and was silent for a minute. Finally she reached a decision. 'It's a big island when you think in terms of searching every inch of it. We'll leave the children with Janet and I'll come with you and Ross. There must be another spade.'

Barry was doubtful. 'I'm not sure I want you with us. Ross thinks there are more sheep missing, so there could be a few more big plants around. It might be better if you stayed behind.'

Valerie was frightened, but first and foremost she was a mother. She reached for Julia and Jonathon and put her hands on their shoulders. She said with finality:

'These are my children as well as yours, so if there's something out there that's a danger to them – I'm going to help you fight it.'

The weather eased the next morning. The day dawned grey and overcast with low cloud, but at least the rain and the wind had died down. They ate an almost silent breakfast and then set out for the Matheson cottage, Barry carrying a spade over his shoulder. When they arrived Ross quickly found a spare spade for Valerie.

Jonathon made a last-ditch effort to persuade Barry to let him join the adults, but it was squashed like the dozen arguments which had preceded it. Glumly, Jonathon promised to stay with Janet and Julia, but as a consolation prize he was permitted to keep Robbie.

Ross had already corralled any sheep within easy reach, and they spent the rest of the morning rounding up the strays. From now on the sheep would be confined to the corral. Ross was determined to provide no more free meals.

They began their systematic search for deathseed

plants in the afternoon. For Barry and Valerie, although they did not recognize the fact until much later, it was a new beginning, a turning point in their relationship. From now on they stopped pulling apart and began actively working together.

They started with the low valley between the two cottages, Ross working one hillside and Barry and Valerie the other. Fearing that the tenacious little plants might dig down their roots again once they had been pulled up, each of them carried a *kishie*, the plan being to collect the plants in the straw baskets as they went along and then tip the lot over the nearest cliff into the sea.

They filled the baskets much more quickly than they had expected. Now that he was searching the ground at his feet instead of gazing constantly skyward at the wheeling circles of seabirds, Barry was amazed at the number of little blue-flowered plants he managed to find. Most of them were no more than three to six inches high, but here and there they found a bigger one which had started to trap small birds.

When Valerie found the three-foot plant which was growing half-concealed in the heather tangles halfway between the two cottages, her heart seemed to lurch into her mouth. How close she must have passed by it on her walks to visit Janet! She called Barry, who made a determined attack to dig it up, but the tendrils, which were longer than the plant itself, managed to get an immediate grip on his arms, and on the spade. Barry struggled and Valerie screamed. Ross came running from the slope of the far hill, but Valerie did not wait. Forgetting her fear, she plunged in with her spade, chopping wildly at the plant's roots. Once she had loosened the roots, Barry got both hands around the main stem of the plant and threw his weight backward. The plant came up in a thrashing tangle of greenery, but then went limp, defeated.

After that they felt it prudent to hold a conference and make some rules. Valerie was forbidden to touch any plant that was more than eighteen inches in height – she was to leave them all to Ross or Barry. And in the case of any plant approaching a height of three foot or more, the two men agreed to wait until they were both in a position to tackle it together.

The search went on until they had emptied a dozen basket loads of the feebly writhing plants into the sea. Valerie found her back was aching and her hands had developed blisters from the unaccustomed work with the spade. However, by then they had cleared the entire triangle between the paths linking the cottages and leading back from each cottage to the small south cove with the landing quay.

'We'll do the south-west corner of the island next,' Ross decided, as they leaned on their spades for a breather. 'That'll give me one area where it's safe to let the sheep graze. Then tomorrow we'll do the south headland and work our way north.' He looked at Valerie and smiled. 'But I don't think there's any need for you to do any more tonight. You've worked hard enough.'

'I'll stick it out,' Valerie said defiantly. She was beginning to find that working with the spade was preferable to sitting at home and worrying. She made a brave effort to return the smile. 'We're into the nineteen-eighties now. Women are supposed to be equal to men nowadays.'

They worked on through the last few hours of daylight. The south-west part of the island was not too badly affected, except for one small area where they found a six-foot horror which had fed on another of the missing sheep. Valerie recoiled from the gruesome spectacle, but did not dare to turn her back on it. They had already learned that the tendrils had a reach of anything up to twice the height of the parent plant, so Ross and Barry circled the monster warily from opposite sides, keeping a good twelve feet away.

'*Now!*' Barry shouted, and with spades levelled they both charged in and struck together.

The larger plants seemed to have their roots only partially buried in the earth, as though they only went down as far as was absolutely necessary to get an anchoring grip. This left a good third of the upper roots exposed, and gave its enemies a fighting chance. Ross and Barry severed two of the main roots before the giant plant fought back. The dead sheep was completely dried and drained, just a dirty fleece bag of dehydrated pulp and bones, and the plant surprised them by letting it go and bringing all of its tentacles into play. Barry chopped through another root before finding himself helpless in its grip. Ross was immediately entangled.

Valerie stood petrified. A tendril had curled around Barry's body, pinning his arms to his sides, and he was struggling like a fly stuck in the elastic green web of some hideous vegetable spider. Ross was still wielding his spade but he could no longer pull back to get a full swing and his blows were losing their bite. It took him three short hacking blows to cut another root, and then yet another tendril wriggled around his arm.

Ross and Barry were cursing in unison, first in anger and then with a naked edge of fear in their voices. Valerie jerked out of her frozen shock, took a tight grip on her spade, and ran in to help them. The main tendrils were already coiled around the two men so she was able to complete the attack on the roots unmolested. Three minutes later the plant toppled and Ross and Barry were able to untangle themselves. Valerie dropped her spade, flew into Barry's arms, and wept.

For a few moments he comforted her, and then all three of them surveyed the boot-churned battleground and the tangled wreckage of the fallen plant. It had taken all of their combined efforts to bring it down.

Barry voiced the fear they were all feeling.

'That was a close fight. We almost lost. If they grow any bigger than this brute...'

He left the sentence unfinished, suddenly realizing that it would do no good to frighten Valerie. But it was too late. Valerie was already terrified.

Nadia Gavrilova was one of only three children living in Babushskaya. Her mother had left the village to marry and bear her child, but much later when her own mother had become widowed and infirm she had persuaded her husband to come back with her and re-settle. The other children were both boys, two brothers who had been brought back to the village in similar circumstances. Their mother too had to return to help care for ailing grandparents.

Nadia was the oldest of the three children. She was ten, the same age as Jonathon Gordon. Like Jonathon, she had the misfortune to walk into the lurking tendrils of a deathseed plant; but her adventure was fatal. The two small boys had been confined to their own backyard by their cautious mother, and Nadia was playing alone. No one was close enough to hear her dying screams.

The child was missed an hour later when her mother called to her to come in for her evening meal. The men of the village organized a search party, but Nadia was not difficult to find. All the children had been warned to stay away from the roped-off enclosure where Shumilov had set up his field study, and so the search began on the opposite side of the village. The wind had carried the seed spores over the village and the deathseed plant and Nadia were found on the edge of a thicket of elder and wild blackberry bushes.

Nadia's mother became hysterical and her heart-rending shrieks and sobs continued without pause until she collapsed from grief and exhaustion. Nadia's father was equally affected, but his anguish took a more vengeful and violent form. The scientists working on the Khyshtym road were the culprits! Gavrilova had to be physically restrained from seeking out Shumilov and murdering the little professor with his bare hands. Fortunately a working party of soldiers had been stationed in the village to guard the field study site and keep out unwanted visitors, and these were on hand to keep the potentially ugly situation under some degree of control.

Shumilov hurried to the scene, badly shaken, and immediately gave orders for the plant to be destroyed and for the child's body to be retrieved. The job was done quickly by six soldiers with spades. But the villagers were not appeased. Children everywhere are the bright glow of hope in the hearts of their elders, and in Babushskaya, where children were scarce, little Nadia and her two playmates were cherished more than most. Every woman in the village was distraught, and every man was in a grief-stricken rage. First poor old Ivan, and now their darling, mischievous little Nadia. It was too much to bear.

Officialdom once more descended upon Babushskaya. This time it was not only the dreaded Second Secretary of the Regional Party Committee who came, with a host of lesser functionaries; the remote, all-powerful figure of the First Secretary appeared also. At any other time in their lives the people of Babushskaya would have been too cowed, too fearful even to open their mouths, but today they plucked up their courage and made their complaints in strong, bitter and angry voices.

The two commissars listened with serious, grey-jowled faces which revealed nothing of their feelings, until at last the Second Secretary told the villagers curtly to be quiet. Their grievance had been heard and would be considered after further investigation. Some of the men muttered sullenly in the background, but the general chorus died down.

The whole party went to view the uprooted killer plant and the crushed, bleeding body of its victim. There were exclamations of revulsion and horror. Some of the officials simply stared aghast. The First and Second Party Secretaries said nothing. But in the corner of the First Party Secretary's mouth a muscle began to twitch.

They marched upon the field study site, with the entire population of the village trailing behind. Shumilov, Kaznovetsky and Galina were waiting to meet the deputation, but the First Party Secretary paid no heed to the formal introductions. He was staring in amazement at the now enlarged area of the field study site. The ropes had been moved back to accommodate the longer reach of the gigantic deathseed plants, which had now attained heights of sixteen to eighteen feet. They were three times as tall as a man, as high as the surrounding birch trees, a solid, jungle wall of thick, green foliage and snaking, thirty-foot tentacles.

'We were not aware that any of the plants were growing outside the enclosure,' Shumilov was saying apologetically. 'Every day I ordered the soldiers to make a search of the surrounding area to ensure that nothing grows outside the restricted study site. We did not expect the seed spores to carry to the other side of the village. Somehow the plant in the thicket must have escaped detection. Of course, now we will widen the search area to be sure there can be no more accidents.'

The First Party Secretary had barely heard. 'How...' he demanded, 'how did these things grow to such enormous size?'

'We have been... er, feeding them,' Shumilov admitted, 'mainly with cattle and goats. We have made film records of how they strangle their prey. Naturally, we had to determine how far they would continue to grow.'

There were howls of outrage at this, and some of the bolder peasants surged forward, shaking their fists. The Second Secretary barked at them to restore order and the soldiers quickly formed a barrier to hold them back.

Kaznovetsky saw the urgent need for some justification of their work. He said quickly: 'Our experiment is almost complete. As you can see, some of the largest plants are now beginning to wither. We believe we have established the limit of their size, and that like plantoids they will eventually kill themselves off by their own excessive growth rate. They reach a point where they can no longer sustain themselves and must inevitably die.'

The villagers were not impressed by this scientific discovery. Instead they howled for an immediate end to these abominations. The Second Secretary grew red in the face and again shouted for order and silence.

However, the villagers had an unexpected ally. The First Party Secretary was an iron-hard communist and a devout Marxist. His authority was near-absolute and when pursuing work quotas, state taxes and all state dues, his determination was merciless. His loyalty was above all to the state, not to individuals, or villages, or even towns. But in the final analysis he always remembered that the state *was* the people. They had to be bossed, regimented and disciplined for their own good, but they did not have to endure this. In his examination of their plight he failed to see how this continued experimentation could possibly benefit the state. Therefore it was unnecessary. Therefore the people should not be obliged to suffer it. He was aware that these scientists would carry much weight in Moscow, but he was sure of his position. He too had a small daughter, aged ten years with long black curls, very much the same as Nadia Gavrilova must have been when she was alive.

FLOWERS OF EVIL

The muscle at the corner of his cheek twitched again, and when he spoke his voice was hard and flat:

'This experiment must stop. It will end now. *Today!* Every one of these plants will be burned to ashes.'

Shumilov's protests were loud and vehement, but his was a lone voice. Kaznovetsky defended his friend for what was past, but he too was prepared to concede that the field experiment had gone far enough. They still had the laboratory specimens in Moscow which could be brought forward one at a time for detailed study in more controlled conditions; and they also had enough film evidence to justify their proposed expedition to the meteorite crash site on the Tunguska River.

The First Party Secretary turned a deaf ear to Shumilov's arguments, and barely noticed Kaznovetsky's conciliatory urgings. Overruling them both in the same flat voice, he issued his precise orders.

The next morning he was in attendance again to see those orders carried out. The Red Army had been called in, and four massive battle tanks with flame-throwers rumbled up on clanking steel tracks to manoeuvre into positions on all four sides of the enclosed field site. All faced inward, and on the given order the fat muzzles hurled huge gouts of red fire into the green forest of deathseed plants. The monstrous tendrils flailed in death agony as the plants were consumed by the incinerating heat of the fire, and thick clouds of oily black smoke billowed skyward. The onlookers were driven back by the waves of radiant heat and the sickly stench, and within ten minutes there was nothing left within the boundary ropes except a few scraps of smoking vegetation and a patch of charred and blackened earth.

When the tanks had finished, the ground troops moved in. Five hundred infantrymen combed two square miles of the fields and birch woods around Babushskaya, and every tenth man carried a back-pack of chemical tanks linked to a smaller, portable flame-thrower. Wherever the deathseed plants were discovered they were burned out by well-aimed bursts of flame.

In all, three days were to pass before the emergency was declared over, and the officials, and the scientists, and the army all went home. After that Babushskaya was left to an uneasy peace.

Unfortunately, Lairg Island had no army and no tanks, and no sophisticated weapons of destruction to protect it. Only three bone-weary adults with spades, working whatever hours daylight and weather permitted – three adults whose lives depended on their efforts. They searched every square yard, working with grim and dedicated concentration, until they felt they must have discovered and uprooted every plant of every size on the island. At the end of the second day, Ross and Barry decided they could afford to ease up and relax. From now on they had only to keep watch for any seedlings they might have missed in the thick heather, and stamp them out before they grew to a threatening size.

Then came the annual autumn phenomenon, the event for which Barry had waited so eagerly. The birds came, the great autumn migrations from the north, descending on Lairg like an endless rainfall of many-sized and many-coloured wings. Barry was not to know that the arrival of the birds, which he had looked forward to so keenly, was to turn into an unprecedented environmental disaster, bringing with it horrors he could never have foreseen. For him and his family it was to be the beginning of the ultimate nightmare.

CHAPTER FIFTEEN

The first of the great flocks had gathered on a grassy meadow beside a lake, fed by the rushing green waters pouring down in rivers and waterfalls from the high glaciers and snowfields. The early Norsemen had called this country Iceland, shivering in its cold, bleak climate, and populating it only because they had fled there from the rule of a tyrant. The great mountains were permanently capped with ice, and now ice floes were forming at the edges of the lake, heralding the advent of another bitter, frozen winter. The descendants of the early Norsemen would stay in their coastal towns and villages and see that winter through. But the birds were moving south.

The meadow was a thickening carpet of brown, feathered bodies, with more arriving every minute. In the stands of thin birch trees on three sides the branches were weighed down with birds, like spectators on the terraces of some huge, natural stadium. There were thousands of redwings – noisy, gregarious birds of the thrush family, with speckled breasts and a prominent white stripe over the eyes. Mixed in with them were other thrushes, mostly fieldfares, but with a few song and mistle thrushes. A handful of lapwings and snow buntings had been caught up in the general mood of excitement and anticipation, and waited quivering with the rest.

On the edge of the meadow, almost indistinguishable from the multitude, crouched a female redwing with a twisted wing. In the early months of summer, she had almost died when a hunting merlin had swooped like a small, dark-blue thunderbolt from a cloudless sky. It was only the close proximity of the birch trees which had

FLOWERS OF EVIL

saved her from the striking falcon. She had turned into a screen of leaves which had deflected the prey bird's aim. The merlin had screamed in disappointed rage, and more leaves had been dislodged than feathers. One vicious claw had raked her wing, tumbling her down, but the merlin had been forced to twist in flight to avoid colliding with the heavier branches and had ascended with empty talons. The redwing had crawled into the long grass, trembling and bleeding, but mercifully her wing was not broken. Her mate had found her there, and had brought her food until the wing had healed and she could take to the air again, albeit clumsily.

The male was close beside her now, a fractionally larger and stronger bird. His back was a deeper brown than her own, the speckles on his chest darker, and the red bands on the underside of his wings brighter. They had spent the summer together and the bond between them was close. They had built their nest in a tangle of briar bushes and raised three young. The chicks were flown now and the nest was abandoned. Probably their offspring were in the vast flock around them. They did not know. Once the chicks could fly and feed themselves their task as parents was over, but they stayed together just the same.

Suddenly, with no recognizable signal, the flock began to move. The leaders took flight and in a whirl of excited wings, the whole multitude ascended. In one of nature's most glorious and mysterious spectacles, the redwings suddenly filled the sky, circling above the lake and heading south in a huge, ragged V-formation. The female with the twisted wing lurched almost drunkenly before finding a satisfactory rhythm, but her male held back to fly at her side giving calls of encouragement. Through the massed beating of wings and the deafening, flute-like cries of a thousand other birds, she could always recognize the voice and meaning of her mate.

The weather was clear and the icy wind was behind them, speeding them on their way. The flock made good time, like a vast, dark, speeding cloud. Its shadow passed over more lakes and meadows, thin forests of birch trees, snowfields and bleak plateaux of black volcanic rock. The birds were oblivious to the terrain, conscious only of the blind need to head south. The land yielded to heaving grey seas, but the birds flew on without pause.

As the hours passed the weather changed. The wind shifted direction, blowing hard from the east and threatening to scatter them out into the desolate emptiness of the North Atlantic. Responding to deep-rooted instinct, the birds hung together and struggled to stay on course. The flock rose and dipped in its efforts to get above and then below the worst of the taunting winds. As they dipped, the birds flew perilously close to the hostile waves. A few stragglers faltered, touched the wave-tops and were drowned.

Storm clouds loomed directly ahead. The birds had no choice but to fly into the grey-black mountains and were immediately fighting to maintain altitude as the lashing rain fell heavily from above. Many of the birds were tiring now, becoming fatigued by their efforts to fly against the elements, and more and more of them faltered and were hammered down to a watery death in the merciless seas.

The female with the twisted wing began to fall behind. She had courage, and her tiny heart was pumping fit to burst, but the weakened wing was aching and she was losing her rhythm. Now she was dropping earthwards and sagging dangerously close to the waves.

The male came back for her, circling desperately, finding her despite the blurred curtains of rain and taking up his position again, a few inches from her feebly flapping wing. Again he found the breath to encourage her with his cries, but at first the female could not respond.

Her flight path dipped lower until she was only a few feet above the wave crests. The distraught male stayed with her, still urging her upward. If they drowned they would drown together – and perhaps she sensed it. From somewhere she found the will and the strength to try harder. Inch by straining inch, she battled her way upward once more through the rain.

The depleted multitude passed through the barrier of black storm clouds. Emerging from the rain they climbed higher, the stragglers trailing far back. The redwing with the twisted wing was still there, a long way behind but still thrusting southward, with her triumphant mate in constant attendance.

The long hours and the long miles passed by. Night came and despite the pitch-blackness the flock held together and maintained its course. More of the weaker birds were lost, but when dawn came, the bulk of the flock was still intact and the thousands of weary wings were still beating southward. The female with the twisted wing had fallen even further behind, but with her loyal mate still at her side she had not yet succumbed to pain and exhaustion.

They made landfall at mid-day, where their ancestors had always landed through uncounted centuries, on the island of Lairg.

The redwings descended upon Lairg in a sudden snowfall of large red and brown flakes, blotting out the sky with their bodies and wings. They literally fell upon the island, every last residue of their strength drained by the terrible rigours of the long ocean crossing from the north. With dreadful finality they fell like manna from an evilly twisted heaven, straight into the carnivorous clutches of the waiting deathseed plants.

Most of the plants which had escaped the dedicated search-and-destroy sweeps made by the only three fit adult humans on Lairg were small, but with the redwings crashing down helplessly and exhausted on top of them, they had only to close their tiny tentacles and squeeze. The birds had stretched themselves to the utmost limits of their endurance, and Lairg was their goal. They had no reserves left to struggle against any danger which might befall them on arrival. They collapsed in their thousands and died like sacrificial offerings. Just as surely as the journey had squeezed out their strength, so the deathseed plants squeezed out their blood. The birds were too weak to resist.

The female with the twisted wing barely made it. Pain and exhaustion were a thick, smothering blanket threatening to overwhelm her, and without the urgings of her mate she would have given up and perished long before. But now the male's gasping cries became more excited and insistent, and sensing that land was below, she plunged down. She landed only yards from the cottage and flopped like a dead weight to earth. Tendrils stirred casually from a clump of heather and closed around her.

Instantly the redwing began to squeak in terror. The male had landed close beside her and he too emitted pitiful cries. Unable to understand exactly what was happening, he only knew by instinct that once again his handicapped mate was in dire peril.

A tall shadow loomed over the snared redwing. Large, angry, but careful hands reached down and plucked the grasping tendrils away. The heel of a large boot stamped on the deathseed plant and the rescued bird was lifted in a gentle fist.

Barry Gordon stood with tears in his eyes, his entire body shaking with black anger and frustration. All around him he could see the thrushes dropping, and the hungry movements of the plants, lashing out with their tendrils in the thick grass and heather. The birds had no chance. It was impossible to save them all. The redwing he had picked up was no more than a token gesture. He

FLOWERS OF EVIL

felt sick inside and could not bear to watch any more. Bitterly, he turned away.

He took the female redwing with the twisted wing into the cottage. Later, when she had rested, he would take her to the south headland and throw her aloft to continue her journey. As he went inside he did not notice that the male redwing which had accompanied the bird he had saved had been caught by another plant. The male writhed feebly, his beak gaping open and his bright eyes becoming glazed as he slowly died, in company with hundreds of his kind.

The redwings were only the first wave. Every day the flocks continued to descend upon Lairg in a seemingly endless flow of migrants. Their behaviour patterns were different from those of the resident birds. The residents were mostly seabirds who had their nests on the great stacks and the cliffs, and found their food on the beaches or in the sea. Only rarely did they have any cause to touch down on the island itself. The migrants were different, most of them were landbirds, and even the seabirds among them found no room on the already overcrowded ledges of the cliffs. They had no choice but to land on the interior of the island.

The first flocks of swallows, finches and buntings provided an immediate nursery diet for the small deathseed plants which still flourished undetected in the thick heather, and overnight the plants were ready to seize upon the smaller ducks, plovers, terns and waders. Soon even the biggest gulls, geese, buzzards and prey birds were too small to satisfy their appetite. The plants were now growing much faster than Ross, Barry and Valerie, with their limited resources, could stamp them out. Lairg rapidly became a grotesque graveyard of dead, crushed and mangled migratory birds.

CHAPTER SIXTEEN

On the day the mailboat was due, a force ten gale was raging. All through the night the winds and the rain had savaged the island, and when morning came and Barry and Valerie looked out of their bedroom window toward the nearest of the east coves, they could see roaring grey breakers charging up the beach to dash themselves into great spouting thunderclaps of white foam on the tall black rocks. Beyond the breakers, the sea was a deadly maelstrom of surging white-caps, like range upon range of sea mountains, endlessly dissolving and reforming.

The window frames rattled from the violent impact of rain and wind, and they stood well back in case the glass panes shattered and burst inward. Behind them their bags were all packed, ready for departure, but it was obvious they would not be leaving until the weather cleared. The scene before them would be the same in the small landing cove on the south side of the island, and even if the *Island Pride* could fight her way across the open sea, her captain would find it impossible to bring her against the quay without smashing her hull to pieces on the sharp rocks.

Only twenty yards from the window they could see a cluster of the new deathseed plants, already three feet in height, sprinkled liberally with the hideous feathered confetti of dead, crushed migratory birds. It was two days now since they had been able to leave the cottage to pursue their uprooting operations, and Barry hardly dared to think what might be happening on other parts of the island which were out of sight and immediate reach. At their last conference, he and Ross had agreed that it was becoming too dangerous to continue attacking the larger plants, and now they were simply waiting in their respective cottages for the boat to come and take them away. Fed by the endless streams of landfalling birds, the growth rate of insatiable horror plants had accelerated. They were multiplying too fast to be checked. The battle had been fought – and lost.

Barry was bitter on two counts. First he had to abandon all hope of completing his book, since it was no longer safe for any of them to remain on the island. The migration process was to have been the main subject of *Winged Skyways*, and without the relevant text and photographs he had hoped to collect, the book fell apart. Even if he found another island, one which had not been invaded by deathseed plants, he would be too late to pick up the pieces. At best he could only hope to start again when the spring migration came round in six months' time. Meanwhile, the time and money wasted represented a professional setback and a financial loss.

That was one bitter pill to swallow – but the other galled him even more. He hated *losing* to the plants. Looking at his own and Valerie's hands, which were bruised and scratched with scarcely a whole fingernail between them, and then watching helplessly while his beloved birds provided an unending free banquet for the loathsome, alien vegetation, was more than he could stand. It filled his throat with bile and his stomach with a gnawing frustration.

Valerie sensed something of his feelings and she covered one of his clenched fists with her hand. Her touch seemed to ease the tension, and Barry forced himself to relax. He lifted her fingers and stared again at their scars, and then briefly touched them to his lips in a kiss. It was an almost forgotten sign of affection. Their eyes met. A thousand thoughts passed between them, but not a word was spoken. The sound of knuckles rapped on the bedroom door and without waiting for an invitation Julia and Jonathon barged in.

'It's too rough, isn't it?' Julia looked past them through the window at the hostile sea and sky. She was biting her lip and her voice was anguished. 'The boat won't come.'

'Not today,' Barry tried to sound casual. 'But the weather will probably clear up again tomorrow. You know how quickly it changes from day to day.'

'But what if it doesn't, Daddy? The captain thinks we're planning to stay here for another month – he doesn't know we have to get away. He may decide to miss this trip and not bother to come until the boat's due again. And that won't be for another two weeks.'

'Hush now,' Barry put his arm around her and gave her a tight squeeze. 'You're starting to panic without reason. Remember that any day now Janet Matheson's due to have her baby. The captain of the mailboat knows that. He knows that on this next trip he's supposed to take her back to Mainland so she can have the baby safely in hospital. So he'll be out here, just as soon as he's able.'

Julia nodded slowly and felt ashamed. She had forgotten about Janet's baby. Valerie had forgotten too, and for a moment she suffered little pangs of guilt. It was two days since the storms had shut them in, two days since she had last seen the Mathesons. Perhaps Janet was already in labour. She knew she ought to find out, but her heart quailed at the thought of leaving the cottage and walking across the island. When she last saw her, Janet had been confident the baby would wait another week, so perhaps there was no need. Valerie finally decided to wait until tomorrow. If there was no hope of the boat then she would have to pay Janet a visit.

For the next three days the Arctic gales and the powerful north winds continued to batter Lairg Island and

FLOWERS OF EVIL

Valerie was forced to postpone her visit to the Mathesons. Each day was worse than the one before. In between the storms the decimated flocks of exhausted birds fell out of the leaden sky, and the deathseed plants feasted, doubling and trebling in size.

As the days passed, Valerie was not the only one to be concerned over Janet's condition. Isolated in their own cottage on the opposite side of the island Ross watched his wife with apprehension, waiting anxiously for the first signs that the baby had started on its journey of no return. He was cursing himself now for listening to Janet's arguments and allowing her to stay here for so long. They had both known they were cutting things fine and that she should have gone over to Mainland on the mailboat's last trip.

Janet merely smiled at him and made efforts to soothe his strained nerves whenever the subject was raised. Most of her time she spent quietly knitting, although her hands paused often to rest on her swollen belly. With each pause Ross came alert, anticipating the first twinge of pain.

'Relax, Ross love,' she told him for the thousandth time. 'It's not yet, and if it does happen before the boat comes, you know you'll cope.' She laughed and revived the standing joke. 'Just forget I'm your wife and pretend it's one of your prize ewes. There's nothing to it.'

'I almost wish it would come before the boat arrives,' Ross said with feeling. 'What worries me most is that it'll come while you're on the damned boat. Then you won't be in hospital, and you won't have me to look after you either.'

'Ah, well, I'll not be the first Shetland woman to give birth in a boat. At least then we'll know whether he's meant to be a shepherd or a fisherman.' She spoke blithely, but then realized fully what he had said. Her face became alarmed. 'Ross, do you mean you won't be coming with me?'

He spread his hands helplessly. 'There's the sheep, Janet. If I leave – who's to look after the sheep?'

'But you can't stay here alone! Not with these awful devil plants growing everywhere.'

'It won't be for long, love. Barry will make sure the right people get told. The army will have to come out here, or the Ministry of Agriculture and Fisheries, or some such body. Someone will have to come out and deal with the brutes. We'll have the island cleared properly before you're ready to come back.'

Janet stared at him; she should have known. He was an islander, and they clung to their inhospitable old rocks with all the tenacity of limpets. He wouldn't let anything drive him from his home.

'You're mad,' she told him bluntly. 'Mad to want to stay here. But I'm mad too, mad enough to love you – and crazy enough to want to come back.'

He laughed then and kissed her, and they knew it was settled. Robbie looked up from his place by the fireside and uttered a series of short, approving barks, thumping his tail happily on the hearthrug.

It was several hours later when they heard the sound of the ewe bleating faintly above the downpour of the storm. Robbie pricked up his ears, staring at the door and then questioningly at Ross. The shepherd heard it too and his face creased into a frown.

'Damnit, one of the sheep is loose.'

He got up and went to the door. When he opened it, a blast of wind and rain crashed into the cottage. The bedraggled ewe had been pressing for shelter in the doorway and, pushed by the force of the wind, it lurched past Ross before he could stop it. Ross swore. The sheep was standing in the middle of the room, dripping rainwater from its sodden fleece on to their best carpet, and bleating loudly and miserably.

Ross struggled to shut the door for a moment, then reached for his oilskin jacket and trousers hanging on a nearby peg.

'I'll take her back to the corral and find out what's wrong,' he said as he dressed.

Janet bit her lip. 'You'll be careful?'

'Of course I will. Don't worry. I'll leave you Robbie for company.'

'No, Ross. Take Robbie. If there's more sheep loose you'll need him to help round them up. And you'll be back sooner.'

'Aye,' Ross nodded slowly. After pulling up the hood of his jacket and tying the neck strings, he hesitated. He didn't want to frighten Janet with any dramatics, but he knew it would be unwise to go outside without some means of defence. Finally he went to the long wooden cupboard where he kept his tools and brought out a long-handled axe, trying hard to keep the action casual. 'Here, Robbie,' he called.

The collie stood up reluctantly. Ross opened the door again and grabbed at the sheep's wet fleece in an effort to drag it to the doorway. The ewe had no desire to leave the sanctuary of the cottage, but Robbie knew his job. The collie barked and butted the ewe's flank. All three of them moved through the open door and out into the howling storm. Ross closed the door behind them.

Left alone in the cottage, Janet was still biting her lip. She stared at the closed door, and then looked down at the pools of water the sheep had dripped on to the carpet. She knew she ought to mop the water up quickly before the carpet spoiled. It wasn't a cheap carpet by any means, and it had cost extra to have it shipped over from Lerwick. But she was very heavy now and the baby was kicking inside her with painful regularity. She doubted if she could get down on her hands and knees any more, and if she did the baby would get squashed as she bent forward – and that would hurt them both. Ross would be angry with her if he came back and found her on her knees, so it was best to leave it. With a sigh, she returned to her knitting. There was nothing else she could do.

Five minutes passed before the door banged open and Ross returned. His oilskins were streaming water and his face was grim.

'That damned storm has broken down one of the fence sections on the corral. It probably went some time last night, when the winds got up. Now half the sheep have wandered out and they're scattered all over the island. I'll have to fix the fence and round them up.'

Janet looked anxious. A quick look outside was one thing, but to go searching the island for strays with the devil plants everywhere was another. 'Can't it wait?' she protested. 'Leave it until the weather clears. Then Barry will help you.'

'It could be days before the weather clears. I could lose half the sheep by then.' He forced a bleak smile. 'Don't fret now, love. I'll go right on being careful.'

He went back to the tool cupboard to find a hammer and fill his jacket pockets with large nails. Then he went over to Janet and kissed her.

'I've a couple of hours' hard work ahead of me, so rest easy and don't expect me back too soon.'

She clung to his arms for a few moments, but then let him go. She knew the sheep were his livelihood.

Ross went back into the storm with Robbie trailing wet and unenthusiastically at his heels. The rain was still falling in torrents and the knifing winds were strong enough to bowl them over if they should lose their balance. Once out of Janet's hearing, Ross gave way to another bout of bitter cursing, but the words were torn away and drowned in the howling of the elements.

FLOWERS OF EVIL

On the north side of the corral, the fence had been blown inward and one of the main support posts snapped off at ground level; the next had been pulled out of the soil. A full section of the fence had been carried down flat by the two fallen posts, and the sections on either side were left hanging. Ross stared round warily through the downpour to make sure there were no dangerous-sized deathplants lurking in the area and then put down his axe. Taking up his hammer he began the task of knocking the fallen section of fence free of the two toppled poles.

With a spade he dug out the post holes again and then set the poles back in place. One was now a couple of feet shorter than the other, but it was only a temporary measure until he could order some new posts. He backfilled and stamped the earth down hard. The hanging sections of fence he pushed back and nailed on to the posts again without too much difficulty, but the third section was a struggle. Every time he lifted it up into position, the wind hurled him staggering back. Summoning up all his strength, he persisted doggedly until he got the section upright, with his shoulder braced behind it. His hood had slipped back and the rain was streaming down his neck as he awkwardly succeeded in getting the first couple of nails hammered home on one side. After that it was easier going, and he smashed the rest of the nails home in a fit of rare temper.

He stood back to view his handiwork and decided it would hold. He felt better now the job was done – but the really dangerous work was only just beginning. He hesitated over the axe and the spade, but then swapped his hammer for the axe once more. He called to Robbie, who was wisely sheltering in the corral with the sheep who had not panicked when the fence caved in, and together they set out to round up the strays.

The wind and the slanting sheets of rain were thrusting down powerfully from the north. Guessing that the sheep would have taken the direction of least resistance, Ross began his search to the south. Fortunately, this was the area where he had worked hardest to keep the death-seed plants down, so he felt there was relatively little to fear. Even so, he stayed alert and cautious. Lairg was enveloped by the heavy rain clouds and his visibility was reduced to less than twenty yards. He moved slowly, and remembering how fast the plants could grow and how far their tendrils could reach, he stayed well away from any clump of heather or other natural camouflage which could have allowed a plant to develop unseen.

He allowed Robbie to forage ahead of him, trusting to the collie to do the real work of nosing out the sheep. He had to wrestle a bit with his conscience, but it was the only way which made sense. If Robbie were caught by a devil plant, he could move in quickly to cut out the plant at the roots with the axe; but if *he* were caught and unable to use the axe, then there was no way Robbie could help him. He could rescue the dog, but it would not work the other way round. In any case, Robbie was a sharp dog. He had been nearly caught once and he was scared of the plants. He would not let himself be caught again.

In ones and twos and small groups, Robbie hunted out the escaped sheep, and together they herded them back to the safety of the corral. Where Ross could hear nothing above the tumult of wind and rain, Robbie's ears would pick up a faint bleat; or he would smell out the sheep, or find them through simple, unerring instinct. Ross was cold, soaked to the skin, tired and uncomfortable, but he thanked his lucky stars he had a dog as good as Robbie. Robbie could work miracles with the sheep.

As they worked, they saw plenty of deathseed plants, most of them growing in clusters like the beginnings of some menacing phantom forest behind the grey curtains of rain. Ross gave them all a wide berth, but he was

FLOWERS OF EVIL

appalled to see how quickly the plants had grown and how far they had spread. It seemed as if they were absorbing the salt-laden air of Lairg as well as the great flocks of birds, and that the whole of their growth and reproductive cycle could be telescoped into a matter of days, or even hours.

Four of the sheep had already become prey for the larger plants. Ross swore bitterly each time he saw a white fleece trapped in the network of ugly tendrils, but since all the victims were already dead he made no attempt to extricate them. It was more than a one-man job, and it was not worth the risk. He had to think of Janet.

Ross had now made sure there no more sheep to be located on the south-west corner of the island, but allowing for those he knew to be dead, the count was still three short. Grimly he faced the choice between east and north. The next best grazing was on the north side, but it was also the area where he could expect the uncontrolled deathseed plants to be growing most prolifically. For a moment he was tempted to give the last three sheep up for lost. But they were his livelihood and his responsibility. Also, he was an islander born and bred, with the islander's ingrained instinct for battling on in the face of arduous conditions. It was the only way the generations before him had survived. He called to Robbie, and with true island tenacity turned into the teeth of the rain and the biting wind, and moved north.

They found two of the sheep quite quickly, each one crushed in the clutches of a large deathseed plant. By now Ross had passed his limit for blasphemy and could only stand silent, staring balefully, knuckles white around the haft of his axe, fighting back the almost overpowering urge to rush forward and chop the plant down. He had to remind himself that it had taken the full strength of himself and both the Gordons to overthrow a plant this size – and even then it had been a close thing. It would be suicide to try it alone.

He was convinced the last sheep must be dead too, but he was determined not to turn back until he had found it. Robbie had found all the sheep so far, each time leading him to the scene with sharp barks; he trusted Robbie to finish the job. They had moved past the long west cove and up toward the west cliffs when his faith was justified. Robbie was ranging ahead and his barks came back faint but clear on the gusting wind.

Ross felt a moment of elation. He had learned to tell from Robbie's tone whether the sheep was alive or dead, according to whether the dog gave an excited yapping or a hard, angry growl. These yaps were joyous. Ross hurried off in the direction of the barking, but found Robbie on the cliff edge, looking down to where the sea boiled and foamed in a wicked black cauldron a hundred feet below.

'Back, Robbie.' Ross was suddenly afraid the wind would hurl the dog over the edge, and reached a restraining hand for his collar. Obediently, Robbie backed up, turning his head to look at his master with confident brown eyes and briefly wagging his tail.

Somewhere below Ross heard the bleat of the sheep. It sounded close. He got down on his belly, lying flat so the wind could not topple him, and pulled himself up to the edge to look over. Thirty feet below him was a wide ledge eroded out of the face of the sheer cliff. It was not flat, but sloped inward like a shallow V. On it lay the fallen sheep, bleating pitiably. The feeling of triumph which Ross had felt at discovering the sheep alive vanished instantly. For growing from the same ledge only just out of reach of the trapped sheep, was a deathseed plant the size of a bush.

Ross clenched his fists and gritted his teeth with frustration. The sheep had only to make one move from its precarious position, and it would either fall off the ledge into the sea or move into range of the hungry tendrils. If he was to save it, he would have to move fast, he would have to do it alone. There was no time to cross the island and seek help from Barry Gordon.

He eased back and got to his feet, looking round for an anchor point and lighting on a solid-looking outcrop of rocks. They would have to suffice. He called to Robbie and hurried down to the sheep corral to fetch the coil of rope he kept there for rescue work.

In ten minutes he was back with the rope. He passed it twice around the largest of the rocks to make sure it would not slip and tied it with a double knot. Then he tested it by throwing his full weight on it a couple of times. When he was satisfied, he tied the free end around his waist, leaving enough slack to enable him to reach the ledge. Taking the slack in his hand he paid it out, keeping the line taut as he moved to the edge of the cliff.

A glance below showed him the sheep had not moved. He checked that he had enough cord in his pocket to tie its legs, which would be the only way of securing the animal over his shoulders for the return climb, and then began his descent. Robbie watched him with anxious eyes from the cliff top.

Ross had thrust his axe into his belt, just in case his arrival panicked the sheep into the arms of the plant, and the long handle was hampering his progress. The storm was breaking at last, but the rain still drummed on his shoulders and the wind clawed at him, vainly trying to pluck him out into space as he climbed downward. The sea raged and thundered below him, smothering and then receding from the jagged black teeth of the rocks, which waited like spittle-flecked fangs to snap up his falling body. Looking down, Ross was suddenly afraid – but he was damned if he was going to give up and leave another of his precious sheep to the devil plants. Not while there was the slenderest chance of saving it. Spitting out a mouthful of rain and loose dirt, he continued his descent.

Suddenly the axe jammed, the haft wedging into a crevice and pushing the head hard into his ribs. Ross swore, and moved one hand from the rope to shift the axe and free himself. His boots were planted firmly against the cliff face, but the rain had loosened the soil and stones, and abruptly both his footholds gave way and he plummeted downwards in an avalanche of tumbling rocks. The rope burned through his right hand and he was unable to check his fall. The end of the rope secured around his waist brought him to a halt, but in the same second he hit the ledge. His leg had twisted awkwardly beneath him, and he heard a brittle snap and felt the blinding agony of breaking bone. His scream was ripped up from his bowels and forced out through bared teeth into the gleeful wind.

He had landed immediately beside the sheep, which bleated in panic and made a scrambling effort to back away. The waiting deathseed plant whipped out a tendril, snared the terrified animal by its hind leg, and drew it remorselessly to its doom.

In the fall Ross had dropped his axe and seen it spin away, lost in the nightmare of wave-pounded rocks below. Now he lay crumpled on the ledge with his smashed leg twisted beneath him, almost fainting with pain, and watching helplessly while the struggling, shrieking sheep was crushed. In moments the animal's red blood began to drip and spurt through the white fleece and ruptured skin.

On the cliff top Robbie was equally helpless, unable to do anything more than utter wild, ferocious barks, and run to and fro in futile agitation.

CHAPTER SEVENTEEN

After two hours of waiting alone for Ross to return, Janet was beginning to feel real fear. She could no longer concentrate on her knitting, and simply sat in her chair staring at the door, listening to the fury of the storm and praying for him to come back. After four hours she was almost out of her mind. Her head ached and her stomach churned, and her fingernails had drawn blood from the palms of her hands. The storm had eased, but it soon would be nightfall and she knew Ross should have been home. Even if the job was taking longer than he expected, he would have called back at the cottage to let her know. He was not a thoughtless man, and he knew she would fret. Something had happened to him – and she could only fear the worst.

At any other time she would have gone out to look for him, but the weight of the baby held her back. She did not want to lose the baby, and she knew Ross would not want her to lose the baby, but it was becoming increasingly difficult to sit and do nothing. Finally she went to the door and opened it. The rain blasted in, soaking her, but she stared unheeding toward the corral. Long ago, she had heard the faint sound of hammering, but now there was nothing. She could not even see the corral through the grey curtains of storm. She shivered, wondering which way he might have gone in search of the sheep, the sheer hopelessness of her plight bringing her near to tears. She closed the door and went back to the fireside to throw on more peats and try to steam herself dry.

She had given up all hope, when she heard Robbie's bark, and her heart jumped with relief. She ran back to the door, expecting to see them together, but when she opened it there was only Robbie standing alone, barking and whining with his tail between his legs.

She stared over the dog into the rain, her heart beating fast and a prayer tumbling from her lips, but saw nothing. She was drenched again but hardly knew it. The fire was warm in the hearth behind her, but Robbie made no attempt to enter the cottage. He merely looked up at her dejectedly and whined.

'Where is he, Robbie?' she had to ask, even though the dog could not answer. 'Where's Ross?'

Robbie whined again and drew back from the door. He took a few steps into the storm and then looked back over his shoulder.

'I'm coming,' Janet said. 'It's all right, I'm coming.'

She pulled on her raincoat, fastening the buttons top and bottom with fumbling fingers but unable to stretch the belt around her bulging waistline. Then she struggled into Wellington boots and hurried out of the cottage, urging Robbie to lead the way. She was bare-headed, and in her haste she left the cottage door swinging open.

Robbie loped ahead of her, stopping frequently to let her catch up, and never getting out of her sight. Twice he stopped with a warning growl, baring his teeth and backing into her to bring her to a stumbling stop. Each time she saw a deathseed plant looming in the rain. They were the first she had seen, but Ross had described their unnatural size and their long, menacing tendrils, and even in the grey murk they were unmistakable. Janet stared at them with revulsion, and blindly let Robbie lead her past, praying that Ross had not fallen foul of them.

When Robbie stopped for the third time she thought at first it was for another devil plant. She stared ahead, but saw nothing. The wind flayed her and she tasted the salt spray in the rain and realized she was on the west cliffs. She heard the booming of the sea far below and took a step back to be safe. Robbie went up to the very edge of the cliff, head bowed looking downward, and uttered a series of anguished barks. Then Janet saw the tight-stretched rope still secured to the large rock and stretching down over the cliff edge. At last she understood what had happened.

Hope flared desperately in her breast – the hope that after all he might only be hurt. She got down on her knees on the wet grass, ignoring the acute discomfort of her heavy belly, and keeping one hand on the rope as a safety line, she crawled up beside Robbie. Taking a deep breath, and fighting back the thought that the rope might have snapped and there would be nothing to see, she pushed her head forward and peered down over the edge.

Thirty feet below her was the ledge with the deathseed plant, and embraced in its merciless coils she could see a white fleece and yellow oilskins. The plant had taken a sheep, and her husband. Both were almost still, stirred only by the wind, their struggles long over. Janet screamed, but Ross did not answer. She saw a glimpse of his face, as white as a seagull's breast with a rivulet of red running from his mouth, and a strangling tendril curled tight around his throat. She screamed again and drew back, falling face down upon the wet grass where her body was wracked and heaved by uncontrollable, soul-tearing sobs.

The black and white collie stood over her, a loyal and patient sentinel in the rain. Ten minutes passed before her sobbing eased and Robbie lowered his head to nuzzle her cheek. Slowly Janet sat up, distraught but beginning to recover her own instincts for survival. Ross was dead, but the unborn baby inside her was still alive. She had to live too, if only for the baby. She struggled to her feet and stumbled away from the dangerous, crumbling edge of the cliff.

FLOWERS OF EVIL

Unable to bear the thought of going back to her own home without Ross, she ran blindly for the second cottage on the far side of the island. It was further to run, but the Gordons were her only source of human company and sanctuary. For the first few minutes Robbie held back, trailing at her heels and stopping several times to bark his disapproval before catching her up again. Then he gave up, recognizing his new duty, and ran beside her.

Her terror-stricken flight across the island was a continuation of her nightmare. The rain had almost stopped, but the winds lashed her as she fled and her flapping raincoat slapped viciously at her legs. A grey sea-mist blanketed the island and the light was fading fast, the thickening shadows and threatening darkness adding to her fears. Frequently she fell, her feet slipping on the wet grass or stumbling over the rough terrain. Bruised, battered and winded, she picked herself up each time and hurled herself bodily onward.

She was making a direct line for the Gordons' cottage, cutting across the centre of the island, and without Robbie to head her off she would certainly have come to grief in the clutches of the deathseed plants lurking in every dense clump and thicket. But thanks to the dog's sharp intelligence and instinct, she was saved a dozen times. Robbie would knock her sideways to change her direction and so prevent her running headlong into the waiting predators. She screamed each time she saw the thick tendrils writhing in the gloom, and several times they lashed out in narrowly missed attempts to catch her.

Despite her clumsy shape and weight, pure desperation was driving her on. That and Robbie racing at her side, barking loudly and fending her off whenever danger threatened. She swerved past massed concentrations of the deadly plants, some of them towering as tall as trees above her head. At times it seemed as though the whole

FLOWERS OF EVIL

island was alive with the evil, swaying tendrils, snaking in and out of the thick, drizzly mist like forked Satanic tails from some grey hell. They were the serpent-headed Medusa of Greek mythology, the multiple heads of Hydra, leering horribly on every side. They were the blood-sucking ghouls, phantoms and vampires of every primitive superstition, reaching out and combining in one ghastly, mind-swamping reality. Janet was no longer living one nightmare. Instead, it was as if a million nightmares had been dredged up to plague her from the blackest depths of her subconscious.

In her panic she was more animal than Robbie, running like a tormented rabbit with its eyes and wits removed. Her heart was pumping fit to burst in her chest, and it seemed as though her lungs were on fire with the agony of trying to gasp in enough air to keep her moving. The blood was roaring in her head as though that too was liable to explode at any moment, and a white-hot pain was knifing into her side. The pain in her stomach had intensified, and she felt that if she paused for only a second she would be violently sick and abort the baby.

She was in sight of the Gordons' cottage when her luck ran out. She had come over the brow of the low hill now and seen the blurred mist-shrouded outline of the cottage below her. Her chest heaved and she panted for breath, and she lurched forward over the last sixty yards of downward slope. But as she tore down between two thickets of deathseed plants, she overbalanced, plunging head first down the incline, her body twisting as she fell. Even in that moment a basic instinct was at work, preventing her from landing full on her belly and killing the baby. She hit hard, and slid down the wet grass on her shoulder and hip.

The tendrils of the deathseed plants were a double nest of cobras, waiting to strike. On her left the longest tendril of the biggest plant reared up and lashed for-

FLOWERS OF EVIL

ward. The seeking tip just reached its target and quickly curled around her left ankle in a vice-like grip. In another second she would have been drawn into the parent plant, but on her right another tendril struck. The second plant secured a grip on her right wrist and pulled. Janet was held between the two monster plants like the prize in some hideous tug-of-war. She felt an excruciating pain at her hip and shoulder as though her limbs were being torn out of their sockets. Her screams were loud, piercing, and hardly human. Beside her, Robbie leaped frantically up and down and added his own hysterical barking to the uproar.

Inside the cottage, Barry and Valerie were both at work in the kitchen. Food stocks were running low, and Barry was gloomily opening a tin of corned beef while Valerie chopped up a cabbage – the last of their fresh vegetables. They both knew that if the weather did not break and let the mailboat through soon, they would all be very hungry.

Jonathon and Julia were in the main living room, putting together a large jigsaw puzzle. It was a picture of horses in a meadow, very much like the meadows in Surrey, and it was making Julia feel miserably homesick. She was thinking wistfully of the stables where she spent most of her spare time, and the ponies she used to ride. Jonathon was simply bored. They had put the puzzle together twice before and it was getting too easy. But there was nothing else to do. A whole week of being shut in by the awful weather had exhausted all their indoor pastimes. Now everything was a bore.

Which was why Jonathon stared frequently through the window, scanning the grey skies hopefully for the first minute crack of blue, and wondering what the huge cat-whisker plants were doing on the hidden parts of the island. In his day-dreams, Captain Killer and Blood-Axe, and all the rest now battled cat-whisker plants as often as they joined in combat with all their other enemies. So it was Jonathon who saw the shadowy figure appear briefly on the hill top, only to fall and be snared between the two clumps of deathseed plants.

For a second he thought he was in a private world of his own imagination, and that it was a Viking or a commando who had come over the hill. Then faintly he heard the screams and the barks.

'It's Robbie,' he shouted. 'Robbie's out there. And someone's with him. It must be Ross or Janet. The plants have got them!'

Julia rushed to his side at the window. She could see nothing clearly, just a flurry of vague, struggling movement halfway up the slope of the hill, veiled by the tattered curtains of mist. She pushed open the window and the screams automatically shot up in volume. Julia's face turned white.

'Daddy,' she cried. 'Daddy, come quick. I think it's Mrs Matheson. Please, Daddy, *please!*'

Barry came out of the kitchen at a run. He paused for a split-second at the window, staring out over Julia's shoulder. 'Oh, God,' he said in horror.

'Help her,' Julia begged. 'Daddy, do something. *Help her!*'

Barry was already moving to the door. He had anticipated the need for a weapon and several days ago he had honed the blade of a large axe to a razor's edge. The axe was kept standing by the door and he snatched it up on the way out. With long, desperate strides he ran up the hill.

Valerie had followed him out of the kitchen, with the large vegetable knife still in her hand. If she had stopped for one moment to think about it, she would never have found the courage to step outside, but Barry had already gone and Janet's screams were too blood-curdling to be ignored. Valerie shouted at the children to remain inside and then plunged out to follow her husband.

As soon as he got close enough to see what was happening, Barry came to a dead stop, almost tripping over the dog which rushed under his feet. Janet was suspended between the two clumps of plants, held by the longest tendril of the largest plant on each side. The tendrils of the lesser plants were thrashing violently in their attempts to reach her, but they would not succeed until she was torn in two. Feeling sick with horror and helplessness, Barry could only stand and stare. It was obvious that if he cut either of the tendrils holding Janet, he would simply be giving the victory and the meal to the other plant, which would reel her body in and grasp her with its remaining tendrils before he could strike another blow.

Then Valerie bumped into him from behind. He turned to push her back and saw the glint of steel from the heavy kitchen knife in her hand. Suddenly he saw a chance.

'Val, you've got to help me – and we've got to do this right. Move in closer, and when I give the word cut off the tendril holding her wrist. I'll have to chop the tendril at her foot in the same moment, otherwise we'll lose her.'

Valerie nodded. Her mouth was dry and her body was bathed in cold sweat, and she had to fight the impulse to turn and run away. Keeping a close watch on the other tendrils, measuring their length and taking care to stay out of range, she moved in closer to Janet. Barry closed in and raised the axe on the other side of the helpless woman. Janet had stopped screaming now. She had fainted.

'*Now!*' Barry snapped.

Valerie chopped down with the knife. It took her three blows before the tendril holding Janet's right wrist was severed, and immediately Janet was dragged off to the left. But before her body had been pulled more than a few inches, Barry struck down with the axe. The tendril around Janet's ankle parted. On both sides the cheated deathseed plants were whipping the earth and sky in demented fury, powerless to prevent their victim being lifted under the arms and hauled hastily away from their clutches.

'Take the axe,' Barry said. 'I'll carry her inside.'

Valerie took the axe from him and with both hands free he knelt down to hoist the unconscious woman into his arms. It was a struggle to get her up, but he made it, and they hurried back to the cottage. As they drew nearer they moved more slowly, for there were now a large number of deathseed plants growing close around the cottage. They had forgotten the danger in the heat of the moment as they rushed out to rescue Janet, but they returned with more caution. Getting in and out of the cottage had become a dangerous business, and it was the main reason why Barry kept the axe sharp and handy.

Robbie followed them into the cottage, and when they were inside Valerie bolted and barred the door behind them. Barry laid Janet carefully on the rugs in front of the fire and sent the children scurrying upstairs to fetch pillows and blankets to make her more comfortable. They removed Janet's saturated outer clothes and towelled her dry. Jonathon returned as an interested observer, but Valerie sent him into the kitchen to boil a kettle for a hot drink.

Five minutes passed before Janet's eyelids flickered. By then she was wrapped up in blankets and propped up on pillows. She opened her eyes and her stare was glazed as she looked wildly around her.

'It's all right,' Valerie calmed her. 'You're safe now.' She offered a large, steaming mug. 'It's hot cocoa, with a stiff shot of brandy. Try some. It'll warm you up.'

FLOWERS OF EVIL

'No,' Janet pushed the mug away. 'I can't drink spirits.' She closed her eyes again and shuddered, but not at the smell of the cocoa. She was seeing a memory. 'Oh, Ross,' she sobbed. 'My poor Ross.'

'Where is Ross?' Barry asked gently. 'What happened to him?'

'He's dead,' Janet told them wretchedly. 'I don't know how. He fell over the west cliffs and a devil plant got him.'

Barry's face went tight and stony. For a few moments he was unable to speak, but then he forced his locked jaws open. 'I'll go and find him. There may be a chance. If I hurry I could be in time.'

He started to get up, but Janet grabbed fiercely at his arm.

'No,' she said. 'He's dead. I saw him. It's too late.'

'Then I'll get his body back. I can't just leave him to one of those filthy –'

'*No*,' Janet repeated. Her fingers were hard as eagle talons around his bicep and she pulled herself up to stare into his face. Her eyes were haunted. 'Don't you understand? He's dead. And if you go out there they'll get you too. The whole island's smothered with them. My husband is dead. My baby's father is dead. I don't want to see your wife without a husband too – or your children without a father. It's not worth it. Ross wouldn't want it. I don't want it either.'

Barry hesitated. Janet opened her mouth to say more, but then her face creased and she fell back upon the pillows with a moan of pain. Her whole body arched in a sudden spasm and she moaned again. Her hand dropped from Barry's arm and she clutched at her belly. Barry looked baffled and turned to Valerie.

'She's right,' Valerie told him. 'It wouldn't do any good for you to go out and look for Ross. If he's dead you can't help him. Besides, we've got another problem. She's going into labour.

Two hours later the baby was born. The shock Janet had received, together with the violent exertions of her flight across the island, had brought on her labour pains. The contractions were short and sharp, at ten-minute intervals to begin with, but soon coming at a more rapid rate. Fortunately, there was plenty of time for Valerie to get organized. The complaining Jonathon was sent to his room, and allowed to take Robbie with him, and Barry and Julia were ordered to boil up gallons of hot water and make a search for all the available clean blankets and towels.

They had brought with them an extensive first-aid kit, complete with handbook, and Valerie read the chapter on childbirth carefully, steeling herself for her role as midwife. According to the book, the golden rules were to stay calm, reassure the mother that everything was normal, and allow nature to take its course in conditions of scrupulous cleanliness. Valerie read the chapter twice and hoped it was all going to be that simple.

As they were reluctant to move Janet now that the pains had started, they compromised by spreading clean sheets underneath her. Valerie scrubbed her hands for the prescribed four minutes and then pulled on sterile rubber gloves. Barry scrubbed down the wooden table top, so that Julia could lay out the hot water basins, towels, cotton wool and gauze, surgical scissors and three lengths of string, which had all been sterilized by ten minutes of boiling in a saucepan.

After that it was mainly a matter of giving moral support and comfort to Janet until the baby appeared, and urging her to rest as much as possible between contractions. The cramp-like pains came more quickly and lasted longer, while Janet moaned feverishly, her face glistening with sweat and tears. Whether the tears were for herself or for Ross, it was impossible to guess. After one of her more violent contractions a small gush of blood-stained mucus showed, the first positive sign that the baby was on its way.

Outside the cottage, a new gale had whipped up. Racing winds hurled themselves across the island and slammed into the cottage walls. Rain continued to pour down in torrents, and it was obvious they were in for another long night of storms.

While the window panes shook and the thatch rustled, out in the wild darkness beyond there were more sinister scratchings and scrapings. It sounded like the rustle of foliage upon foliage, and rain drumming on large leaves – all the sounds which might be expected in a tropical forest during the monsoon.

Something smacked against the window. Valerie was holding Janet's hand and Barry was supporting her head. Both of them were fully occupied with the task of soothing their patient. Julia stood back, trying to be both out of the way and yet within call if she was needed to fetch or carry. She turned her head to look at the window. Then something smacked at the glass again, and she saw it was a tendril.

Her heart froze. 'Daddy,' she shouted in anguish. 'The plants are trying to break in.'

Barry looked up. He started to tell her she was imagining things, but then the tendril hit the glass for the third time and he saw it clearly, momentarily flattened against the glass.

'It's impossible,' he said. A few hours ago there had been nothing growing that close to the window, he was sure. He could not believe his eyes. Then two tendrils flailed at the window together, and he had to accept that it was not impossible. It was happening.

'They can smell the blood,' he realized, looking down

at Janet. 'God help us, they can smell the blood.'

'Shut up,' Valerie told him curtly. She had to concentrate on one job at a time, and even if Barry was right she did not want Janet alarmed. Janet contracted again, gritting her teeth to suppress another cry of pain, and her waters broke. With the gush of fluid that had surrounded the baby there were pink traces of blood.

'The baby's coming,' Valerie said calmly. 'Don't hold your breath now, Janet. Try to keep your mouth open and take short breaths. That's the best way to help the baby out. Ease it out slowly.'

The baby's head was emerging. Barry watched it, uncertain whether or not to interfere. Valerie pushed him out of the way.

'Leave it to me. I've got the gloves. The baby should only be supported. It musn't be pulled.'

'At least it's the right way round,' Barry said thankfully. He had been terrified of complications. His relief was short-lived. There was a sudden crash of breaking glass, and Julia screamed.

They all jerked round. Even Janet, wild-eyed and gasping, had to twist her head to see what had happened. She echoed Julia's scream.

The window had shattered inward and a tendril was groping inside. It stretched toward the helpless woman at the moment of birth, drawn by the scent of fresh blood, but its reach was a yard too short. It began to wave viciously in its frustration.

Barry jumped to his feet, ducked under the tendril, and ran to the door to pick up his axe. Turning back to the window he aimed an accurate blow which sliced off the tendril and dropped it, harmless but still squirming, on to the floor. Another tendril wriggled in through the broken window, dislodging more fragments of jagged glass. Barry struggled to free his axe, which was embedded deep in the windowsill, and chopped again. The second tendril fell, but there was a third to take its place. Behind his back Barry heard the other window on the far side of the room shatter inwards and Julia scream again.

The baby's head and shoulders were clear now and Valerie was supporting it carefully with both hands. 'One more push,' she urged gently, and Janet strained again. With a fast, final rush the baby was out. Valerie smiled with triumph. 'It's a boy. Janet, you've got a boy.'

'For Christ's sake, clean that blood up,' Barry yelled as he dashed from one side of the room to the other. 'It's driving them crazy.'

Valerie looked round and saw him wielding the axe with fast, powerful blows. Another large tendril and a shower of smaller ones rained like deadly green mambas to the floor, before he had to race back across the room once more to the other window.

'Hold them off,' Valerie said. 'We can't rush this.' She was ice-cold with fear, but she was determined to concentrate on everything she had read in the book. She must be careful not to drop the baby; she must be careful not to stretch the cord; and she must be sure the fluids drained away from the baby's mouth and nostrils so that he could breathe.

'Hurry it up,' Barry begged. 'We've got to get her upstairs and out of reach of these things.'

Mercifully, the afterbirth came quickly, but with it came more blood. Outside, the deathseed plants were beating the walls of the cottage in a frenzy, but now it was mostly rain and wind blasting through the broken windows. When a tendril did find its way through, Barry was quick to slice it off.

As soon as it was possible, they carried Janet and the baby upstairs to their bedroom. There Valerie finished the final, tricky tasks of tying and cutting the umbilical cord and cleaning up mother and child, then urged Janet

FLOWERS OF EVIL

to sleep. Exhausted by all her ordeals, Janet soon closed her eyes and slid into deep unconsciousness.

But for the Gordons there was no sleep at all. They stayed awake and listened to the storm and the deathseed plants clamouring outside the cottage walls.

CHAPTER EIGHTEEN

'They can move,' Jonathon said, in the bored, matter-of-fact tone of an expert who could have supplied the information long before, if only he had been asked. 'I've watched them coming down the hill. It's only a little bit at a time, so unless you watch them for a long time you can't see it. They sort of wriggle a root forward, and then dig it down again. Then they move another root forward, and so on. It's all one root at a time, ever so slowly. It's a bit like watching a clock. The hands don't move but they get round somehow. Cat-whisker plants are the same. I couldn't see how they moved until I started watching the roots.'

It was daylight. The storms had blown over, the sun was shining brightly from a clear blue sky, and the seas around Lairg were calm and gently sparkling. But it was a prayer answered too late. They couldn't go outside. The whole family was gathered at the window of the main bedroom, looking down through the glass at the tight cordon of deathseed plants which had formed around the cottage.

Barry looked at his son in exasperation. 'Why on earth didn't you tell me?'

'I would have done,' Jonathon was both righteous and affronted, 'but Mum said she was sick of hearing me talk about cat-whisker plants, and she didn't want to hear another single word.'

Valerie remembered the outburst and could not deny it. At the same time she shared Barry's irritation. Jonathon had a disconcerting habit of turning their reproaches against them. 'Jon, you knew perfectly well what I meant. I wanted you to stop saying the *same* things over and over again. I didn't mean that if you noticed something *new* you weren't to tell us.'

'Oh,' Jonathon remarked briefly, but his tone said more. It implied both surprise and innocence, suggesting he had only shut up because he had been told to, and that it was her fault for not explaining herself properly.

Valerie was tempted to smack him, but Barry put a pacifying arm around her shoulders.

'It's all right, Val. It wouldn't have made any difference even if we had known. It just explains how so many of them appeared so quickly. I suppose it also explains why their roots are only partly buried. I should have noticed it myself.'

'But why are they moving?' Julia asked. 'Why are they shutting us in?'

'That's obvious, silly.' Jonathon was scornful. 'They're after us. We're food for them.'

'*Ughh*,' Julia made a groaning sound and shuddered. She moved closer to her parents.

'Stop it, Jon,' Barry ordered sharply.

'But he's right, Daddy, isn't he? They are after us?'

Barry hesitated, but there was no way he could disguise the fact. He said slowly, 'I guess they are, but that doesn't mean they'll get us. We'll find a way out.'

'But how? We can't even go downstairs.'

It was true. During the night they had heard more ground-floor windows breaking, and at first light, when Barry had cautiously stepped downstairs, he had found broken glass all over the floor, and every window frame blocked by green leaves and foliage. The tendrils had penetrated everywhere, searching and feeling. Barry had his axe in his hand, but it would have been dangerous and hopeless even to try to clear the invading greenery. He had backed up the stairs again and reluctantly informed his family that they were trapped in the upper bedrooms.

'At least the weather's changed,' Barry said at last, answering Julia's question by stressing the only hopeful sign. 'The mailboat should get here sometime today. They'll be able to help us.'

'The mailboat only has a crew of three or four men.' Valerie didn't want to be a prophet of doom, but they had to face up to the full seriousness of the situation. 'They won't be enough to help us. It's a jungle down there.'

'They'll be able to go back to Mainland for more help.'

'But it all takes time, Barry. And these things grow so fast. Look at those tendrils straining to reach up here. Soon they'll be able to reach, and they'll be breaking these windows. And once they get into the bedrooms there's nowhere else for us to go.'

Barry looked down at the waiting plants. It was like a close-up aerial view of a jungle, but no sun-steamed swamp forest had ever been as sinister, hostile and hungry as the waving green blanket below. His face became grim.

'As a last resort we'll set fire to the cottage. Flames and smoke must make them recoil. Then we can break out at the last moment.'

'What about Janet and the baby?'

Barry turned to look at the pale face of Janet Matheson, who was still fast asleep in the big double bed behind them. The baby was sleeping peacefully in the large, towel-padded kitchen drawer they had improvised as a cot.

'We take them with us, of course.' He spoke simply as though a helpless mother and child presented no real problems.

Valerie smiled, and felt comforted by his confidence and strength. Suddenly she felt that if any man could get them all out of here alive, then Barry would do it. She hugged him close, and was glad of his answering squeeze.

FLOWERS OF EVIL

A flicker of guilt marred the moment, as she found herself thinking of Simon Lancing. She had almost cured herself of the habit of making endless comparisons between her husband and her absent lover, but when she did make them now her conclusions were reversed. Ever since the deathseed plants had threatened their lives, it was Barry who had shown up the more favourably. Somehow she could not imagine Simon fighting off the deathplants with an axe, or proving such a determined defender of her children. Barry was still the rough diamond, but he was the stronger and more capable man of the two. She had been forced to revalue them both, and Simon's party manners, flattery and fine clothes would have been no use here.

The ordeals she had shared with Barry had made them closer than ever before, re-uniting them as a family. The past might not be wholly forgotten, but at least it seemed a long way behind them now. Apart from the one furious fight soon after they had arrived on Lairg, there had been no recriminations. Barry seemed prepared to forgive and forget. It was more than she deserved, and she loved him for it. She wondered if now was the right time to put her feelings into words. But just then Jonathon interrupted.

'Look, Dad!' His exclamation cut across her thoughts. 'Look at the birds.'

Barry and Valerie both looked. The blue sky over the high north end of the island was filled with beating wings, as the latest wave of migrants strained to reach landfall after their exhausting ocean crossing. Most of them glided down on the air currents, but some literally tumbled out of the sky, without even the strength to flap a wing. Hundreds of them landed directly on to the dense thickets of deathseed plants which dominated every part of the island.

'They're ducks,' Julia said. 'Big ducks.'

'They're too big for ducks,' Jonathon argued. 'They're geese.'

'You're both wrong,' Barry informed them, 'They're divers. See the big ones with the black heads and the bands of white spots on the black wings? They're great northern divers. They have their breeding grounds in Iceland, and fly south for the winter. The brown and white birds with the red mark at the throat are red-throated divers. They must have come down from Iceland too.'

All conversation in the bedroom died into frozen silence as the divers began dropping down on to the thick blanket of foliage encircling the cottage. The great northern divers were large, web-footed birds with a wing span of almost five feet. The red-throats, though smaller, still made a plump, juicy and very substantial meal. The tendrils curled around them almost lazily, as if knowing there was no need to hurry – none of the birds would be capable of taking off again until they had rested. In a slow, grisly spectacle, the birds were being remorselessly slaughtered. Within minutes, Barry could count over thirty struggling bodies, whose vainly beating wings and terrible quacking and wailing made Julia cover her ears and run away from the window.

Barry closed the curtains. They would only torture themselves unnecessarily by watching the birds being crushed. Already the drama had underlined the warning Valerie had already voiced. The deathseed plants were growing too fast, and with this heaven-sent feast the plants could only go from strength to strength. Very soon the longer tendrils would be able to reach the upper floor windows. They would have to find some means of escape swiftly, or they would never escape at all.

Another hour passed before Barry made his decision. He waited for Janet to wake and persuaded her to take some milk and cereal for breakfast, knowing she was going to need all the strength she could muster. Then he gathered them all around him and told them what he planned to do.

'We're going to have to set fire to the cottage. I've wracked my brains, but there just isn't any other way. We've got to get out. Every minute the plants are getting bigger and pressing closer. Which means that every minute we stay here lessens our chances of getting through them when the time comes. We can't wait for the boat to arrive. We've got to go now – and fire is our only weapon.'

Janet's face seemed almost as white as the pillows on which she lay. They had given her the baby and she pulled it tight to her breast. 'We can't go outside until the boat comes. Where could we go? My cottage won't be safe. Nowhere on the island is safe. The devil plants are all over Lairg.'

Barry understood her fear. She had already made one terror-stricken flight across the island and one more would be too much. He said gently, 'We don't have to go far, just down to the nearest beach. The plants certainly can't grow on the rocks, and they don't seem to like the sand. So far I've never seen one on any of the beaches. If we can get there it'll be the safest place to wait.'

'But what if the boat doesn't come? If the weather turns bad again?'

'Those are risks we have to take. The only certain thing is that we can't possibly survive in this cottage. The plants have got us trapped. By tomorrow the tendrils will be able to reach into every corner of every bedroom.'

'I agree the house isn't safe any more,' Valerie said slowly. 'But setting fire to it? I'm not sure about that. We could burn ourselves alive if we wait too long – and the plants could still get us if we run out too soon. It's a drastic step to take.'

'It's our only choice,' Barry said firmly. He didn't want any argument or the kids would pitch in and they would end up convincing themselves that it was hopeless. A half-hearted attempt would be bound to end in total disaster. To survive, they had to believe in their chances and commit themselves fully.

'What we have to do is to prepare our line of retreat first. We can't get out of the doors or any of the ground floor windows, because they're all blocked tight by the plants. They're thick below this window too. But I've checked in the other bedrooms, and I reckon there's a way out from Jonathon's bedroom. There's a gap there that the plants haven't filled in yet, and they're not too thick on either side.'

'I can't climb out of the bedroom window,' Janet protested.

'We'll help you. It's not too high, and we'll make ropes out of the sheets and plenty of knots for handholds. It'll be okay.'

Janet looked unconvinced, but Barry knew he had to sweep all their doubts aside. He went on quickly, 'When we've got everything ready, we'll set fire to all the ground floor rooms. Then we all go into Jonathon's bedroom and close the door. We seal the door top and bottom by stuffing towels into the cracks, and that should hold back the worst of the smoke and heat for a good twenty minutes. If things go right, the flames and smoke will pour out of the broken windows downstairs and drive back the plants close to the outside walls. Then we climb out of the window, through the gap, and make our run for the beach.'

'What about Robbie?' Jonathon implored. 'Robbie can't climb down a rope.'

Barry glanced at the black and white collie curled up patiently on the floor beside Janet's bed. Robbie lifted his nose from his forepaws and his ears flicked.

'Robbie comes too,' Barry said. 'Dogs are like cats, they can jump from a height and land on their feet.' He tousled Jonathon's head. 'You won't have to worry about Robbie.'

He paused, ready to squash any further arguments, but there were none. Without giving them time to think of any, he rushed them straight into action.

'Right then, let's get on with it. Jon, take Robbie into your bedroom and collect up all the sheets from your bed and Julia's bed. Val, you and Julia help Janet to get dressed. Take her and the baby into Jon's room. Make up some packs of food and blankets to take with us in case we do get stranded overnight on the beach. I'll go down below and start the fires.'

They all looked back at him hesitantly, but then Valerie drew a deep breath and followed his lead. 'Okay, Barry, but be careful. I'll get things organized up here.'

Barry nodded and went out. He picked up his axe and made his way very cautiously down the staircase to the ground floor, stopping halfway to let his eyes become accustomed to the gloom. With foliage screening every window there were only a few bars of sunlight filtering through. The peat fire in the hearth glowed dimly but was almost out. The interior of the cottage was no longer homely and comforting. Instead it was a dark, menacing cavern, filled with shadows and infiltrated by green stalactites hanging loosely from every opening. As they became aware of Barry's presence the stalactites began to move, rearing up and straining toward him.

Barry watched them, noting the positions of the longest tendrils, measuring their length and calculating where it would be safe to move across the floor. Realizing how few safe areas were left, he felt his mouth go dry. In the few short hours since he had last taken a look, the plants had crowded in still further, almost choking out the daylight. It was almost as though they were trying to crush the cottage itself. Sweat trickled down Barry's spine in a creeping, chilly rivulet.

When he had marked out his path he went over it at a run. The tendrils lashed at him but failed to reach. The table was in his way, but he scrambled over it rather than risk going round. He reached the kitchen doorway and skidded to a stop. A tendril lashed through the door and he ducked. The tendril slapped the door post, but Barry wheeled and struck with the axe, chopping the tendril short. Shaking itself as if in pain, the injured limb withdrew.

Barry peered into the kitchen. The window over the worktops had caved in and more tendrils and foliage had spilled inside. There was one other twelve-foot tentacle, the size of the monster he had just chopped, draped over the sill, making any safe passage through the kitchen impossible. Barry gritted his teeth and made a swift attack. Two powerful blows with the axe severed the two dangerous tendrils where they passed over the windowsill, then he hastily retreated out of reach of their smaller brothers.

Cautiously he peered into the lean-to extension. It was partially collapsed under the weight of the deathseed plants outside, and more tendrils had penetrated through the cracks under the outer door and under the eaves. Again he made quick, rushing attacks with the axe to remove the most threatening of them.

The paraffin for the night lamps was stored in the extension. He grabbed the two full cans which were left and carried them back into the main building. For the next ten minutes he worked hard with the axe, smashing up the mainly wooden furniture into heaps of kindling. He made the piles as close as he dared to the broken windows where the plants were pushing inside. All the newspapers, books and other inflammable materials he could find he added to the bonfires, splashing paraffin liberally on top.

He paused, breathing hard to study his handiwork. Satisfied for the moment, he went into the kitchen and packed two of their rucksacks with all the food supplies which remained. He carried them upstairs and found the rest of his family gathered with Janet and the baby in Jonathon's bedroom. They had fashioned a sufficient number of sheets into knotted ropes and were tying up rolls of blankets to take with them when they made their escape.

'All set?' He asked.

Valerie nodded. She was standing by the window and her face was troubled. 'We're ready, but I'm not sure. . . . It's not much of a gap.'

Barry moved up beside her and looked down through the window. Sure enough, the gap had narrowed since he had last looked at it. The space through the deathseed plants was less than four feet wide now, and many of the tendrils on either side were long enough to span the full width. But it was the only gap there was. Everywhere else around the cottage the cordon was thicker and the plants were taller.

'I know it's risky,' he admitted. 'That's why we need the fire. There's no other way.'

He gave her shoulder a squeeze, smiled briefly at Janet and the children, and hurried back downstairs before they could offer any further objections.

In the darkened living room he emptied out the *kishie* and divided the unburned peats between his three bonfires. The only task left was to light them. He raked out the glowing remains of the fire in the hearth until he had stirred it into life, then shovelled the burning embers on to each mound of paraffin-soaked wood and paper. The bonfires flared instantly into crackling sheets of flame.

Barry worked his way backward and waited on the

stairs. For a few seconds he watched as the interior of the cottage was illuminated in a red glow by the flickering firelight, holding his breath until he saw the tendrils at the windows start to withdraw from the growing heat. More sunlight, and consequently more air and oxygen, poured in through the broken panes of glass to fuel the fires, which now began to spit and roar more fiercely. With relief Barry saw the last trailing branches and foliage pull away completely from the nearest window. It was working. Choking on the smoke-laden air, he began to back up the stairs.

After closing the door at the top of the landing, he snatched the pillows off Julia's bed and stuffed them into the wide gaps at the top and bottom. He wanted the fire contained on the ground floor for as long as possible. Finally, he went into Jonathon's room and repeated the process of sealing the door against drifting smoke and heat. His family and Janet watched him silently, white-faced, but now the die was cast. They had no means of extinguishing the fire he had started. There was no going back.

Barry dragged the foot of the heavy box bed over to the window. With the axe he knocked out a couple of the bottom planks so that he could pass the ends of the sheet ropes through and secure them. After that there was nothing they could do except watch and wait.

They stood in a close group at the window, looking down at the narrow lane through the deathseed plants below. Janet held the baby against her breast and shushed it when it cried. Robbie stood beside her and tried to lick at her hand.

Gradually it became hotter in the small bedroom, and despite the padding at the door slender ribbons of smoke began to filter through. Robbie barked anxiously and Jonathon patted his head and spoke to reassure him. They could hear the fire roaring beneath them, and remembered the heavy wooden beams in the ceiling beneath their feet. The beams were now burning and more smoke was filtering up through the cracks between the floorboards. The heat became uncomfortable.

'Don't worry,' Barry told them. 'It'll be a long time before the beams burn through and the floor collapses. We've still got a good twenty minutes.'

'Look at the plants,' Jonathon said. 'They're pulling back!'

Dense clouds of black smoke, laced with red flames, were now pouring out of the ground floor windows of the cottage. From where they stood they could see that the deathseed plants outside one of the windows were blackening and burning. Each plant was now writhing in agitation, stretching its foliage and tendrils away from the scorching heat of the fire.

Barry stared intently at the plants immediately below. They too were leaning back from the heat, and he could see the roots clawing at the earth as they tried to move away. Unfortunately, their rate of movement was too slow, and the fire was building up too fast. It looked as if the plants would not be clear by the time the fire forced the humans to make their escape.

'When we go, I go first,' Barry decided. 'I'll take the axe and do what I can to clear the way. Julia, you come next. You can help Janet down while Mum helps her out of the window. Jon, you hold the baby until Janet's down. Then you and Mum come last. Okay?'

They all nodded. The heat was becoming unbearable and sweat trickled down their faces. The thickening smoke irritated their throats and nostrils and Julia began to cough. Soon they were all coughing and their eyes smarting. Robbie began to bark and shift about in panic and Jonathon hung on to his collar.

'Stick it out,' Barry urged. He knew that they had to give the plants as much time as possible to pull back; but if they waited too long they could be overcome by smoke and collapse in the fire. The roaring beneath their feet was becoming fearsome and suddenly a new and more ominous crackling broke out to the left above their heads.

Barry looked along the outside wall and saw immediately what had happened. The flames licking out of the ground-floor window to their left had curled upward and ignited the thatch at the eaves. In racing tongues of red, the flames were now spreading fast through the thatched roof. Soon the whole lot would come crashing down. Barry dared wait no longer.

'Let's go,' he snapped, and threw open the window.

Grabbing the tied-up blanket rolls, he threw them one at a time over the heads of the plants on to the clear ground beyond. The two rucksacks full of food followed, and then he gathered up a startled Robbie in his arms. Before Robbie could bark or Jonathon could protest, he hurled the dog out with all his strength. Yelping as he landed, Robbie hit down on all fours just out of reach of the plants, and scuttled frantically away.

Next Barry threw out the two sheet-ropes, dropped his axe through the window, and slithered down after it. He jumped the last few feet and snatched the axe up again as though his life depended on it, as indeed it did. He had already marked out the biggest plants on either side, and now whirled into them without a moment's pause. Fortunately, all the plants were leaning over backwards, shielding their murderous tendrils from the fire, and as they arched over they exposed their thick, central trunks liked bared necks to the blade. Barry hacked into them, the axe-blade making a wicked silver blur, arcing in a lightning figure-of-eight as he cleared the gap on either side. Gasping at his father's speed, Jonathon found time to reflect that not even Blood-Axe could have done it better.

Valerie decided to ignore Barry's order of descent.

Keeping the big, triangular kitchen knife in her grasp, she slid quickly down the rope to help. She knew that if Barry were caught by the tendrils there would be no hope for any of them.

She was not needed. Barry had already hacked out a path and came back shouting for the others to follow quickly. Janet climbed out of the window, helped by Julia, and Valerie caught her as she dropped the last few feet. Julia leaned out of the window with the baby and Valerie opened her arms. Julia dropped the baby into them. It howled with fright and Janet snatched it back to her breast. After grabbing both women and steering them at a run to safe ground, Barry went back for the children. First Julia, and then Jonathon dropped into his arms. The deathseed plants beyond the immediate area he had cleared seemed to sense what was happening and the longer tendrils flicked over the shorter plants between, snaking out over the escape route. Barry forced the two children down low and they made a desperate crouching run through the narrow avenue.

When they could stop safely and look back, all of them were gasping for clean air, and sweat and tears were dripping down their smoke-grimed faces. Jonathon's knees were quaking and Robbie stood beside them all, barking furiously. The cottage was blazing from end to end, the thatched roof sending sparks and flames streaming upward like a huge torch. The deathseed plants caught close to the inferno were shrivelling and burning, and the roasting smell of blood-gorged foliage hung thick and nauseating in the air.

Barry picked up the bedrolls and food packs and handed them round. 'Come on,' he said wearily. 'Let's get moving.'

There were more deathseed plants blocking the path which led to the south beach, so they picked their way carefully down to the nearest of the east coves. They had

FLOWERS OF EVIL

to follow a zig-zag route between more thickets of the predator plants, but reached the cove without mishap.

Here, Barry calculated they would be safe, for a short while. The food and blankets they had brought would help them to survive for a few days. But their biggest problem was the lack of shelter, and the ominous rain clouds were building up again on the horizon. He prayed there would be no more storms to keep the mailboat from reaching them. A few more like last week, and they would all be dead of exposure within hours.

On the landward hillsides, he could see the plants formed up in almost military ranks, and wondered how long it would take for them to close up and drag themselves down to the beach. He could only hope they would not cross the sand. Because with their backs to the sea, the trapped party were running out of escape routes.

CHAPTER NINETEEN

At nine o'clock in the morning, hot sunshine was steaming dry the grey roofs of Lerwick, and the port was bustling with activity. The foreign fishing boats from Iceland, Norway, Sweden and Holland which had sheltered from the past week of bad weather were eager to be gone. The local fishermen were glad to put to sea, and the oil industry supply boats and the inter-island ferries also had their schedules to maintain. The hungry seabirds wheeled in white circles over the sound, which was suddenly alive with the chugging beat of engines.

Alistair Mckenna had eaten a good breakfast – two fresh, sweet mackerel with several slices of thickly buttered bread – and was whistling cheerfully as he hurried down to the quay. His father had left the house an hour before him, and by now the *Margaret* was on her way out to the fishing grounds. It was a good-to-be-alive day and Alistair could hardly wait to feel the deck of the *Island Pride* creaking beneath his feet again. It was a fine feeling to be going back to work and back to sea after the enforced stay ashore.

When he stepped down on to the mailboat's deck he was surprised to find the vessel silent and apparently deserted. The engines were not running, nor was there any sign of his crewmates. Puzzled – he knew he was not that early for work – he made a quick search. Finally he put his head down the engine-room hatchway and found all three of them, captain, engineer, and an older deckhand, crouched over the engines, which were partially stripped down.

'Morning, Skipper,' Alistair sang out. 'Morning, Hughie. Morning, Tom.'

The three men looked up, smiling a little at the lad's eagerness. The captain and Tom both returned the greeting, but Hughie, the glum-faced engineer, looked even more fed up than usual. He was streaked with oil and grease and when he glanced up it was only to grunt briefly. Hughie's love-hate relationship with his engines was definitely tilted more to the hate side this morning.

Alistair wrinkled his nose at the oily fumes coming up from the cramped spaces below. How anyone would want to go to sea buried in a dirty, foul-smelling engine room he could not imagine.

'What's wrong?' he asked.

'She won't start,' Tom answered.

There was a long silence while the engineer peered at different parts of the engine in turn, poking irritably with a screwdriver. At last he put the tool and his handlamp down and banged his fist upon his forehead. He was a God-fearing Bible-reading man, and it was his substitute for swearing.

'It's got me baffled,' he confessed to the captain. 'All the most likely faults I've eliminated twice over. I'll just have to take her down a wee bit further, clean out all the oil filters and make some more checks. We'll not be sailing today. Maybe not tomorrow either.'

The captain, a dour and patient man accustomed to delays both mechanical and elemental, knew his ship and he knew his crew. The engines were old and ailing, and Hughie was a stubborn man who did not admit defeat easily. He clapped his engineer sympathetically on the shoulder.

'Do your best, then. We've no outward passengers today, so it'll hurt no one if we postpone sailing till tomorrow. It's just an awful shame now the weather's turned in our favour at last.'

Hughie and Tom nodded solemn agreement. They discussed the problem for a few more minutes, and then

FLOWERS OF EVIL

the captain climbed out of the hatch to give them more room. Alistair stood back to let him pass. The captain paused and regarded his youngest crew member.

'Sorry, young Alistair. You'd best take another day of shore leave. We won't be needing you until tomorrow.'

Alistair walked slowly back along the harbour wall, feeling dejected. But his spirits did not remain down for long. He decided to go round to *Brave Viking* to see how his own boat had fared during the storms, and his stride quickened. A few minutes later he was on the opposite side of the harbour wall, looking down at the eighteen-foot green and white cutter riding easily on the light swell. She looked unharmed, but he climbed down on to her deck and gave her a thorough check over, just to make sure.

He rolled back the cockpit cover and went down into the small cabin. It was locked, but he had his own keys. His gaze went automatically to the fishing rods clipped securely to the bulkhead. He was tempted. He had the day off and the weather was fine. His food for the day was packed in the small haversack he carried on his shoulder; thick cheese sandwiches, lovingly prepared by his doting mother. The urge to put out to sea was strong. The salt was tingling in his blood.

Before taking the boat out alone, he normally had to ask permission from his father, who had a more experienced eye for the weather. But his father was no longer there to be asked. Hesitating, he went back on deck and studied the sky. He had taken *Brave Viking* out before on days like this. After careful consideration, he decided there was no reason why his father would not have given permission if he *had* been asked. His mind was made up.

He checked the fuel gauge, found the tank was full, and started the engine, smiling at the ease with which it fired first time and turned over. He pitied poor old Hughie. After casting off the mooring lines and easing the throttle half-open, he headed the *Brave Viking* out into Bressay Sound.

Soon the island of Bressay was behind him and the cliffs of Mainland were growing smaller on his port side. He thought of stopping the engine, putting out a sea anchor and trying his luck at the fishing, but the breeze was fresh in his face and he was enjoying the movement of the boat. It would have been fun to put up the sail, but he was not allowed to sail unless his father was there to help. So he kept the motor running and pointed her bows to the open sea.

Soon his thoughts of fishing became mingled with other thoughts – thoughts of a pretty face with blue eyes and long gold hair. Over the past two weeks Julia Gordon had played the imperilled heroine role in nearly all his daydreams. He remembered how he had asked her to come fishing. She had not said yes, but that was only because that awful little brother of hers had interfered. The main thing was that she had not said no either.

His face creasing with concentration, Alistair tried to recall every inflection of her voice, every body signal, and every sparkle of her eyes and her smile. She liked him, he was sure of that. It was only her brother who had forced her to move away. If he were just to call at the island, casually and ask her again, then perhaps she would come after all. By now she would be heartily sick of being cooped up by the bad weather.

In the end, he never made a positive decision to go to Lairg; it just so happened that he was already more than halfway there, and never made a decision to stop or turn back. *Brave Viking* seemed to have a will of her own, bounding effortlessly over the waves, and now he was this close it would cost him nothing to pay the island a visit. After all, it would be the only Christian thing to do. The folk on Lairg had been cut off for two weeks and might be in desperate need of something. Janet Matheson was expecting a baby; and the Gordons were strangers, who might have come ill-prepared for the rigours of island life. He could explain to them all why the *Island Pride* had been delayed, and take back messages to Lerwick.

Lairg appeared slowly, a solid bulwark of black-edged green rising out of the blue sea. Alistair steered tentatively for the south cove landing quay, but then changed his mind. He wanted to see the girl, but he didn't want it to look as though he had come all this way *especially* to find her. No – he'd go to the Matheson cottage first. It would be more natural and neighbourly to show concern over Mrs Matheson and her baby. Afterwards he could walk over to the second cottage and casually ask Julia if she would like to spend an hour or two fishing. Perhaps, if he was lucky, Julia would be visiting the Mathesons and he would bump into her accidentally; then it would seem much more like a chance meeting. After this complicated feat of reasoning, Alistair changed course and headed for the long west beach nearest to the Matheson cottage.

As he moved the boat in closer to land, he saw the thick column of black smoke rising from the centre of the island – his first indication that something was wrong. He stared at the smoke with narrowed eyes, trying to understand its meaning. It was far too thick for normal chimney smoke from the hearth fire, and he wondered if someone was burning rubbish. He puzzled over it, until the sound of the sea crashing and swirling over the dangerous black rocks brought him back to the present. First he had to concentrate on bringing *Brave Viking* safely into the long west cove.

The wind was blowing from the north-east, so he was approaching the sheltered side of the island. He shut down the throttle as he entered the bay, put the engine into reverse for a few seconds to bring the boat almost to a stop, then let the gentle swell of the waves carry her forward until the bows grated on the shingle bottom. Then he switched off the engine and dropped his anchor over the stern.

As he slipped over the side, wearing his tall seaboots, the waves washed up above his knees, and he waded ashore quickly, not waiting to be caught by a big wave which might have flooded his boots. He looked back once, and saw that, relieved of his weight, *Brave Viking* was now riding an inch or two higher in the water. Satisfied, the boat could come to no harm, he strode up the beach, sand and pebbles crunching under his feet.

He saw the strange new plants immediately, as soon as he had climbed over the tumble of boulders at the top of the beach. They were growing everywhere, individually and in large groups, and the sight of them made him gape. In the Shetlands, trees were a rare sight, since the lack of shelter and the bitter winds gave them no chance to grow. Apart from grass and heather the islands were mostly bare. Yet Lairg seemed to have become a forest overnight.

Alistair stared all around and scratched his head. For a moment he wondered if he was dreaming, or if he had somehow arrived at the wrong island. This place was more like something out of the tropical south seas than one of the Shetlands. Then the dispersing column of smoke caught his eye again, and he saw now that it was coming from the second cottage on the far side of the island. That was the first mystery to be solved, and the only way to find answers was to find the people who had been stranded here.

He could see the Matheson cottage clearly, just two hundred yards up the low valley, and he had to pass it on his way to the Gordons. He decided to call there first. Perhaps Ross or Janet would be at home and would be able to tell him what had happened. He walked up to the cottage slowly, with a growing feeling of apprehension. In spite of the sun he felt strangely cold. There was a crawling, shivery feeling at the back of his neck, as though he were being watched. Yet the island seemed deserted except for the profusion of weird new plant life. Instinctively, he gave the plants a wide berth.

He reached the cottage and found the door swinging open. He called Ross Matheson by name and tentatively looked inside. The cottage was empty. He went further inside and shouted up the stairs, but there was no answer. He stood frowning. Even if Ross was out with the dog tending the sheep, Mrs Matheson should have been here. Then he guessed the answer. Mrs Matheson was close to having her baby, so Ross had taken her over to the other cottage where Mrs Gordon could look after her.

It did not explain the open door though, or the plants, or the smoke. It was all very queer. Alistair had a sudden urge to hurry back to the open air.

He started to head down the valley to the second cottage, but then he saw the corral where Ross sheltered the sheep in bad weather. He stopped in amazement. One end of the corral had collapsed and was almost buried from sight under a multitude of the huge plants. They were the biggest he had yet seen, a great, strangling profusion of greenery in which some of the plants reached up to twenty feet in height. He was reminded of pictures he had seen of ancient civilizations after their temple and palace ruins had been re-discovered by explorers. The only difference was that in the pictures it had taken centuries for the jungles to smother the crumbling edifices of stone, while here on Lairg it had taken less than two weeks.

Another strange thing caught his eye; clumps of greyish white, like sludge snowballs or tufts of dirty cotton, were caught up in the green tangles. He moved closer to investigate, taking care not to go too close to the collapsed end of the corral, and with sudden horror he realized what they were. Each white patch was the wool fleece of a dead sheep.

At the sound end of the corral there were two loosened and broken planks, smashed out from inside as though some panicking and terror-stricken animal had hurled its weight against them. Alistair peered into the gap, and as his eyes accustomed to the gloom, he saw that the far end of the corral was choked with the menacing green foliage, and that more than a score of sheep had perished in the tight-curled tendrils.

Quickly he realized his own danger, and turned to run. As he did so, a tendril struck through the gap in the planks and fastened round his foot, tripping him up and bringing him crashing down to the ground. He screamed, finding himself being dragged back through the hole in the corral fence. He grabbed the edge of the hole as he was pulled through and hung on with all his strength. He shouted for help, but then another tendril tightened in a whiplash around his waist and began to squeeze the breath out of him.

Alistair fought desperately for his life, kicking and struggling as the plants tried to drag him further into the corral. More tendrils were stretching out for him now, writhing and straining in the gloom, but as long as he could keep his grip on the fence planks he could stay out of their reach. The timbers were creaking loudly, and he saw with horror that the nearest fence post was leaning inward. The most alarming creaking was directly above his head, and looking up he saw that the plank to which he had anchored himself was being torn away from the rest of the fence. The nails were slowly pulling out of the cross timber.

Terror filled his heart. He was being stretched and crucified on a rack more agonizing than any devised in a mediaeval torture chamber. Slowly but surely he would be torn in half and his arms and his trapped leg pulled out of their sockets. Either that, or the fence plank would give way and he would be dragged into the hungry wall of foliage.

He took the only chance he had and let go of the plank with his right hand. With all of his weight now hanging on one arm the pain in his left shoulder joint was excruciating. Tears flooded his eyes, as he used his free hand to snatch for the heavy bait-cutting knife he kept sheathed at his hip. He pulled the knife free and slashed at the tendril around his waist. The tendril was tough, as resilient as rubber, but mercifully he had kept the knife blade razor-sharp. The tendril parted and the severed end dropped away.

The pull at his waist was weaker now, but he was still trapped by his left foot. He tried to reach the second tendril with his knife but could not bring the knife into effective use while his body was being stretched taut. Neither did he dare release his one remaining handhold on the creaking plank. He squirmed helplessly and with the heel of his right boot he tried to kick away the tendril locked on to his other foot. As he twisted, his left foot moved inside his seaboot. He twisted, kicked and wriggled the trapped foot frantically, and suddenly it was slipping free, out of the boot. He crawled out through the hole in the fence, sobbing and terrified, and leaving his long rubber seaboot behind him.

As soon as he could stand, he backed away from the corral and the house, keeping to the open ground where there were no plants near. He looked back along the direct route to the beach and his boat, and sweated as he saw how close he had passed to some of the plants on his way up to the cottage. Now that he studied them more closely he could see the scores of dead seabirds caught up in their tendrils, like unplucked poultry hanging in a series of obscenely overgrown butchers' windows, and realized how narrow his escape had been.

His curiosity about the plants, about the mysterious column of smoke, or the fate of the people who had been left behind on this nightmare island, had vanished. All he wanted was to get away, to get back to his boat and escape to the open sea. However, the direct route back to the beach looked too dangerous, and he did not fancy trying it again. Looking for another route, he could see that the hillslopes leading to the higher part of the island offered more open spaces, so hoping to circle round to the beach, he moved off, walking awkwardly with one seaboot and clutching his sheath knife firmly in his sweat-slippery hand.

Picking the safest path through the clumps of death-seed plants, he eventually came out on to the west cliffs. But on the way he had seen more of the monsters which had fed upon the scattered sheep. And when he had looked over the cliffs to see how far he had been forced to detour from the beach, he had seen the drained corpse of Ross Matheson crushed in the tendrils of the large plant on the ledge below.

Alistair was only fifteen, and the horrors were piling up too fast for him. Gripped by panic, he fled along the cliff edge and began to scramble down over the steep black rocks to the beach. He cut and bruised his stockinged foot, but ignored the sharp stabs of pain. In a series of long, reckless jumps over the last piles of boulders, he finally reached the beach, landing in a sprawling heap face-down on the sand. The impact knocked the wind out of him and drove sand into his face and eyes. He clawed his way up, spitting and gasping, and then limped across the last few yards of hard-packed sand and shingle to the edge of the sea.

Without waiting to catch his breath, he waded out to *Brave Viking* and hauled himself aboard, immediately dragging up the anchor and starting the engine. He backed the boat out into the long shallow bay until he had room to turn, then swung her bows round hard and tight and headed for the open sea.

Behind him there were heavy storm clouds moving up from the north, blotting out the sunlight over Lairg. The fickle weather was worsening again, and the seas were rising. More gales were on their way, but the sea was a familiar enemy which Alistair knew how to fight. Right now he believed there could be no storm, hurricane or tempest, which could be in any way more terrible than the devil's work he had witnessed on Lairg Island.

CHAPTER TWENTY

At the bottom of the North Sea, forty fathoms below the heaving green waves, the Soviet trawler *Yenisei* lay on her side on a bed of rippled sand. The Arctic gales were whipping up the surface, but at this depth there was only cold, dark stillness. No tide or current moved in this part of the ocean and the *Yenisei* rested in watery solitude and peace, a drowned ship of dead souls lost in a vast fluid tomb.

Every member of her crew was a fish-nibbled corpse, but not everything aboard the sunken ship was dead. Barnacles and weeds had started to grow on her decking and hull, and fish swam silently in and out of her portholes and through the flooded holds and cabins. And there was something else – something which had come down with the ship, but had not drowned.

A large and curious codfish swam slowly down to the wreck. A twitch of its fins and tail propelled it through the open door of the wheelhouse and for a few minutes it investigated the floating bodies trapped inside. After feeding on them it withdrew and continued lazily down from the bridge and past the upper deck cabins. Something stirred in the grave: a thick green tendril snaking out from one of the sunken cabins. It curled around the fat codfish and drew it bulging-eyed and struggling into the black hole of the cabin doorway.

The deathseed plant did not need air or sunlight, and it had survived under the sea. All it needed to thrive was salts and blood, and the cold, thin blood of a fish, although not as sustaining, was an acceptable alternative to the warm blood of a bird or mammal. Already the plant was adapting to its new underwater environment.

FLOWERS OF EVIL

At first, the blood from its crushed fish victims had drifted away before it could be absorbed by the hungry roots and leaves. But now the plant was learning instinctively, and the luckless codfish was completely enveloped by the large, smothering leaves before the crushing process began. The plant was no longer able to feed at the roots, but the leaves were fast developing improved sucking surfaces to absorb the blood and keep the alien growth alive.

Meanwhile the seeds were drifting loose in the ocean, aimless until they encountered underwater currents or tide movements to speed them on their way. They were as prolific on the sea bed as they were on land. They would grow larger in the sea, and eventually, as Shumilov had discovered with the land-based variety, their own huge appetites and growth rate would kill them off. They would absorb too much of the salts they devoured and collapse under their own weight.

But in the meantime they were taking root on the ocean floor and propagating in a new form of deadly seaweed. Steadily the plants were advancing to more shallow waters.

In his small boat Alistair Mckenna had put a thousand yards of sea space between himself and Lairg Island, and only now was he beginning to feel safe. He eased the throttle down and looked back, and as the boat lost speed it began to wallow heavily in the rising seas. The black thunderclouds were looming larger over the island, and the strengthening winds were making the boat difficult to handle. The storm had gathered itself in the north during his hair-raising adventures on shore, and now it was bearing down on him fast.

Alistair knew the only sensible thing was to open the throttle wide, pray that he could outrun the storm, and race back to Bressay Sound, before the full force struck.

Every sea-bred instinct screamed at him to flee for shelter. But at the same time he was haunted by his conscience – and by a pretty face. Julia was just a lass, no older than he was himself, and if she was still alive, then she and her family must surely be in desperate danger on that terrible island. But he was terrified to return.

Another mighty battle began within him. He could run for Mainland to fetch help, but perhaps no one would believe his incredible story. And even if he was believed, the fast-approaching storm might only be the forerunner for another whole cycle of gales which could cut off the island for another week or more. By the time any help could get back to the island it would be far too late.

Alistair chewed at his lower lip, trying to conquer his inner fears. He remembered his daydreams, of rescuing his beautiful blonde-haired princess from danger. Now that the danger was real, not imaginary, he was funking it. He was running away from the island leaving her behind. The conflicting dream images and the stark reality tormented his mind. He called himself a craven coward, and then insisted just as vehemently he was not. Finally he swallowed hard to bring his stomach under control. He opened up the throttle and carefully brought *Brave Viking* round, aiming her bows back at Lairg.

He began to circle the island, keeping an anxious eye on the threatening north horizon. The smoke from the Gordons' cottage had been dispersed by the winds, but maybe if he rounded the south headland he might be able to go in close enough to see what had happened. He knew he would not dare to land again, but he convinced himself that as long as he kept a barrier of sea between himself and the shore he would be safe from the loathsome horror which had taken over the land.

The Gordons and Janet Matheson had watched the

FLOWERS OF EVIL

gathering storm clouds with sinking hearts. The weather was against them yet again. After temporarily escaping from the deathseed plants, it seemed that the biting winds and icy rains were coming back to finish them off. Their plight looked hopeless. Julia was near to tears, Janet wept for her baby, and even the irrepressible Jonathon was at last subdued.

Their move to the beach now looked to have been a mistake, and Barry tentatively suggested that perhaps they should try to cross the island and reach Janet's cottage. It was possible that with no one in the cottage, the deathseed plants had not yet surrounded it. It might give them a few more days of refuge before the plants sensed their presence and were able to drag themselves up to the walls. But Janet flatly refused to take any more risks with her baby. Barry then suggested he should try to scout a safe route alone, but both Valerie and Janet combined to hold him back, afraid that once he moved inland they would never see him again.

Frustrated, Barry tried to make the best of their situation. He selected a group of rocks midway between the breaking waves and the top end of the beach where the deathseed plants were lining up. There was a hollow between the rocks where the whole party could just squeeze in, and although it would give no overhead shelter from the rain, the rocks might shield them from the worst of the freezing winds. All they could hope to do was to huddle there together under their blankets. Their shared body heat might just keep them alive through the storm.

Janet settled down in the hollow between the rocks with a blanket round her shoulders and cuddled the baby. Robbie crept up close beside her and looked hurt when she stopped him from pushing his wet nose too close to her child. Valerie stayed with them, stroking the dog and making strained conversation, trying to stop Janet from sinking any deeper into apathy.

Barry set Jonathon and Julia to work searching for driftwood, with the vague idea of putting up some sort of tent made up of blankets. Even if they didn't find any substitute tent poles at least the search would keep their minds occupied. Jonathon also suggested they should gather wood for a signal fire and Barry was quick to approve. Anything positive which kept them busy was good for morale.

While the children hunted along the beach, he watched one of the larger deathseed plants moving toward the cove. It moved painfully slowly, as Jonathon described, groping forward and dragging itself along, one root at a time, but in five minutes he was sure it had moved as many inches. The larger the plants were, the more positively they seemed able to move. This one was aiming to block off the path from the burned-out cottage to the beach, and remove any chance of their returning inland.

Bitterly, Barry returned his attention back to the beach, knowing it would do no good to let the others see how badly he was worried. He moved among the rocks, kicking over pieces of flotsam, but not finding sufficient for even one tent pole. Jonathon returned from the next cove with his arms full of smaller pieces for a fire, but every one was heavily soaked with sea and rainwater. With no dry materials to help ignition Barry knew they would never burn, but he praised his son for a job well done.

The wind was rising, stinging their faces with the first drops of rain, and the waves were growing bigger and angrier as they crashed down on the beach. Behind the breaking waves the seas were grey-black and swelling ominously. Far out on the blurred horizon a lightning bolt flashed down, splitting the sky in white forks and briefly turning the black clouds red and purple. Seconds later, the thunder cracked over their heads and rumbled away like cannons booming on the far side of the island.

There was no chance of the mailboat coming today, and Barry knew it Even if it had left Mainland during the calm it would be turning back by now. The captain would know he could never hope to put safely into Lairg once the storm hit the island.

Grimly he turned away from the hostile sea and put his arm round Jonathon's shoulders. 'Come on, Jon, we'd best join the others in the shelter.' He looked down the beach. 'Where's Julia?'

'Over there.'

Jonathon pointed to the far end of the cove, where Julia had climbed up on to the highest point of the rocks. She was gazing out to sea with her fair hair streaming in the wind. Barry guessed she was looking for the mailboat.

'Julia,' he yelled. 'It's no good. The boat won't come near in this weather. Come down and take cover.'

Julia heard the cry. She looked round and acknowledged with a hand signal, knowing her voice would be smothered by the roar of the sea and the wind. On her left the sea was smashing on the rocks, hurling spray over her, and on her right the surf was pounding up the beach. Her heart sank again – she knew her father was right. She stared for another lingering moment out to sea. The grey, rain-streaked horizon was empty. There was no sign of a boat. A gust of wind almost blasted her backwards from her sentry point, and she turned to scramble down to the beach.

Barry and Jonathon had already taken cover. In a few more moments, Julia would have joined them and the whole party would have been hidden behind the windbreak of the rocks. But as she turned, Julia saw a flash of green and white colour emerging from behind the south headland. She swung back to face the sea, straightening up and staring, hardly daring to believe her eyes. It was a boat – a boat she recognized. Her heart sky-rocketed upward and jammed in her throat. She was choked with joyful relief and temporarily speechless.

'Daddy,' she screamed as soon as she could find her voice. 'It's a boat. It's Alistair! It's Alistair in *Brave Viking*!'

She began to jump wildly up and down, careless now of whether she might slip and fall, or whether the cheated winds might blow her over. She shouted until she was hoarse and waved her arms frantically above her head.

Alistair was tight-lipped as he steered *Brave Viking* out from the leeward side of the headland, butting her bows into the full force of the heavy seas. The small boat bucked beneath him and he was hard-pressed to keep his footing on the heaving deck. He held fast to the wheel, fighting to keep to his chosen course. He knew immediately it would be worse than foolish to take the boat anywhere near the tall stacks and the high north cliffs. It would be suicide. Even if there were people alive at that end of the island, there would be no way he could help them or take them off. A quick look at the east coves and the burned cottage, that was all he dared risk; then he would have to make a fast run for home. Even now he feared he had left it too late and the storm would catch him on the open sea.

For the first minute after rounding the headland he was too busy trying to control the boat even to look toward the shore. Then the wind dropped briefly and he had only the sea to contend with. Bracing himself, he strained upward on tiptoe as successive lifts of the waves gave him broken glimpses of the small chain of the coves. The beaches were all bare beyond the boiling foam, but he did not know whether he was glad or sorry. He had done as much as he could. Now there was nothing left but to turn away.

He stretched himself again for a glimpse of the cottage, and saw it briefly through the first squall of rain. The thatched roof had burned out or caved in, and only the stone walls were left standing. All around the cottage were huge carnivorous plants like the ones which had eaten Ross Matheson and his sheep. Alistair shuddered and looked away.

As he took a last look at the beaches, it was then he saw the desperately waving figure perched on the dark rocks at the south end of the first cove. His heart stood still, and the fear gripped him again. It was her, Julia! There was no mistaking her slim figure and fair hair. She had been partially hidden from his view as he rounded the headland and he had almost missed her.

He steered the boat closer to the shore, and as he did so the winds caught up with him again and the rains broke. He could see more people running now, four or five of them, hurrying from the rocks to joint her. The boat was rearing up and down beneath him, and Alistair had to ease the throttle back and try to hold her steady. If he was not careful she could be carried up the beach, grounded, and pounded to pieces in a matter of minutes by the thundering waves. And she would be broken up even more quickly if he let her be flung against the sharp rocks on either side.

He was close enough now to recognize the people on the beach. The big, bearded man was Julia's father. The two women were her mother and Janet Matheson. The awful little brother was there, and the other running figure, he now realized, was the Matheson's dog.

Alistair was in a terrible dilemma. He knew that if he tried to bring *Brave Viking* on to the beach she would be smashed to matchwood. The sea here made a furious contrast with the calm bay on the west side where he had landed earlier. At the same time, he knew that if he left these people here they were doomed. The storm howling behind him was brewing up into a big one, and if the huge seas which would soon be driving right up the beach did not sweep them all away, then they would be pushed into the waiting tendrils of the deathseed plants, which now formed an impenetrable barrier at the top of the narrow strip of sand.

The people on the beach were all shouting, but all he could distinguish above the tumult of the sea and wind was the demented barking of the dog. Alistair shouted back in an effort to explain why he could come in no further, but he was wasting his breath.

However, Barry understood. He turned and grabbed Valerie's arm.

'He can't bring the boat in any further. It's too dangerous. We'll have to go out to him. I'll take you first.'

'No,' Valerie protested, rain pouring down her frightened face. 'The children—'

'Our friend out there has his work cut out holding the boat,' Barry shouted back. 'The first one I put on board has to be able to help pull up the others. You're the strongest. I'll come back for the children.'

Valerie allowed herself to be dragged to the sea's edge, then looked back with the white foam surging around her thighs, her face anguished.

'It's all right, Mum,' Julia shouted bravely. 'We're okay.' She put her arms round Janet and Jonathon and held them tight.

'Quickly,' Barry urged. 'We can't hang about.'

Valerie went with him then and they waded out into the breaking waves. The seas were freezing, almost stopping their hearts, and Valerie's teeth were chattering within seconds. A wave smashed her off her feet, but Barry held her. She could not get her feet to touch bottom again and swam desperately with Barry still walking beside her. The next wave broke over her head, the salt water forcing its way into her mouth and nose, and she felt panic and thrashed frantically with arms and legs. She was drowning in the roaring darkness of angry water. Barry hauled her up again, urging and encouraging as they struggled out to the boat. Then he lost his own footing and for a moment they were both floundering, with the white hull lurching toward them on a wave and all but smashing into their faces. Barry reached up to get a grip on her gunwhale and pushed Valerie up over the side. She tumbled into the well of the cockpit and sprawled there trembling, sea water streaming from her clothes.

Barry let go immediately and fought his way back to the shore. He was breathless when he reached the beach and simply pointed at Jonathon. He had thought of a better way of transporting the others, and crouched down on his knees, indicating to Jonathon that he should climb on to his shoulders. Jonathon did so and Barry gripped his son firmly below the knees and straightened up. The rain-heavy wind almost blew them over, but Jonathon clasped both hands around his father's head and hung on.

Barry waded out into the sea again, and this time he moved slowly, straining to keep his footing. The surf boiled around his thighs, around his waist, and finally up to his armpits before he was through the breakers. A few more slow, cautious steps and then the boat came to meet him. Valerie leaned out of the cockpit and plucked Jonathon from his shoulders, dragging the boy safely aboard.

Meanwhile Alistair was fighting the controls for all he was worth, bringing the boat forward for the few vital seconds when it was needed, and backing her out again as soon as he could. He reversed the engines and with the power roaring and the screw-blade thrashing, the *Brave Viking* slogged her way back from the white jaws of danger. Barry was already on his way back to the shore.

He brought Julia next, again carrying her out on his shoulders. Alistair watched, biting his lip, and again he let the boat ride forward in the hollow of a wave, just far enough to allow Valerie to snatch Julia from the hungry sea.

Barry struggled back to the beach again, and now he was weakening. He felt as though the waves had pounded his body to a soggy pulp and his legs threatened to buckle. He moved up to Janet and crouched down before her, waiting for her to mount his shoulders. She stared at him with fear-crazed eyes and backed away. The skirts of her dress and the corners of the blanket gathered round her were flying in the wind. Curtains of rain and exploding spray swirled between them.

'I can't,' she sobbed. 'I might drop the baby.'

'Hang on to me with one hand,' Barry told her. 'Hold tight to the baby with the other.'

'I can't do it. I'm afraid.'

'You can and you will. If you can't do it for me, then do it for Ross. It's his baby.'

Janet's face was a mask of terror and misery. Barry reached for her arm and pulled her toward him. 'For Ross,' he repeated, and crouched again.

Awkwardly, Janet threw one leg astride his shoulders. He got her settled comfortably, making sure she was well balanced and had a firm grip on the baby. Then he straightened up. They swayed in the wind, Janet sobbing loudly. Barry could feel her thigh muscles squeezing fiercely at the back of his neck, and his own thigh muscles screamed in silent protest at her added weight. He turned and staggered back into the sea.

This was his fourth trip, and his hardest. The waves beating into his face had mounted in fury, and he was fast losing the last remnants of his strength. Three times he was almost swept off his feet and forced to stand fast and brace himself until he regained his balance. His legs wanted to fold under him and there were despairing moments when he knew he would never reach the boat. Then at last he was through the breakers again and the boat was thrusting up to meet him. As Julia leaned out to snatch the baby from her faltering arm, Janet screamed and toppled sideways into the sea. She kept screaming until Barry reassured her that Julia had the baby safe on board, and only then were they able to get her up and over the gunwhale in her turn, Barry pushing from below, Valerie and Jonathon heaving from above.

Barry had just started to climb up behind them, when Jonathon wailed through pent-up tears.

'We're leaving Robbie behind. Robbie's still on the beach.'

Barry looked back. He had forgotten the dog, although he realized that its frantic barking had been sounding in his ears ever since they had spotted the boat. Wearily, he lowered himself into the sea and went back again.

Mercifully Robbie was not as heavy as Janet. Barry succeeded in getting the collie over his shoulders, holding a forepaw with one hand and a hind leg in the other. Robbie kicked and jerked in momentary alarm, but then became still, whining fearfully in Barry's ear. Barry carried him out to the boat and heaved him aboard.

Willing hands helped drag him up and over the side. With the boat wallowing dangerously under his weight, he slid down into a gasping heap in the well of the cockpit and collapsed there, utterly exhausted and momentarily helpless.

Alistair crashed the engine into reverse once more and gave full power to the throttle. With the propellor blade churning, *Brave Viking* battled her way out stern first, inch by inch. The small cutter was overloaded and struggling low in the water, and the waves were breaking over her gunwhales. Julia found a bucket and began to desperately bail out the water slopping around their feet.

Alistair knew that once he was clear of the cove he would have to bring the bows round and head her south, and that that would be the moment of maximum danger. So far he had not exchanged a single word with any of the folk he had rescued and had put all his mind to managing the boat. He waited for a gap between the biggest waves, and prayed. Then he brought the boat round.

Brave Viking lurched and rolled. Julia and Janet screamed, and all of them grabbed at the gunwhales and held on. Barry was pitched across the deck and Valerie made a lunge for him as he fetched up against her feet, locking her fingers on the loose hood of his anorak.

For thirty petrified seconds it seemed that the cutter must turn turtle. Alistair heaved on the wheel, swinging her bows further round to complete the circle. The next wave was already rearing over them and only just in time Alistair brought the bows head on to meet it. The sea poured over the windscreen of the tiny wheel-house and cascaded past in a solid waterfall on either side.

Alistair breathed again as they rose through it, but he breathed too soon. As the boat planed down into the hollow behind the wave, a tendril suddenly broke through the surface of the sea. For a moment it flailed toward the storm-lashed sky. Then it slapped down on the gunwhale on the port side. The boat tilted over as the undersea plant gave a powerful pull, threatening to spill them out.

Alistair was stunned, frozen by shock. If Neptune himself had appeared from the depths with a forked trident, he could not hardly have been more dismayed. Behind him the women were screaming and the dog was barking. The deck angled steeply beneath their feet, sending them slithering down toward the tendril. Fear and the will to survive pumped blood and movement into Alistair's muscles, and instinctively he reached for the sheathed knife at his hip. But he could not hold the twisting wheel with only one hand. With another big wave looming up to starboard, he had to give up the effort to reach the knife. He clamped both hands on the wheel again and fought to keep *Brave Viking* afloat.

Barry was still sprawled breathless on the deck, but Valerie had seen what Alistair was trying to do. She lurched forward and pulled out the knife from the sheath at the boy's hip. Turning, she attacked the grasping tendril and cut it away.

The deck levelled out, but they were still immediately above the groping plant on the sea bed. It had sensed the vibrations from the boat's engine and was striking out in blind hunger, searching instinctively for prey. A second tendril snaked up dripping from the waves and lashed close to Janet and her baby. Janet shrieked and fell to the bottom of the boat, clutching the baby to her bosom. The tendril groped toward her and Julia struggled to drag her clear. Valerie moved forward, aiming slicing blows at the tendril with the short knife. All of them missed.

'Get down into the cabin,' Alistair yelled. 'All of you get into the cabin.'

The cabin door was beside the wheel, and Jonathon was the nearest. He got the door open and scuttled inside. Julia pulled at Janet, while Valerie continued her attempts to sever the tendril. The long green arm seemed to sense that Janet was out of reach and changed direction, snaking toward Valerie. Valerie stepped back, recoiling as the tip of the tendril passed within inches of her face. She tripped backward over Barry's legs as the boat tipped on a rising wave, and a howling gust of wind finished the job of hurling her into the sea.

Barry had struggled to his knees. He felt the hard kick against his legs and looked back in time to see Valerie disappear over the side. For a few agonizing seconds he saw her wave her arms frantically in an effort to regain

FLOWERS OF EVIL

her balance and drop the knife. The blade thudded point first into the deck in front of Barry's face.

She was gone before he could grab her, but her despairing cry was enough to drag up the last reserves of his strength. He pushed himself up and retrieved the knife from the deck. Alistair had shut down the throttle to hold the boat back as soon as he realized he had lost a passenger, but the tendril from under the sea was still swaying dangerously over the open cockpit.

'Give her full speed,' Barry ordered. 'Get the boat clear!'

And then he turned and dived over the side.

Again Alistair was torn, but Barry had made the decision for him. The tone was an echo of his own father, and in a storm Alistair had the good sense to do exactly as he was told – and do it quickly. He opened the throttle again and *Brave Viking* thrust forward, moving out from under the tendril, but leaving Barry and Valerie behind.

Julia clawed her way out of the cabin, grabbing at the wheel and his arm. Her wet hair was plastered over her white face and she was hysterical.

'Alistair, you can't leave them. *You can't!*'

'Your father said get clear.' He was almost hysterical himself. 'If we lose the boat we'll all drown.'

'But you must go back. *You must!* Look!' she pointed desperately. 'The tendril's going back into the sea.'

Alistair looked back. The tendril was indeed pulling back beneath the wind-tossed waves. He bit his lip and made his decision, shutting down the throttle so as to allow the boat to maintain her position.

'We can't go back,' he repeated. 'But we'll wait for them. They have to swim to us.' He stared back over his shoulder. 'Where are they?'

Julia ran to the stern of the boat, searching the heaving grey, rain-lashed waves. But there was nothing. Robbie stood beside her, barking furiously, and automatically she took a hold of his collar. The tears flowed hot and anguished down her cheeks.

Barry had surfaced, but for a few moments all he could see was the rain splashing hard into the wave tops in front of his face. *Brave Viking* had pulled away and he saw no sign of the tendrils or of Valerie. He trod water and twisted his body round to search in all directions. Panic gripped him. The icy Arctic seas chilled his body and a terrible numbing fear froze his soul. Then he saw her. She was being tossed up on a wave crest a dozen yards away; her arm was waving weakly and her mouth was open, but no sound came out – she was choking on great mouthfuls of sea-water.

Barry struck out toward her with a fast over-arm crawl, hampered by the weight of his clothes and the battering force of the waves. He shouted her name and saw her look toward him. Then a wave rose between them and they were both plummeting down into separate hollows. Barry swam with all his strength and the intervening wave passed over him. He spluttered out a mouthful of salt water and blinked his eyes clear. Valerie was only six yards away, struggling to reach him. But just as they closed the gap by half, a tendril rose out of the sea behind her and curled almost lazily around her waist. Valerie screamed and was pulled under.

Barry did not hesitate; still gripping the knife in his right hand, he immediately took a deep breath, filling his lungs, and followed her down. As the sea closed above his head he kicked back strongly. For a few seconds he could not see her in the watery grey gloom. The salt stung his eyes and he was practically blinded. Instinctively he squeezed his eyes shut, then forced them open again. For a moment he could make out nothing at all in the swirling grey depths, then he saw her blurred, struggling form, almost within arm's reach.

FLOWERS OF EVIL

Two more powerful kicks and he had a hold upon her right wrist with his left hand. He pulled himself past her and came face to face with her bulging eyes. She was drowning, and he knew he had only seconds to save her. The plant was now dragging them both steadily down to the sea bottom, and more tendrils were wriggling out to meet them.

Barry entwined his legs around Valerie's to hold her, and succeeded in changing his grip without letting go of her, locking his left arm tight around her body just below the armpits. Now he was able to use the knife in his right hand to slash at the tendril around her waist. His slow-motion underwater blows had no effect, so he changed his tactics and tried to saw the tendril through. Mercifully, the plant was also slow and uncertain in its undersea environment, and lacked the lightning speed and accurate aim of those on land.

For what seemed an eternity they twisted and struggled. Another tendril fell past Barry's face and missed. His lungs were bursting and the blood was roaring in his head. They were dragged almost within reach of the lesser tendrils of the gigantic undersea plant before the blade finally cut through and the tendril around Valerie's waist was severed. Barry dropped the knife and concentrated the last of his fading strength and consciousness into swimming back to the surface.

Now there were more tendrils reaching for them through the sea, but none of them secured a hold. Barry was almost blacking out as he broke through the waves and gulped greedily for air. The red and black mists cleared from his brain and he struggled to hold Valerie's head up. She was unconscious, but he prayed she was still alive. He looked for the green and white boat, saw it fifty yards away and began to swim toward it.

Julia saw them and shouted to Alistair, who calculated

the risk and took it, turning the boat in the heavy swell to pick them up. Janet entrusted her baby to Jonathon and crawled out into the cockpit to help Julia haul her parents aboard.

Valerie slumped senseless on the deck. Her face was grey and she had stopped breathing. Barry knelt over her and tilted her head back to clear her airway. Covering her mouth with his own he began to blow air into her lungs.

With all of them on board, Alistair opened up the throttle and headed away from the horrors of Lairg Island. After clearing the south headland, he set his course for Mainland across the open sea, leaving the storm behind them to vent its full fury upon Lairg.

After five minutes Valerie's grey colour had improved, and soon after she was breathing again without help. Barry felt a huge relief and at last the blackness descended. He keeled over and fell beside her, exhausted and unconscious.

CHAPTER TWENTY-ONE

They were lucky, for the storm was blowing from north-west to north-east, and by running due south they were able to race out of its direct path. The seas remained rough and the gusting winds and rain squalls accompanied them all the way back to Mainland, but the worst of it passed behind them. With the help of some expert seamanship, Alistair was able to bring *Brave Viking* safely into Bressay Sound.

Alistair knew his father would be proud of him. But what was even more pleasing was to have Julia Gordon standing by his side, watching every spin of the wheel in his capable hands with shameless hero-worship in her soft blue eyes.

In the small cabin, Barry and Valerie sat together on the cramped bunk, alone except for Robbie, who was curled up wet, miserable and seasick on the deck at their feet. Jonathon could never be confined for long, and when the rain eased and they entered the sound, Janet had risked taking the baby up into the cockpit to catch the first glimpse of Lerwick. Barry had his arm around Valerie's shoulders, and for a long time she had leaned against him with her eyes closed. They had pulled themselves into that position and remained there ever since they had recovered.

At last he felt her stir and lift her head, and when he turned his face he saw she was looking into his eyes. She had been thinking, but her thoughts were muddled and emotional.

She said hoarsely, 'Barry, you shouldn't have done it.'
He was bewildered. 'I shouldn't have done what?'
'Dived into the sea to save me. I'm not worth it. You

could have drowned too, and the children would have been left alone.'

'I had to save you. You're my wife. I need you.'

'I know,' she said unhappily. 'I realize now how much you really love me and need me. And I love you, and I need you, too. But I don't deserve your love. I've made such a mess of things. I've been such a fool—'

'Forget it.' He closed her lips gently with his fingers. 'It's over now. Isn't it?'

She nodded, and moved his hand away. 'Yes. But it should never have started. I suppose I felt taken for granted, by you and the children. Everything between us seemed old and stale. Then Simon came along. He was young and fresh. I lost my silly head and wanted to throw away everything we had. Then the deathplants came and now I know that what we have together is the most important. Oh, Barry – can you ever forgive me?'

Her tears flooded over her face and he held her close and kissed them away.

'I can forgive,' he promised. 'If you can forget. We'll start all over again. You're never going back to Simon Lancing. And none of us will ever go back to Lairg Island. After all we've been through, our marriage must come out stronger than ever before.'

She became still and comforted in his arms, but after a few minutes she began trembling again.

'Barry, those horrible plants, what if—'

'Shush,' he told her. 'We're safe now and it's all over. When we've told our story, the army can send in a hundred men with flame-throwers – or the RAF can drop a shower of napalm bombs. We couldn't fight them alone, but with all the forces of human technology ranged against them the plants won't stand a chance. They'll be totally burned out.'

And later they were. But even as Barry spoke, far away

FLOWERS OF EVIL

behind the Ural Mountains in the small Russian village of Babushskaya, a remote, unrecorded and very tiny event was taking place. On the edge of a scorched patch of blackened earth, where the flame-throwers of the Red Army had hurled their bright tongues of orange fire, a minute crack had appeared and a seedling was pushing through. In a few days there would be others like it, just as they had first shown themselves on the edge of the black Khyshtym wasteland. And they would grow velvety-green leaves, almost invisible tendrils, and delicate little sky-blue flowers.

In the neat back garden of a white-painted, middle-class home in a small town in Nova Scotia, where the west-bound winds from across the North Atlantic made their first landfall, a child drew her mother's attention to a pretty little flower she had just discovered growing wild. The little girl was a toddler, barely four years old, with long braided pigtails, a heart-warming innocence, and infinite curiosity.

'What is it, Nancy, darling?' asked her mother.

Nancy sat down beside the tiny plant with its eye-catching emerald-green leaves and bright blue-petalled flowers. She examined it with a child's intensity of interest and then looked back at her mother.

'It's a pretty flower, Mummy. Can we put it in a little pot and bring it into the house? Then we can watch it grow with our other spiky plants.' Nancy's tone and her wide-open eyes were hopefully pleading.

'Can we, Mummy? Can we, Mummy? Please?'

All Futura Books are available at your bookshop or newsagent, or can be ordered from the following address:
Futura Books, Cash Sales Department,
P.O. Box 11, Falmouth, Cornwall.

Please send cheque or postal order (no currency), and allow 30p for postage and packing for the first book plus 15p for the second book and 12p for each additional book ordered up to a maximum charge of £1.29 in U.K.

Customers in Eire and B.F.P.O. please allow 30p for the first book, 15p for the second book plus 12p per copy for the next 7 books, thereafter 6p per book.

Overseas customers please allow 50p for postage and packing for the first book and 10p per copy for each additional book.